and **Life** of
Eleanor
Parker

ALSO BY KERRY WILKINSON

Down Among the Dead Men
No Place Like Home
Watched
Ten Birthdays
Two Sisters
The Girl Who Came Back
Last Night

THE JESSICA DANIEL SERIES
The Killer Inside (also known as *Locked In*)
Vigilante
The Woman in Black
Think of the Children
Playing with Fire
The Missing Dead (also known as *Thicker Than Water*)
Behind Closed Doors
Crossing the Line
Scarred for Life
For Richer, For Poorer
Nothing but Trouble

SHORT STORIES
January
February
March
April

THE ANDREW HUNTER SERIES
Something Wicked
Something Hidden

SILVER BLACKTHORN SERIES
Reckoning
Renegade
Resurgence

the Death and Life of Eleanor Parker

Bookouture

Published by Bookouture in 2018

An imprint of StoryFire Ltd.

Carmelite House
50 Victoria Embankment
London EC4Y 0DZ

www.bookouture.com

ISBN: 978-1-78681-254-4
eBook ISBN: 978-1-78681-253-7

SUNDAY

Chapter One

'Life's a lot like a well-made sandwich. The two ends are kinda boring but what truly matters is all the fancy stuff in the middle.'

My father told me this on the day he learned he was ill.

His words flash through me as I splutter awake. Water sprays from my mouth, fizzes out of my nose and dribbles over my chin. I'm blinking, trying to figure out where I am, but it's hazy, dark, and still the water comes. It feels like it's everywhere: spilling from my ears, dripping from my arms and seeping into my clothes.

I finally catch my breath and open my eyes wide enough to see the bright white of the moon splayed across the sludgy curve of the riverbank. The water is underneath me, tickling my toes, gentle dark ripples babbling towards the arch of a familiar stone bridge. With another blink, I know where I am.

The river runs through the centre of Westby, the bridge linking one side of the village to the other. I've lived here my entire life, crossing that stone arch most days.

None of that explains why I'm sitting *in* the river.

I yank my feet roughly away from the water as if bitten by a snake and haul myself to the riverbank, then slide up the mud on my backside. Slushy muck squishes between my fingers as I hug my knees to my chest, trying to figure out what's going on. My exposed skin feels like it's been basted with a slimy film of grease, a Christmas turkey ready for the oven.

I'm cold – *really* cold – half-dressed, drenched, on the banks of a river. It's night and I'm shivering under the darkness.

This isn't how I usually wake up. I'm more of a double duvet and fluffy pillow kinda person.

What's more concerning is that I can't remember how or why I'm here. My red skirt – or at least it *used* to be red – and a spaghetti-strapped top with my favourite denim jacket offers little protection from the chill of the night. It's the sort of thing I'd wear most of the year round. Daytimes, evenings, my house, a friend's house. It doesn't offer any clues as to where I've been.

There's an itch at the back of my mind, a niggling something of utmost importance. Like when I flipped those pages of exam questions last summer, trying to scrape correct answers from a rebellious mind that was determined to wander.

I take a breath but my chest is tight and there's a gurgle, like the final bubbles of a bath disappearing down the plughole. When I roll onto my knees, I slide closer to the water, but slowly – *really* slowly – I scramble up the bank. Mud sticks to my palms and loose twigs and stones scrape at my knees but the further I get, the drier the ground. Eventually I reach a patch of flattened grass close to a gravelly towpath, where I sit and wipe the flecks of grit from my legs and mud from my hands.

It seems obvious now, yet I'd somehow missed that I am barefoot. My toenails are a glossy pink but chipped. There's a spark of recognition, of sitting on my bed and painting them on a morning where sun blazed through my window. It feels recent. Maybe it was yesterday…?

There's still water prickling the back of my throat and I cough more up, deep hacks, wheezing and snorting, until the liquid finally feels as if it's out of my system.

When I clamber to my feet, my head spins and it's as if the river is rushing towards me. Stars flare around the edge of my vision and I remember the first time my friend Naomi and I tried cider. We were barely fifteen and I don't reckon there's any alcohol quite as good as underage, illicit alcohol. Nor anything quite as bad as underage, illicit hangovers.

This feels like that – the dizziness, the confusion and the empty, pained stomach.

Except I know I haven't been drinking. Among the patchwork of incoherent thoughts and memories, there is Naomi's Easter party, where I awoke in her bathroom and vowed never to drink again. Not until I actually turn eighteen. That was April and now it's June. That much I remember.

My phone comes out of my jacket pocket in one piece but the screen – severely scratched long before I ended up in the river – doesn't respond. Jabbing the buttons on the side does nothing to persuade it to come back to life, neither does whacking it on the ground and calling it names. That's the sum total of my IT skills, so back into my sodden pocket it goes.

I untangle the necklace that has twisted itself around my throat, straightening out the coil of white gold links and letting it hang properly. It was a sixteenth birthday present from Mum – an inheritance from a great-grandmother I never met. It's one of the few things I own that's actually worth anything – but that doesn't mean I wasn't royally ripped off. Giving away things you already own shouldn't count as a birthday present. That's re-gifting.

Those things I remember.

Either way, seeing as I still have my phone and necklace, I've not been robbed. But I have so many questions. Did I fall in the river? And where is everybody? It's the middle of the night, so no surprise the village centre is empty, but where are my friends? There was a house, grey fuzzy blurs of being surrounded by other people. There was music, singing, dancing and… burgers with ketchup. Lots of ketchup.

Still the filmy, smoggy haze hangs over those memories. There are shapes instead of actual people. It's like waking up, briefly remembering a dream and then instantly forgetting it.

I try to think of the most recent thing in my memory. Gears turn slowly but there was a car, music, singing and then… I don't know. The river and Dad talking to me about sandwiches.

Using the trunk of a tree, I pull myself up and then wait for my head to stop spinning. I think about cleaning myself up in the public toilet block in the car park across the bridge, but it's not really a place I fancy visiting at any time of the day, let alone in the early hours. It's grim, dank and smells horrendously.

With little other option, I start walking home. It's only a mile or so, a route I've taken hundreds of times – though never in bare feet. Small stones scratch at the bottoms of my feet and I hobble awkwardly up the slope at the back of Westby Church. The clock on the tower reads a few minutes before half-past four and the distant horizon is beginning to burn orange.

I'm never sure when late officially becomes early.

The cobbles leave me oohing and aahing, with even the smoother edges tickling and scraping the soles of my feet. They lead me to the top of a small hill, which opens out onto the back of a new housing estate. Well, new in the sense that I remember when it used to be a field.

It feels like I should be in pain but I'm not. I'm cold and wrap my arms around my front, hugging myself.

There's not a soul out and about, nor a light lit inside any of the houses as I continue through the estate. From nowhere, I realise it's Sunday. It's a ridiculous time for a Sunday morning – *any* morning – and Westby is a ghost town.

After passing through an alleyway overgrown with hedges on either side, I find myself on the road where I live. It's wide, with detached houses and trimmed lawns on both sides. The type of place with neighbourhood watch signs in front windows, Britain in Bloom boards at either end of the street and an army of curtain-twitchers desperate for something – *anything* – to gossip about.

Luckily, given the time of the morning, I will not be a topic of discussion for my early hours walk of shame.

The spare front door key is hidden under the third plant pot out of the eight that sit underneath the bay window, so I retrieve it, unlock the front door, and then put it back where I found it. This isn't the first time I've crept into the house after midnight and probably won't be the last. Hopefully it'll be the only time I leave a trail of water on the welcome mat. That's something to deal with in the morning, either that or deny all knowledge. It's difficult to know if I'll be in trouble.

Mum will be in bed, so I stick to the edges of the stairs, where I know they won't creak, and tiptoe my way up to the landing. The bathroom door is slightly open but the doors to my brother's and mother's bedrooms are both closed.

The trickiest part of any late night/early morning sneak-in is the hop across the hallway. I swear the squeakiest part of the floor moves from one time to the next. One day it's in the centre of the floor, waiting eagerly to croak its annoyance when I put a foot out of place; the next, it's one step away from my bedroom door.

I gamble by walking across the landing as if it was the middle of the day. The floor goblins must be sleeping because there are no giveaway squeaks and I ease my bedroom door open before heading inside. Victory!

The curtains haven't been closed and the rising sun illuminates my room as if it is any other morning. The faded band posters are still fixed to the wall above my bed, my shoes still spill out from underneath, and my double wardrobe doors are open. The usual mix of clothes bomb and floordrobe have slopped onto the carpet. It's now after five and, though I should feel tired, I'm wide awake.

I'm still cold, though.

The clothes I was wearing form a sodden pile on the floor but when I turn to find something warm to put on, I catch a glimpse of myself in the mirror. My wet hair is matted into clumps and there's a slight graze on my ankle.

That's not what scares me, though.

There are dark marks around the top of my chest, not quite bruises but the type of bumps that might easily turn black or purple in a day or so. When I step closer to the glass and run my fingers over my dimpled skin, there is no pain… no anything, really, except the cold. The marks are small and rounded and it's only when I splay my hand across them that I realise they're fingermarks. Four oblong dents and a fatter thumb.

I'm transfixed until another uncontrollable shiver creeps up on me and I turn away, trying to remain quiet. After sputtering more water, I find my winter pyjamas in my bottom drawer – the fleecy ones with teddy bears that I tell myself I'm too old for.

I'm still shivering, so put on two pairs of socks and a thick jumper that was hanging in my wardrobe. There's a woollen bobble hat patterned with grinning monkeys at the back of my underwear drawer, so I bundle my hair underneath and put that on, too.

It feels like I'll never be warm, so I close the curtains and clamber into bed, tugging at the duvet and twisting back and forth until I'm cocooned within.

It's summer and I should be baking but I'm not. I should feel safe at home in my bed but I don't.

Something happened last night and no matter how hard I try to concentrate, it's all a foggy, confusing grey.

When I was young and couldn't get to sleep, Mum used to read me stories – then she'd tell me to close my eyes and rest. Eventually, I'd drop off. Even though I'm not tired, I shut my eyes and will sleep to come, hoping I'll wake with a clearer head. There's darkness but little warmth and then, in a flash, I'm back in the river. There's a hand on my chest, another on my head and I'm battling against the force pushing me down, trying to escape the liquid that's filling my lungs. I gulp for air but there's only water and I'm coughing, gasping, fighting... losing.

It hurts.

I can't breathe and the harder I try to give my body the oxygen it craves, the more water floods between my lips.

It scratches and claws. Nails raking my throat and then...

Then there's only black.

I sit up straight, kicking the covers aside, choking against the water that's no longer in my lungs. I'm twisting and flailing against an invisible enemy, scraping at unseen arms until I realise there's nobody there and I'm still alone in my bed.

The memories are still just out of reach but there are two things of which I'm certain. I didn't *fall* into the river – I was drowned in it and, somehow, despite the fact I'm still here, I died last night.

Chapter Two

Sleep is not my friend.

I eventually pad downstairs and plop myself on the sofa. My phone is still playing dead, much like me, I guess, so I flip open the laptop and start googling. The problem with searching for things like 'resurrection' and 'coming back from the dead' is that there are generally two types of results.

First is the religious websites, because we all know that famous dude whose name begins with a J that rose from the grave. I am many things, some good, some not – but I am most definitely *not* the daughter of any all-seeing, all-knowing, master of creation.

Second is the zombie stuff. There's the slow-moving undead, who flap around, go 'urrrrrgh' and try to eat people; then there's the fast-moving ones, who flap around, go 'urrrrrgh' and try to eat people. I have no desire to either eat anyone or go 'urrrrrgh', so I'm pretty sure I'm not a zombie either.

My searching gets me nowhere and I'm interrupted by Mum stretching her way into the living room. She yawns and it looks like her jaw might dislocate as tears stream from her eyes. She's barefooted but wearing her velvet-like dressing gown with the belt around the middle. It has comfort and warmth written all over it. After a second yawn, she does a double take when she sees me.

'Who are you – and what have you done with my daughter?' she says.

'Huh?'

She nods at the clock above the television. 'It's seven o'clock on a Sunday morning and you – whoever you might be – are awake and on my sofa. My daughter doesn't even know there are two seven o'clocks on Saturdays and Sundays. She'd be in bed until mid-afternoon.'

I close the laptop lid and put it to one side. 'Har-di-har. Who are you and where's my mum? There's suddenly a stand-up comedian in the house.'

She treads closer, fighting back another yawn. 'What's up?'

'Couldn't sleep.'

Mum leans forward and kisses me gently on the forehead. Her long dark hair has been fighting the grey for years but the battle is finally over. It was a stoic resistance but there was only ever going to be one winner. A strand brushes my nose as she pulls away. 'You're cold,' she says.

'I know.'

She frowns, doubling the wrinkles around her mouth, and presses a hand to my forehead. 'You're properly cold. I hope you're not coming down with something.'

'I feel all right, except for being a bit chilly.'

Mum stares at me for a few moments and then steps away, taken over by another yawn. Now she knows someone's watching, she covers her mouth. It's only when she moves backwards that I realise I've felt nothing of what just happened. Her hair didn't tickle my nose. Her hand was on my forehead and yet I felt… nothing. It was as if she wasn't there. I barely have time to consider that before she continues talking.

'What did you get up to last night?' she asks. 'I went to bed, so you must've been late back…?'

She asks casually but the fish for details couldn't be more obvious. There was a time when I had strict curfews and every minor infraction would be punished as harshly as if I was someone who'd escaped from prison.

Those were the days when we didn't get on.

Now, there's an uneasy truce in which I generally do as she asks but, every once in a while, she allows me the odd night off to be a teenager.

'This and that,' I reply. I'd probably not tell the entire truth even if I could remember. Parents have to be kept on their toes. If adults think their kids are angels, it'll only be a bigger disappointment when it turns out they're not. Better to set the bar somewhere in the middle and then surpass expectations.

'How did you get home?' she asks. 'Did Robbie give you a lift back?'

'Yep.'

'Good – you know I don't like you walking home in the dark, especially with everything that's going on around here.'

'I know, Mum. We've had this conversation.'

I give her my best huffed annoyance stare and she nods. 'I'm putting the kettle on. Do you want some tea?'

'Please.'

'Anything to eat?'

I have no appetite but it must've been hours since I last ate, so I nod and mutter something about toast. Mum offers a weak, consoling smile and then disappears into the kitchen. I'm still envious of the dressing gown.

When she's gone, I try pinching myself – first my neck and then my wrist. I can definitely feel something, although the skin on my wrist takes a second or two to slide back into position. There's no springiness, like there would usually be.

Hmmm…

Google offers little help. I try searching for 'cold skin' and 'feeling chilly' but it turns out I could have anything from a minor cold to full-on cancer. 'Unspringy skin' throws up the name of a grunge metal band, plus a bunch of adverts for menopausal women. Not much help. Considering the entire wealth of human knowledge is online, the Internet really can be incredibly unhelpful.

I delete the search history, wipe any cookies from the past ninety minutes, and then turn the laptop off. It's probably overkill but the last thing I want is my brother asking why I'm looking up stuff about life after death.

I walk through the kitchen and tell Mum I'll be right back, then head up to my room. My phone is on the dressing table but still won't do anything other than glare back at me with a blank, unforgiving screen. When I jab the sharp end of a hair clip into the SIM card slot, a sliver of water dribbles out and when I shake the phone, there's a gentle sloshing sound.

Our relationship has been fractious at best, peppered by over-zealous autocorrects (the phone), unfortunate incidents of being dropped (me), frequent instances of a dead battery (the phone), a broken camera flash (I'm blaming the phone), out of focus pictures (also the phone), and that time I swear I sent a message to Naomi, only to discover it was actually directed to my brother. Thankfully, there was nothing incriminating, but it was definitely, one hundred per cent, the phone's fault.

Despite our differences, I almost feel sad that our relationship has run its course. In all fairness, it was always likely to end in an instance of human-on-phone violence, but I never thought it'd be quite like this.

My wardrobe is something of a shrine to everything I've ever owned. Mum calls it hoarding but that's because she's always watching those TV channels packed with real-life documentaries with people who are super-skinny or super-fat. She saw one about this guy who has never thrown anything out and suddenly she's convinced I'm a hoarder just because I like keeping the boxes that go with things I've bought.

At the bottom of my wardrobe there are rows of pretty shoeboxes, each with their own memory of what I bought and where I bought it. Behind that are more boxes, including – luckily – the one from my old mobile phone. Inside is a charging cable, plug, manual and, thankfully, the phone itself. The screen is scraped and battered, plus there's a chip of plastic missing from the top left corner but, as soon as I insert the SIM card from my other phone and turn it on, the device pings to life.

Hoarding 1. Mother 0.

As the welcome message swirls, I remember why I hated the damned thing. It's slow to do anything and trying to type on the minuscule screen always left me feeling as if I had bloated whale thumbs.

Hoarding 1. Mother 1.

While the phone continues to do whatever it is it's doing, I head back downstairs. Mum's on her way up, still yawning as she tells me she's off to get ready for work but that there's tea and toast on the table.

If this is what being up for seven in the morning means, I could really get used to it.

By the time I get to the table, the old phone has finally woken up. It's bleating about not having much battery but then that was another of the reasons why it has spent the last year and a half in the bottom of my wardrobe instead of my pocket. It was *always* low on battery. It craved an electrical hook-up like a YouTuber craves attention.

I'm hoping for a flurry of messages that might help clear the haze of the previous evening but there's nothing. Literally nothing. My old conversations are lost to the river water and I'm left staring at a blank page as if I'm a friendless loser.

Hoping to cheer myself up, I bite into the toast – but the moment it touches my tongue, bile begins to build at the back of my throat. My stomach lurches, sending a noxious taste into my mouth that makes me want to be sick. I rush to the kitchen sink but the contractions give way to nothing but a pair of syrupy, rancid burps.

Back in the living room, I examine the toast, looking for flecks of mould, but it seems perfectly fine. When I smell the bread, it's as if there's nothing there. That's when I realise that the living room usually has an undercurrent to it. In the plug socket next to the kitchen door sits an air freshener, with a pool of yellow liquid in a glass bulb. The power is on but when I sit next to it, I can still smell nothing. It is only when I lie on my front and press my nose against the device that I can sense the merest hint of lemon.

I sit up again, resting my back against the wall, and peer back towards the table. I have no sense of taste and almost no sense of smell. When my mother touched my forehead, I felt nothing. I can hear and I can see – but only having two of five senses is a worry to say the least. Landslide elections can be won with forty per cent of the vote, yet my politics teacher claims forty per cent on an exam is a bad mark. Talk about a hypocrite. Other than that, forty per cent of anything is not a good result.

Anyway, the fact I'm calm about all this is almost more of a concern than my missing three senses. I should be freaking out, going crazy, panicking about what's wrong with me – and yet I'm not.

Instead, I have the steady, calm realisation that I died a few hours ago.

It's hard to explain how I'm so sure of this. It's like when a person is hungry. It isn't a conscious thought, it's a feeling. Nobody needs to be taught what it's like to be thirsty, they simply know.

That's how I'm aware of what's happened to me. Knowing that as a fact gives me a calmness I should not have.

When that's the morning you've had, anything after that has to be a bonus.

Chapter Three

If there was any question about the state of my hearing then it is immediately dispelled as my phone erupts into a symphony of beeps and vibrations. It's a message from Naomi, but nothing that could help decipher my confusion over what happened last night.

Dont 4get linner @ the deck. Pick u up @ 3

The time on the message reads a few minutes after midnight and, after reading it through twice, memories begin to stir. Linner is our word for a mixture of lunch and dinner. Brunch is a word, after all, so why not linner? Mum was right: often I sleep in until after lunch at the weekends and then, if we're organised and we can scrounge a lift, Naomi and I will head off somewhere for linner. I remember asking her to send me the message so that when I woke up in the morning – *this* morning – I'd remember our plans.

From nowhere, a handful of yesterday's memories splurge into my mind… primarily, shopping with Naomi.

Westby is a small village, in which a little old lady named Mrs Patchett runs the only clothes shop. Her fashion sense lies somewhere between going-to-church chic and lying in a casket for the rest of eternity. The shortest skirt she's ever stocked is something that looks like a tattered old curtain and tickles the ankles. Unsurprisingly, it's still unsold and in stock. Langham is the closest town, the place where we go to college, so there are at least a few places where people under the age of retirement are catered for.

Yesterday, Naomi and I caught the bus to Langham and then mooched from shop to shop, trying things on and generally not buying anything. It's basically free training for the salespeople to help a *potential* customer find stuff that fits, give an opinion on how it looks, and then watch that *non*-customer walk out the door. As I've said many times before, Naomi and I should be paid for our staff-training service.

That was late Saturday morning and early afternoon but after that, everything remains blurry.

Mum reappears in the living room, battling with the button on her jacket and rushing around. She brushes her hair quickly in the mirror next to the kitchen door and talks at me over her shoulder.

'Don't forget your Uncle Jim's coming over later to look at the ceiling fan,' she says.

'You really can stop calling him "Uncle" now. We know he's not our real uncle. It was kinda cute when we were kids but I'm seventeen now.'

She stops and turns to face me properly. I think she winks but she might have a blob of make-up in her eye. 'You'll always be my babies. Anyway, I'll call him and say you're up and about. He might come over earlier.'

'Okay.'

She looks at the toast on my plate. 'Are you eating that?'

The very thought brings the taste of bile to the back of my throat again. 'In a bit.'

'Good – make sure you look after yourself.'

'I will, Mum.'

'And don't let your brother sleep too late. Tell him he's got revision to get on with if he wants to go to university. You, too. Don't think I've forgotten that you've got exams as well…'

She's facing the mirror, so I roll my eyes without getting a huff in return.

'… Don't spend all day outside, especially if you're coming down with something. If you do go out, make sure you're either with someone, or you get a lift home. I don't want you out by yourself. Don't forget that Hitcher fellow people have seen around the village…'

Another eye-roll. There's always something.

'… And be nice to your brother.' Mum turns to face me this time, widening her eyes, letting me know she's serious. 'It's a year since… Sarah.' She lowers her voice at the name. 'Do some work, keep warm and…' She sighs and takes a breath, tugging at a strand of hair she's just straightened. 'Ellie…'

'What?'

'It's just… with me and Jim. You know you and your brother will always be my number one, don't you?'

She tilts her head and it's difficult to know what to say. I could be awkward, could roll my eyes again, but I'm not a complete cow. Deep down, I know what I should do. I smile gently and nod. 'I know, Mum. I love you, too.'

It's what she wanted to hear and she grins, holding my stare for a second, before it's all go again. She wrenches the brush through her hair a couple more times and then fumbles around in the kitchen for her keys, muttering under her breath. She can't find some form or another she needs for work and then hunts around the cabinet at the back of the living room, all the while talking to herself. After re-losing the keys and then finding them once more, she pokes her head around the door to say goodbye. She hustles along the hall, accidentally bashing her bag into the door, and then opens the catch with her teeth because both hands are full. Then she's finally gone.

Sarah.

How did I forget?

What happened to Sarah has been a shadow over our village for the past year. There hasn't been a day where I've not thought of her and yet, for some reason, she had completely slipped from my mind this morning until Mum mentioned her. Some of the things that happened before I awoke in the river are clear memories, others have disappeared and are only stirred when I get a jolt of a name or action.

I know the story but I'm not sure if I trust my memory completely. Google is again my friend and a search for 'Sarah Lipski' throws that iconic picture of her onto my screen. Her hair is long butter-blonde, with a gentle curl that loops over her shoulders. She's smiling for the picture-taker, her blue eyes bright and youthful, even though she's squinting slightly into the sun. Behind her, there's a blur of grass. To anyone else, it's an anonymous garden or a park but to those of us who knew her, it's the green at the front of Westby Church.

This image is the one that ended up all over the television news, the newspapers and the Internet. When most local people hear Sarah's name, this is the image they have of her.

In two days, it will be exactly a year since Sarah Lipski drowned in the River Westby. Her body was discovered a hundred metres or so along the bank from where I pulled myself out a few hours ago. She was a year older than me, the same age as my brother.

She was also his girlfriend.

As well as the photo of her smiling on the green, there are others of her with my brother. As soon as Sarah's body was found, people had gone trawling their social media trails, with the photographs splashed all over the papers and TV. Once they're out there, that's that. Suddenly these pictures that were only taken to amuse a handful of friends are now being pored over by strangers.

Ollie and Ellie. Ellie and Ollie.

There are only thirteen months in age between my brother and me. Much as I hate to admit it, we look ridiculously alike at times. Ollie's dark hair grew long through last year, curling around his ears and jutting out to the side. It worked for him but I thought about cutting mine short so that we didn't look so similar. In the end, after everything that happened with Sarah, he shaved his head anyway.

That's how I picture him now but these photos are reminders of a different time. I scroll through the ones of Sarah, stopping on those that include my brother. There is one of them at a Halloween party – him dressed as a vampire, her as a long-nosed, green-skinned witch. There is another of them on the beach – Ollie with his pasty white chest and thin covering of dark hairs, Sarah slim and tanned in a tied brown bikini. One more has them at some festival. They're both covered in mud, Sarah giving the V sign for peace, Ollie wearing a straw hat.

They're grinning in every photo, enjoying being young and in love.

After Sarah's body was found, the police looked to Ollie. It's always the husband or boyfriend, isn't it? They must've been arguing about something and he snapped. Did she want to break up with him? Had he caught her with someone else? Did they fight? Did he have a secret girlfriend on the side? Was it about money? Did they do drugs? Did he get angry if he'd been drinking?

Why did you do it, Oliver? Why? Why? Why?

The police questioned him for days, largely because he didn't have an alibi. They had been out in his car, barely two weeks after he'd passed his test. He'd dropped her off at her home and then, for a reason he could never explain, gone off for a drive. I mean, people go for drives all the time, don't they? I don't get it myself but then I can't drive. Anyway, the next thing anyone knows, Sarah's in the river.

There was no proof Ollie did anything, yet no proof he *didn't* do it. Being arrested is guilt enough in some people's eyes. Who needs a trial, a judge or a jury when someone *looks* like they might have done it?

In the end, he was released because the police had no evidence to keep him in. They never formally arrested anyone else, though, and because her killer is still unknown – still out there – Ollie has spent the past year living with those sideways glances and muttered under-the-breath remarks.

There goes the girlfriend-killer.

It's taken twelve months but people have gradually moved on. My brother went back to college and immersed himself in work and football.

As I stare at the image of Ollie and Sarah, what should have been obvious suddenly hits me. Sarah was drowned in the River Westby a year ago. Last night, it happened to me as well. If the same person was responsible for both attacks, then who is there that connects Sarah to me?

Who, except for Ollie?

Chapter Four

I continue staring at the photo because I'm not sure what else to do. Ollie and I were close when we were younger. With a little over a year between us, it was easier to play games with each other than it was to go out and find new friends. We'd run around and invent competitions in the garden, or on the yard at the back of my father's newsagent in the village. For a while, we were inseparable.

Things changed, though I suppose siblings usually drift apart once they become teenagers. Well, the normal ones do. I'm always suspicious of those grown-up brothers and sisters who claim to be best friends – or, worse still, mothers and fathers with their daughters and sons who go around telling everyone what great mates they are. It's too weird for words. Family and friends are *supposed* to be different – that's why they are different words.

We've had our niggles but, for the most part, Ollie and I have lived our own lives.

I turn away from the photos and try to come up with anyone else who might link Sarah to me. If I really think, there are plenty of people because she's only a year older than me. We lived in the same small village, went to the same school, shopped in the same places – and so on. But no matter how long and hard I think, I know nobody links us more directly than Ollie. She was his girlfriend and I'm his sister. How much closer can it get?

My memories might be sketchy but it can't be him who attacked us both. I know it can't. I've seen everything Ollie went through over the past year and it's hard to believe anyone could fake that grief.

If I'd been sleeping at home instead of at Naomi's the night Sarah died, I might have heard Ollie arrive back at the time he insists he did. I've thought a lot over these months about how much I wanted to give him an alibi but couldn't. Mum feels the same, too – not that she'd ever talk about it. She's such a heavy sleeper that it's long been a family joke that she'd doze through erupting volcanoes, meteor strikes and earth-quaking lightning storms. It was all very funny until the one time when Ollie could have done with her waking up as he got in.

Or perhaps he never got in at the time he told the police…?

'Shush.'

I'm talking to myself but it doesn't stop those dark thoughts from scratching away.

Not only that, I'm alone in the house with him.

With a shake of my head, I flip the laptop lid closed once more and then pick my cold toast up from the table. It goes in the kitchen bin, uneaten, and then I start searching through the cupboards. Above the counter-top is a biscuit barrel that we've had for as long as I can remember. There's a blueberry muffin at the bottom, the stump stale and hard, the top soft and squishy.

I have to press it to my nose to be able to smell even a hint of it. When I do, all I get is a sense of earth, of mud. It reminds me of an old PE kit that I accidentally left in my schoolbag one summer. By the start of the next term, it reeked of fusty, stinking dirt.

After returning the muffin, I try sniffing more things around the kitchen. Cookies, jam, a jar of Marmite, mustard, an apple, cheese from the fridge.

Everything smells the same – as if I'm lying face-down in a field, my nose to the ground. I nibble at the cheese but it tastes the same as the toast and again I feel sick. I end up spitting it into the sink and washing it away.

It tastes of nothing, smells of nothing – water is the only thing I can keep down. I drink a mugful and then a second, wondering if it'll be enough to keep me alive – or in whatever state I'm apparently in.

Before I leave the kitchen, I flick through the pile of paper and cardboard destined for the recycling. Mum always stacks these things next to the kitchen bin, largely to remind Ollie and myself to do the same. I pull out a copy of the *Westby Weekly News* and stare at the photo of the man on the front. The headline reads: 'VILLAGE ON ALERT OVER POST OFFICE BREAK-IN' – which is enough to send most of the residents into meltdown.

Westby is a place in which very little ever happens. If it weren't for the easy bus ride into Langham, it'd be a nightmare for anyone to grow up here. It's the type of place where people are born, live and die, while barely leaving a fifty-mile radius. A long journey is the hour it takes to get to the coast; the highlight of the year is the Medieval Street Fayre every July; a major talking point is whether the grass on the green near the church needs to be cut.

According to the newspaper – which Mum buys religiously every week, even though it's all on the Internet for free – someone smashed through a back window at the village post office last week. He or she didn't manage to steal anything, yet the break-in is enough to cause 'major alarm'.

There's a photo on the front page of a man with scruffy dark beard and moustache, plus hair to his shoulders. It's one of those police sketches that look like it's been drawn by someone who has never seen an actual human being.

This is the so-called 'Hitcher' Mum was talking about.

According to the report, he is so-named because someone saw a similar man thumbing a lift a mile or so outside the village last month. It might be the same man, it might not be. Either way, there's nothing in the story to specifically link this person to the break-in, or anything else as far as I can tell.

In truth, this sort of suspicion is reserved for anyone who looks a bit different, or turns up in Westby out of the blue. A few years ago, one of the girls in the village decided to start dressing as a goth and people would cross the road to avoid her. Not everyone, of course – but a single person is one too many.

As I scan through the Hitcher story, it doesn't take long to realise what nonsense it all is. The first witness is Mrs McKeith, one of the village gossips who owns the pharmacy. She blabbers on about seeing a suspicious man in the alley at the back of her shop – and that's it. She's probably been dining out on the story all week.

The second witness is no surprise, either.

Rebecca Watts is one of a trio of girls in my year at college who act like they run the place. That's partly because they do. The three of them all have long black hair, which is why they're collectively known as the Ravens. I'm not sure who came up with the nickname – it might even have been one of them – but they've had it since they were about fourteen.

When Sarah's body was discovered and the media came calling, everyone knew they were after someone vaguely attractive to stick on screen. Up stepped Rebecca the Raven. She sobbed for the cameras, her sixteen-year-old breasts hoiked up as if on a winch, lips pouting like they'd been pumped full of collagen… which they might have been.

I doubt she and Sarah had shared more than a dozen words with each other – but no one seemed to care and it's not as if any of the reporters checked. The Ravens crave attention and, after Rebecca's performance, she and Sarah had become best friends ripped apart by a dreadful crime.

Here she is now, having apparently seen the Hitcher on her way home from college. Her photo is on one of the inside pages of the paper and I think it's the same one they used throughout last summer – all tits, teeth and sucked-in stomach.

I read the story twice but am not sure what to think. It's so flimsy but perhaps it was this long-haired, bearded bloke who drowned me in the river? It wouldn't explain what happened to Sarah last summer, yet it's surely better to think that this mysterious loner could be a potential killer than it is to suspect my brother.

After returning the paper to the pile, I turn and find myself eyeing the cooker. It's wide and white, with a silver extractor fan at the top. The type of thing seen on some cooking show. Mum bought it brand new a few years ago as a Christmas present to herself and cleans it thoroughly at least twice a week. It's like therapy for her. There's rarely a time when it's not sparkling. She enjoys cooking.

Well, *enjoyed*.

The past year has taken its toll on her almost as much as Ollie.

Even with all my layers of clothing, I'm still cold, so I turn on the gas and click the ignition button. There's a gentle whoosh and then the ring of flame burns blue. I stare at it, watching the fire dance, but when I hold my palms near, I feel nothing. I turn the heat up to its hottest, making it flare higher, hearing it sizzle with energy, but still none of the warmth seeps into my fingers.

It is then that I feel like doing something stupid. My hands are practically in the flames anyway, so what would happen if I actually touched the fire? Will I be able to feel the heat? Will I burn? Can I be hurt?

If I'm dead but I'm not, then what am I?

The blue at the base of the flame licks into the orange at the top as the gas continues to hiss. I close my eyes and lean forward.

Chapter Five

The door handle behind me snaps down and Ollie appears in the room. I flick the stove off and turn to see him in a pair of boxer shorts, with a baggy T-shirt. He doesn't bother to stifle a yawn as he eyes me suspiciously.

'Why are you up?'

Perhaps he heard me up and about, maybe he checked my room – or Mum might have woken him earlier for some reason. Either way, there's no surprise that I'm here in front of him. If he *had* been the person holding me under the water a few hours ago, wouldn't he be more shocked by my miraculous reappearance?

Ollie cricks his neck and stretches his arms high. He's a little under six foot, seven inches taller than me, and his fingers scrape the ceiling.

When I don't answer, he nods at the stove. 'You cooking?'

I tell myself I never believed it was anything to do with Ollie anyway. 'I'll make you something if you want.'

He bobs on the balls of his feet and his eyes narrow. 'What's the catch?'

'No catch.'

'Then what do you want in return?'

'Eternal gratitude? The knowledge that I'm the greatest sister you could ever have?'

He peers around the kitchen, focusing on the back door, and then turns back to me. 'There must be something going on.'

'Nothing's going on!'

'Then why are you volunteering to make me breakfast?'

'Because I'm a nice person – and an amazing sister.'

His head tilts and then he starts to nod slowly. He doesn't seem convinced by how marvellous I am, by which I should probably be offended. Eventually he cracks into a small smile and rubs his hand across his shaven head. 'All right. I'll have beans on toast if it's going. Bit of brown sauce wouldn't go amiss, either.'

'All right – I'm not your slave.'

'You said—!' I grin at him and he stops mid-sentence. 'Thanks,' he adds.

'Don't get too used to it.'

At some point a couple of years ago, one of Mum's friends lent her a diet book that was packed with gory details about the evils of salt, sugar and pretty much anything that tastes good. Ever since, she's filled the cupboards with healthy things because she's convinced we'll all die a horrible, painful artery-clogged death otherwise. That's offset by the fact that she does occasionally give into the devil and buy things like blueberry muffins. I guess she figures the reduced salt and sugar in the baked beans she buys allows her the odd cake as a compromise.

I plop two slices of gluten-free bread under the grill – it always comes out better than when the toaster gets involved – and then empty a can of low-fat, lower-taste baked beans into a pan and turn the stove back on. Ollie is still in the doorway, leaning on the frame and tapping away on his phone.

I'm not sure I've ever made him breakfast, aside from tipping some cereal into a bowl, but it feels satisfying to be doing something normal.

Ollie doesn't look up from his phone when he next speaks. 'You look awful, by the way.'

'Thanks a lot. I'm cooking you breakfast, remember.'

He still doesn't look up. 'Why are you wearing so many clothes? It's boiling out – that's why I couldn't sleep.'

'I was cold. Mum reckons I'm coming down with something.' Ollie's eyes dart towards me and then his food. 'Don't worry,' I add. 'I'm not going to give you the plague.'

Ollie slips his phone into the waistband of his boxers and yawns again. 'What time did you get in?' he asks.

'After Mum had gone to bed.'

Not a lie.

He smirks. 'Tut tut.'

'You?'

'Early. After I saw you in Langham, I pretty much came home and didn't go back out.'

'What time was that?'

He shrugs. 'I saw you at about half-three, so after that. I don't know.'

The beans are smouldering, so I give them a stir and then flip the toast.

At Ollie's prompting, the events of yesterday are beginning to return. I'd gone shopping with Naomi in the morning and then we'd hung around in the main park in the centre of Langham. It's a sprawling mass of green, with a small boating lake at one end, a mini-golf course and a bandstand. There was some sort of fête going on and the sun was high and bright. There were lots of local stalls, with people selling jam, cakes and crafts. That's not really our thing – but we were perfectly happy to sit in the shade, tap away on our phones and quietly take the piss out of passers-by.

That's what you call a quality afternoon.

Not that I've ever understood that saying. When has anyone ever *literally* taken the piss? And why – and where – would they be taking it? Who's going around with tubs of their own piss ready for other people to take? And if people *are* going around giving away their piss, aren't they the winners in that situation? If a person is going to make fun of somebody else, wouldn't it be better to *give* them piss? That way, the subject of the joke ends up *with* the piss, while the person doing the laughing has *given away* the piss.

Anyway…

'I don't remember seeing you,' I reply.

Ollie shakes his head. 'You were with Naomi, heading off towards the lake with a large carrier bag and a bottle of…' He tilts his head again. 'I thought you'd stopped drinking…?'

'That cider was Naomi's.'

He shrugs, pretending he doesn't care. I know he does. I remember heading towards the water because Naomi wanted to cool her feet in the lake. She'd bought a bottle of cider in the offy close to the college that serves pretty much anyone, ID or no ID. I don't know what we did after that. It feels like a puzzle where I'm missing half the pieces. Every now and then, someone will give me more bits and I'm able to slot things together. I probably need to talk to Naomi.

I nod towards the living room. 'Mum says Jim's coming over to fix the ceiling fan.'

Ollie wafts his T-shirt. 'Good.'

We share a momentary look of mutual understanding. Neither of us is under any illusions about the nature of Jim's – *Uncle* Jim's – relationship with our mother. We've known him forever, even if it's only recently that things between him and Mum have, ahem, escalated.

With little else to talk about, I turf the toast onto a plate and then tip the beans over the top. I hand the plate to Ollie and then dump the dishes in the sink, saying he can clean up. As he disappears into the living room, I head upstairs to the bathroom.

When Ollie said I looked awful, he wasn't being mean – he was stating a fact. Under the bathroom's bright white light, the reflection of my skin in the mirror looks even greyer.

I wonder if the lifeless dull skin is worse than the sprinkle of angry red spots I used to get on my chin when I was thirteen or fourteen. The acne seemingly appeared every time I was nervous, which only made me more anxious, meaning I spent the best part of two years rubbing any number of 'miracle' lotions and creams into my skin. None of them worked and, in the end, the spots went away. I wonder if this drab colouring will disappear too.

My hair is naturally a slightly red shade of brown but now it looks faded. It feels crispy, as if I've sprayed too much hairspray and not brushed it out. The areas under my eyes are a purply-grey, making it look like I had a black eye a few weeks ago and it's only now healing. Changes in a person's appearance are usually so subtle that staring at a reflection day-to-day is not enough to notice the little things. It's only when looking back to old photographs – or even those taken a few months before – that differences become apparent. Faces become thinner or fatter, hairlines and styles change, clothes fit in different ways.

What's so shocking is how quickly my appearance has altered. From yesterday to today, my cheeks have sunken, my face has thinned. It looks like I've gone on one of those Hollywood crash diets of eating nothing but seaweed and rabbit poo, washed down with a glass of my own urine.

Maybe that's what happens with all these people giving and taking the piss!

After a dash to my room and back, I apply a few dabs of make-up to my cheeks and under my eyes, if only to give myself a bit of colour.

I try not to overdo it and, though I still don't look like myself, I'm just about passable. I definitely looked worse on the day I woke up hungover in Naomi's bathroom. I wet my hair and tie it into a ponytail. It still looks like I've slept in a skip but it's as good as it's going to get.

When I open the curtains in my room, I shrink away vampire-style from the beaming sun and vast blue sky. I should be warm but feel nothing but cold.

Even though I'm not massively organised when it comes to clothes, I do move things around based upon the seasons. It's not exactly winter, spring, summer and autumn; more hot and cold. All my cold-weather stuff has been shoved to the back of my wardrobe, so I have to hunt through piles of things I've not worn in months. I eventually settle on a thin but warm base layer, with a long-sleeved T-shirt over the top and a pair of shorts that are underneath tights and jeans. I'm going to look overdressed given the weather but it could be worse – the village goth used to wear a long black leather coat during the summer.

I text Naomi, saying I'll meet her at Tape Deck – or 'the Deck' as it's better known – and that there's no need to pick me up. After that, I grab a shoulder bag and then head downstairs. Ollie is sitting at the dining table, fork in one hand, phone in the other. His thumb is a blur as he types. He has devoured the majority of his breakfast and has orange baked-bean juice clinging to his chin.

'I'm going out,' I announce.

He peers up, though his thumb continues to tap the screen.

'Right.'

'Mum said to tell you to do some revision.'

'Whatever.'

He turns back to the remains of his breakfast but I know it's bravado. I cross to the table and rest a hand on his shoulder, squeezing gently. 'She also told me to be nice to you because of...'

For a moment, I think he's going to shoot back with something sarcastic but he slumps a little lower in his seat and puts his phone face down on the table. He sighs and wipes his chin, whispering a barely audible 'cheers' before he pulls away.

Chapter Six

Living in Westby can be dull at the best of times but during the long, dark winter months, it's no fun at all. Everything except for the main road through the village centre becomes covered in a layer of frost. Because there are so many trees, ancient stone walls and buildings, that ice can hang around for months. It's like living in a perpetual shadow.

I should be warm today. It's a beautiful morning, the type that brings the village to life. All those fields that are out of bounds during those frosty months are blooming, the trees are bright and green, and all the tiny, labyrinthine lanes and paths that weave around the houses are accessible once more. When I was younger, this was the time when Westby would become my playground. I could spend an entire day outside with no money and yet still find a way to amuse myself. Admittedly, a phone with unlimited data is much more fun but still…

I head towards the village centre, but take no particular path, sometimes doubling back on myself so I can remain out of the shade and in the sun. I'm still cold and have little feeling in my exposed fingers. An older woman walking her dog nods and smiles at me. I can't remember her name but nod back anyway.

There's a small play park next to the newest estate in the village. Kids are shrieking with glee on the swings, roundabout and climbing frame. The noisy little sods. I stop momentarily to pluck some blades of too-long grass that'll have the parish council up in arms, holding it to my nose, though there's no smell.

When I reach the village centre, I stop at the back of my father's old newsagent. At one point, when I was still a kid, it was one of Westby's focal points. It is sandwiched between a café and Mrs Patchett's clothes shop, with a cobbled pavement at the front.

One of my earliest memories is sitting on the floor inside, helping my father sort the magazine subscriptions. Villagers had their own cardboard folder in a pull-out cabinet behind the serving counter and I'd match the name on his list to that month's magazines and then file everything away. He gave me fifty pence a time for helping which, in retrospect, means I was royally stitched up. He should have been hauled away on child labour charges.

Not that it was about that: it was nice to spend some time with my father.

It was almost three years ago that he died, a little after turning fifty. His newsagent once sold a bit of everything but those types of places gradually went out of fashion, even in our small village. The shop went out of business a year or so before he died of heart disease. Mum maintains he died of a broken heart having run the place for thirty-odd years – but, well, I don't know… is that even a thing? I think she was more heartbroken than he was about the shop. She was the one who used to rant about chains and big companies muscling in. Dad simply shrugged and said that was life.

Honestly? I think he was right. He was right about a lot of stuff. Starbucks announces it's moving in, the weekly paper goes into crisis mode, villagers reckon it's the end of all humanity – then, six weeks after it opens, they're all in there sipping skinny lattes and marvelling at the breadth of the menu. Wondering why it took so long for a national coffee shop chain to move in. It happened with the Tesco Express, too.

Residents were off down the High Street with placards, marching and protesting as if living here is worse than some war-torn African state. They were talking about boycotts, chaining themselves to railings and whatnot. The moment it went up, they were in there buying lottery scratch cards and pints of milk.

I think some of the people from around here – particularly those who've been here the longest – live for that drama. When Sarah died a year ago, it was like Christmas for them.

My father's shop was bought by a developer who started to convert it into flats before running out of money. If I'm honest, despite ridiculing other people who live here, I feel a twinge of sadness whenever I see the building in the sad state it currently lies. The front doesn't look too bad – except that the windows and doors are filled with wooden boards. It's a far cry from the toys my dad used to display.

I head past the shop and follow the main route towards Langham. It's three or four miles from Westby, along a road that quickly becomes surrounded by tall hedges and overgrown trees. Buses run every hour but, on a day like this, it's a pleasant walk. Before what happened to Sarah, village kids would think nothing of mooching through the lanes and fields to Langham and then catching a bus back later. There are all sorts of trails along the river and through the nearby woods but I've barely used them since Sarah's body was found.

Suddenly, today, I'm filled with a strange sense of invulnerability. What's the worst that can happen to me now? I've already been drowned once and I'm still here.

I've not been much of an explorer in the recent past but, at the moment, I'm looking for something – anything – that might spark my senses. I developed very mild hay fever a few years ago but the cut grass on the side of a farmer's field does nothing today. Sunshine dapples through the trees on the edge of the woods, creating a wonderful show of light and dark – but it feels like I'm a girl in a painting. It's there, it's beautiful – yet it's only in two dimensions. There's no smell, no texture, no taste.

When I check the time on my phone, I realise I've somehow used up the morning and so I head back towards the main road and follow it towards Langham.

The cafés in Westby tend to be vintage-style tourist traps, with dainty cups that come with saucers. I'm not sure when or why saucers were the in thing – but I've pretty much resolved that the places that use them are not for me.

Tape Deck is a café/diner/hangout on the side of the road halfway between Westby and Langham. Despite being a bus ride or up to an hour's walk away, it's long been the main spot for teenagers from both places to hang around.

Except for a pair of people carriers close to the main doors, the car park is empty when I walk onto it. Tape Deck is a single-storey building that was once a petrol station. Whoever owns it built an extension and then painted everything in the style of an American diner – or what I assume is an American diner. I've only ever seen them on TV or in movies. The towering light-up board at the front that used to display the price of fuel now lists each week's food specials. Today's is apparently a corned beef hash burger with sweet potato fries, which sounds amazing until I remember that trying to eat makes me gag.

After eyeing the board with a sigh, I head through the double doors, passing rows of Formica tables that are bolted to the floor. Two families are sitting at the front, chomping through burgers and fries. Four girls, four boys, two sets of parents in perfect symmetry.

The counter is at the far end of the restaurant, with a wide board across the top displaying the menu. Off to the side is my favourite reason for coming here – rows and rows of audio tapes in their cases, the colourful sleeves pointing outwards. They're stacked fifty or sixty high in long rows that run most of the length of the wall. Because whoever runs this place must have a severe case of OCD, everything is in alphabetical order, with 10CC – whoever they are – in the bottom left at one end, and ZZ Top – whoever they are – in the top right at the other. Underneath the tapes is a sign reading: 'RIP Sony Walkman: 1979–2010'.

In truth, I had no idea what a cassette tape was before I started coming here. Neither, I suspect, did many of the customers. When I once told this to Mum, she frowned and muttered something about 'kids today'.

Tape Deck only plays music from the time in which cassettes were mass-produced, meaning I've discovered all sorts of bands and singers I would never have found otherwise. I love the colours, too. The wall is a mosaic of rectangular shapes and shades. Naomi and I can spend ages slouching in one of the side booths running through the names of the artists and then looking them up on Spotify.

There's no sign of Naomi, so I head to the counter and scan the menu, thinking about the things I wish I could eat. Before I can say anything, the lad at the till stammers something at me I don't catch. When I turn to him, he is staring straight at me, eyes expectantly wide. He has black hair that is parted dodgily to the side, with a slim peppering of dandruff. He's leaning slightly at an angle.

'You want the usual?' he asks.

I have no memory of what 'the usual' might be but it seems as if he knows me. I have a vague inkling that I know him too – or at least that he's some sort of acquaintance. He's looking slightly over my shoulder, afraid of making eye contact. Behind him, there's a slight chatter from the kitchen.

'Sounds good,' I nod. 'Can I have some water, too?'

I pay and he hands me a bottle of water, then stares at his feet while he tells me my food will be right out. I'm still not sure what I've ordered but I'm going to try to eat something again.

After sliding into one of the booths next to the wall of tapes, I take out my phone just as a familiar blue Vauxhall pulls into the car park. One of the back-wheel hubs is missing and there's a crusty shaving of rust on the front door. It feels like someone's ringing a bell in my ear as my mind goes into overdrive, putting the pieces together.

A young man steps out of the driver's seat. He has spiky dark hair and is wearing sunglasses, with a football shirt, loose shorts and flip-flops. Mum asked if Robbie gave me a lift home and I said yes. I wasn't sure but didn't want to argue. This is Robbie and the Vauxhall is his car.

I know the girl who gets out of the other side – Naomi. She's my age and we've been friends for, well… ever. She's one of those girls whom everyone would instantly think was some blonde Barbie princess if she could be bothered. As it is, she's wearing a retro gaming T-shirt with a picture of a Gameboy on the front, plus knee-high stripy socks, Converse and denim shorts. She has thick-rimmed glasses and pigtails, with a Hello Kitty satchel angled across her chest. When she sees me in the window, she waves and starts to skip across the car park. Robbie towers over her but when he notices me, he stops on the spot and frowns. He scratches his head before catching himself, realising he's being watched, and then follows Naomi, hands in his pockets, making quick glances in my direction.

When she gets inside, Naomi slips into the booth across from me. She's smiling, full of fun and games. Robbie stands with his palms pressed on the end of the table, staring at the tapes on the wall behind us and saying nothing.

Naomi peers up at him and then shrugs. 'Have you two fallen out?' I look at Robbie and he looks at me – then it suddenly dawns a moment before Naomi explains herself. 'I mean, you are still going out, aren't you?'

Robbie's my… *boyfriend*. How did I forget? The moment Naomi mentions it, those memories of him and me flood into my brain. Of course he is. He's still giving me a strange look, though. His eyes are narrow, his brows dipping and meeting in the middle. Before I can move, he leans forward sharply and pecks me on the forehead, then slides in next to me.

Naomi doesn't seem to have noticed anything untoward. She twirls one of her pigtails, eyeing the rack of tapes on the wall. 'Why'd you walk?' she asks.

'Thought I'd try to clear my head.'

She nods. 'Fair enough. Ben's not here, by the way. He's got to work on his parents' farm today because he was out yesterday. His dad's on one *again*.'

Ben… Naomi's boyfriend. I have the full picture now. Naomi and Ben; Robbie and me.

'What happened to you last night?' she continues. 'The last I saw, you and Rob were driving away.'

I turn to Robbie, but he's only half looking at me as he peers out the window. So Mum was right – he *did* drive me home. Was he the last person to see me before I ended up in the river?

I nudge him with my elbow. 'What happened last night?'

He shrugs. 'Not much, we—'

'All right,' Naomi interrupts. 'I don't need to know the gory details.'

Before she can say anything else, the lad from the counter approaches with a tray of food. He glances quickly at Naomi and then looks away again, before sliding the tray across while not looking me in the eye.

'Do you want your usuals?' he asks.

'Yes for me,' Naomi replies.

Robbie pats his stomach and grimaces. 'Just some water.'

The server risks a momentary look at me but instantly spins away when he realises I'm watching him. I notice his name tag this time – 'ASH'.

'He *so* fancies you,' Naomi says as she pinches a piece of chicken from my tray. My 'usual' is apparently some sort of chicken salad with chunky croutons. Looking at it makes me feel sick, so I sip my bottle of water instead.

'Who?' I reply.

'That Ash guy – the server. He's always staring at you when he thinks you're looking the other way.'

'He doesn't fancy me.'

'Robbie?'

Naomi turns to him but his attention is still out the window.

'Huh?' he replies.

She waves a dismissive hand towards him, says to forget it and then points at my tray. 'You not eating?'

I start poking at the salad with a fork, lifting a shred of lettuce part way to my mouth and then lowering it. 'I'm not that hungry.'

Naomi steals another bit of chicken as I rotate the food around, giving the impression that I might be eating some. When nobody's looking, I slide small amounts into napkins, which I ball up at my side. If I were one, it'd be textbook anorexic behaviour.

Without warning, Robbie stands, clutching his stomach. 'I've gotta go to the toilet,' he says, before dashing towards the back of the restaurant. In the momentary silence, I dispatch a pair of croutons into a napkin, unseen by Naomi.

'What's up with him?' she asks.

'I have no idea.'

'Did you argue last night? He was quiet when he picked me up and he's being weird now.'

I try to act casually, as if I haven't noticed how guiltily he's behaving. My memory is such a sieve that I don't want to jump to conclusions – but he was apparently the last person to see me and now he can barely look at me. Is that how someone would behave if they'd literally seen a ghost?

Naomi sits up slightly straighter as she nods over my shoulder. She speaks while barely moving her lips. 'Don't look now – but the Ravens of Doom have just walked in.'

I don't need to turn because three girls idle along on the far side of the restaurant and then stand next to a booth diagonally across from us.

Rebecca Watts is in the building.

She has her pair of sidekicks with her, too. Her long black hair has been combed perfectly straight and she has a fringe that rests in line with her flawless eyebrows. When she notices Naomi and me, she moves towards us, the other two at her side.

'Aren't you warm in all that?' she asks, dripping with disdain as she nods at my clothes. 'Is it two-for-one in Oxfam again?' She has one eyebrow cocked, a talonic nail angled in my direction.

The names of the other two swirl into my mind as they giggle girlishly. Rachel definitely dyes her hair to match Rebecca's colour, while Rochelle, who has creamy dark skin, is probably natural. They all have matching fringes, not to mention designer bags hooped over their shoulders, identical red nails, ludicrous heels given the weather and venue, plus colour-coordinated summer dresses. Rebecca is in red, of course, because she needs to stand out the most. Rachel's in blue and Rochelle is in white. Together, they could be a human tricolour.

I roll my eyes towards her and shrug. 'What's it to you? Tired of being Sarah's best friend, so you started making up bearded men to get in the paper?'

Rebecca glances quickly towards the families at the back, making sure nobody is listening in. She lowers her voice to a hiss. 'I *did* see the Hitcher, *actually*. He could've abducted me. He could be a rapist. Just because you'd have to *pay* someone to shag you, doesn't mean you have to be jealous.'

Rochelle, who lives across the road from me, oohs as Rachel wags a finger. I can sense Naomi ready to leap into battle, so I reply quickly. 'Sorry, are you talking to me, or menstruating on the floor?'

I nod at Rebecca's feet and she glances down quickly at the clean surface, before fixing me with a ferocious stare. She spits her response: 'At least I'm not a rhino-faced slut with a murdering psycho for a brother.'

She doesn't wait for a comeback, pirouetting on her heels and stomping off towards the counter, wicked witches at her side.

When they've gone, Naomi snorts into her hand. 'That was a bit harsh,' she says, trying to keep a straight face.

'Me or her?'

'Kinda both…'

That's hard to deny. Although my memory is patchy, Rebecca and I do not get on. Part of that is because of the social standing that Naomi and I had at school and now have at college.

The Ravens are part of the cool crowd that generally run the place and whose lives will peak between the ages and sixteen and eighteen. They might not know it, but this is as popular as they will ever be.

At the other end of the scale is the computer lot, who will end up making millions and managing the very people who currently make their lives miserable.

Somewhere in the middle of all that is Naomi and me. We sort of… exist, which is fine. Aside from Rebecca, because of the way she treats everyone else, I hold no grudges. In a year's time, I'll be doing my exams and then I'll be getting on with the rest of my life. In a few years, I won't even remember most of these people. Strangely, I do remember a time when Rebecca and I were, well… friends. I was sitting next to her in a maths class when we were twelve. She started her period and I had to take her to the nurse. Now it's the one thing I have to throw in her face when she acts like a cow. Not literally. Whether that makes me any better than her someone else can decide.

Naomi is drumming her fingers on the table. 'So, er… why *are* you wearing so many clothes?'

'I was cold. Anyway – last night. I don't remember much.'

It's not the smoothest of segues, but Naomi goes with it.

'I didn't realise you'd been drinking. Were you really that bad? Perhaps someone spiked you? Remember that Karen girl last year? She reckoned she'd been spiked but I heard she was putting it on to try to get sympathy from that Jason guy. Anyway, what do you remember?'

Naomi has spoken so quickly that it takes me a moment to figure out what she's asked. 'I remember being in the park with you in Langham. You had that bottle of cider.'

'That's all? You must've been proper out of it. You don't remember Helen's party? Her mum and dad are on holiday, they're due back today, so we went over for a barbecue and pool party. Well, paddling pool. Big paddling pool. Still a pool, though.'

At the mention of Helen's name, I know who she is. She's been in our year throughout school and now college. We've never been great mates but nod to each other and say hello. There's that stat about ninety per cent of human interaction being non-verbal but I reckon at least half is nodding and saying, 'hello' or 'all right'.

Naomi has her phone out and is flicking through the images. She turns it around to show me a photo of someone bombing into the paddling pool, then thumbs the screen sideways to bring up a second image. Robbie's on the corner of a sofa and I'm on his lap, sipping a can of fizzy Vimto. We're both grinning, gazing into each other's eyes, but I have no memory of it happening.

'Was this last night?' I ask.

'You don't remember?'

'Not all of it…'

The Ravens clump down on a booth across the aisle from us and I feel the death stares punching through the air.

Robbie returns moments later, hunched over us, palms again on the table. He seemingly can't look at me as he gazes through the window towards his car. 'I'm really not feeling well,' he says. 'I'm going home. Are you all right to get the bus back?'

I shrug but Naomi says it's fine. Robbie frowns at me once more, then pecks me on the top of the head before heading outside. We watch him go and then Naomi leans in, whispering so the Ravens cannot overhear.

'He's acting weird,' she says. 'What *did* you get up to last night?'

Chapter Seven

Naomi doesn't seem convinced when I tell her that I'm not sure why Robbie's acting strangely. When her food arrives, she lets it go, polishing off her salad and then mine. When we're done, we ignore the Ravens and head outside. It's Naomi's idea to walk home, so we do, following one of the trails back to the village. Naomi talks a lot, largely about how we only have two more weeks of college before we go on leave for our end-of-year exams. She wants to know what I'm going to be up to for the rest of the summer, saying her mum wants her to get a job. When I know what to say, I reply properly. I fudge it when I don't.

Before long, we're passing the 'Welcome to Westby' sign and then we're at the bridge that crosses the river.

I stop, peering down at the water. In the daylight, it seems clearer than I remember from the previous night. A pair of adult ducks is next to the bridge, quacking away as a small fleet of ducklings glide past. There is no one around except us, though a low chatter of giddy children carries on the breeze.

Naomi is at my side, leaning over the bridge and watching the baby ducks. 'It's a year since Sarah, isn't it…?'

'Yeah.'

She turns, hoisting herself up so that she's sitting on the low wall, facing away from the water. I join her and neither of us speaks for a minute or so. I knew Sarah through Ollie – and Naomi knew her through me. It's tenuous but that doesn't take away from the impact when someone who is in a person's life most days is suddenly not there any longer.

'We should do something,' Naomi says.

'Like what?'

'I dunno. They're doing that candlelight thing in a couple of days, but that's not Sarah, is it? Imagine if you died – how would you want people to remember you: some solemn candle thing, or a proper blowout?'

I open my mouth to answer and then remember the water in my mouth, my nostrils, not being able to breathe. It feels too close to think about.

'Sorry,' Naomi adds, 'I didn't mean—'

'It's okay, I know what you were saying.'

'So… we should do something to remember her by. Perhaps ask your brother?'

'I don't think he'd be interested. Some people still think he might've… well, y'know…'

Naomi hums in reply. 'I'll talk to a few people and see if we can think of an idea. It's the longest day tomorrow, so we can probably come up with something.'

She swings her legs and then kicks off from the wall, landing on her feet. One of her socks has slipped down to her ankle, so she hoists it up and turns towards the village centre. She lives on one side of the bridge, I live on the other.

'I've gotta get going,' she says. 'Mum and Dad are having a family barbecue and I'm not allowed to miss it. Not if I want some peace, anyway. Dad'll go bonkers if I'm late.' She nods aimlessly towards the village. 'You all right by yourself? I dunno if Rebecca made it up but everyone's going on about that Hitcher bloke.'

She glances to the water below and I know she's thinking of Sarah.

'I'll be fine,' I reply.

'See you at college, then.'

It had escaped me that I'm supposed to be at college tomorrow. It feels so strange after the way I woke up this morning.

'See you there,' I say.

She starts to walk away and then stops, turning to face me again. She tugs on one of her pigtails and then presses her lips tight before speaking. 'Are you and Robbie going to make up?'

'I didn't know we'd fallen out.'

'There's something going on between you. You should fix it – he'll be off to uni in September and then, well… I dunno.'

I smile thinly back at her and say I'll talk to him, then she turns and heads off along the towpath, not looking back.

Robbie's a year older than us, and Naomi is right. In a few months, he'll be escaping the village and we'll still be here. My thoughts are so jumbled that I don't know what to think. Naomi told me to fix it, but I don't know what to fix. Robbie's the one who was looking at me strangely and then rushed away from Tape Deck. What did I do? More importantly, what happened last night?

The adult ducks waddle away after the little 'uns, leaving me by myself on the bridge. I stare down towards the river and, for a moment, it feels as if everything that happened was a dream. The water in my mouth and nose, the barefooted walk home, that sense of someone's hands on my chest and head, pushing me under. Then I spot the dirty trail up the side of the riverbank from where I hauled myself out of the water.

I pass across the bridge and edge around the bank until I'm overlooking the spot where I climbed up. There's a rounded splurge of flattened earth from where I sat halfway up, trying to figure out where I was and what was happening. I tell myself the patch of land isn't *that* big because my arse isn't *that* big.

Before I know what I'm doing, I'm a third of the way down towards the water. I can see the imprints of my hands in the muck, plus a deeper pool where my heel mushed into the ground. The lower I go, the wetter the earth, until I'm level with my arse print. As I continue, my foot slips and I need to cling onto a clump of roots to stop myself tumbling feet-first into the river. I stop and take a breath, peering towards the water. Now I'm lower, it seems to be moving quicker, babbling and jabbering away from the village.

Without thinking, I take off my shoes and multiple socks, then I remove my tops and jeans until I'm wearing only a pair of shorts and long-sleeved base layer. I tread carefully closer to the water until I'm low enough to dip my toe in. I'm already cold but the water is colder. I'm shivering, knees touching awkwardly as my feet bow out. I force myself to continue waddling penguin-style into the water. The riverbed is soft, with slivers of grit and who knows what else digging into my feet. Still I continue moving as the water comes over my ankles, my knees. When it touches the bottom of my thighs, I stop. The current isn't strong but I'm not a great swimmer – ironic, huh? – and I'm not that tall or heavy either. After dragging myself out of this river, it'd be pretty stupid to find myself struggling in the water again.

I stand with my legs wide enough that I have as firm a base as I'm going to manage and then close my eyes. At first all I can see is darkness but then I can taste the water again, feel those hands on me. My head's whirling and I'm spinning, falling, choking… except that I'm not. When I open my eyes, I've not moved. I'm still standing near the middle of the river, staring towards the bridge.

The water has a slight silty brown hint to it but I can still see most of the way through it towards the bottom. There are stones and twigs, plus probably less savoury things, such as glass. I've been stupid in wading out and yet I was drawn to the spot. Lured, perhaps.

Crouching slightly, I embrace the flow of the river, leaning against it for balance. I squint through the water trying to look for my shoes from last night. I know I was wearing a silver, strappy pair of flats when I was out with Naomi, yet they weren't on my feet when I came to my senses. They could have been washed downstream, or they might be somewhere around me on the riverbed. It's not the shoes *specifically* I'm concerned about, more that they might hold a clue as to what happened.

I step sideways like a crab, still pressing against the flow for balance, then keep moving until the water level starts to lower. There is no sign of my shoes, no sign of anything other than the type of muck that'd be expected on the bottom of a river. When the water dips below my knees, I turn and start side-stepping towards the opposite bank, where my clothes are.

I'm a little past the deepest part when my foot snags on something. At first I think it's an old piece of string or rope, perhaps some sort of seaweed – or is it named riverweed? I take a few more steps and then lift my leg, balancing on the other until I hook the object from my big toe. It's soaking wet, making the leather heavy, but it's undoubtedly a bracelet of some sort. The moment I clasp it in my hand, I feel the water in my mouth once more, the panic beginning to rise – only this time I have a clear vision of a person's hand holding my head under the river.

His or her fingers are splayed wide across my forehead, thumb on one temple, little finger on the other. I'm being pushed down deeper as I reach up and claw at the person. The only thing I manage to snag is something tied to their wrist. I tug as hard as I can, trying to free myself, but it's no good. All I manage to do is yank the bracelet from their wrist before my fingers loosen and the small leather strap floats to the bottom of the river.

Chapter Eight

I stare at the bracelet, knowing it belonged to whoever drowned me. There are three interwoven strands of light brown leather plaited together, with intermittent knots every centimetre or so. There are no particular identifying marks – no logos or initials – and it is plain enough that it could belong to a man or a woman. I trace my finger across the rougher underside and then try to smell it, but it gives me no clues. I have no idea to whom it might belong, although it's hard to know anything for sure seeing as my memory's got that whole Swiss cheese vibe going on.

From what I remember, it doesn't seem like the type of thing Robbie might own. He's into sports, specifically football, and doesn't wear any jewellery. I'm not sure about Ollie. He went through a phase of wearing beaded necklaces and bracelets a couple of years ago when he thought it looked cool. He must've cleaned his mirror at some point because he stopped going out with them and I've not seen them since. Thankfully.

'Ell…?'

At the sound of my name, I turn and look up to the bridge. There's a lad with sandy short hair and a mucky palm that he's using to wave at me. This is Ben, Naomi's boyfriend.

'Why are you in the river?' he calls.

'There was, er, a duck struggling and I, um… helped it.'

Even with no time to think, it's a woefully poor effort at an excuse.

'A duck?'

'Yeah, it, er, swam off in the end.' I nod towards the other side of the bridge where the adult ducks and ducklings are swimming in circles. He looks over his shoulder towards them and then back to me.

'Do you need a hand to get out?'

He doesn't wait for an answer, moving to the side of the bank where my clothes are and edging down carefully. A couple walk past hand-in-hand, slowing as they get level with me. They're nearing retirement age but still look fit and agile in hiking boots and slim softshells. I don't recognise them, so they're likely some of the tourists that pass through at the weekends in the summer months.

'Do you two need a hand?' the man asks, turning from Ben to me.

Ben hesitates but I'm already wading towards the bank. 'Just cooling off,' I say – which is a far better excuse than some nonsense about rescuing ducks. The man offers a cheery wave and then continues along the path with his wife.

As soon as I clamber out of the water, the chill hits me worse than before.

'You're shivering, Ell,' Ben says.

He slips down the bank until he is on the edge of the river. He spins in a circle, muttering something about a coat – even though he doesn't have one and it's warm.

I wrap my arms around myself, stuttering 'I know' before he steps closer and pulls me in for a hug that does nothing to warm me and only gets him wet. I push him away and then brush the worst of the water from my legs and wring out the liquid from the bottom of my top. Ben watches as I start to dress myself, putting on layer after layer until the only things left are my shoes. As I hold them in one hand, Ben reaches down and pulls me up by the other. He has a hand on my lower back, guiding me back to the top, where I sit on the path and put on my shoes. It's a little squelchy but at least I didn't cut myself on any of the rubbish at the bottom of the river.

Ben sits next to me and scratches his head. 'What was all that about?' he asks.

'I told you, there was a duck and—'

'I thought you were with Naomi and Rob?'

'I was. We were at the Deck but Robbie wasn't feeling well, so he drove home – then we walked back. Naomi has a family thing, so here I am.' I pause for breath and then add: 'I thought you were working today?'

'I am – Dad's got me helping out rebuilding one of the barns but Mum's trying to do some baking for the shop and she's run out of sugar. She sent me out to pick some up.' His excuse sounds more made up than mine until he points to a bag of sugar on the path next to him. He nods across the bridge. 'C'mon, the farm's only five minutes away. Let's go get you a towel.'

We cross the bridge once more, looping around the car park and then following a narrow lane. Barely a minute later, the trees begin to cast a darker shadow, almost growing into one another as they create a tunnel of threaded branches. We head through an easily missable gap in the bushes onto a gravel-strewn path, where the tall hedgerows quickly give way to a low verge, before opening into a vast expanse of green, brown and yellow.

Ben remains a step or two ahead, walking quickly and not making small talk. There is a steady *scrunch-scrunch-scrunch* of our footsteps until we reach an open metal gate that would normally stretch across a wide driveway. There's a circular blue sign to the side that reads 'Fairbanks Farm & Shop', with a painting of a sheep underneath.

The driveway leads to a courtyard peppered with dried mud. A pair of huge barns is directly ahead, with a large two-storey house off to the side. Ben leads me along a cobbled path that rings a pristine garden until we reach a small cottage, when he fumbles in his pocket for a key. He unlocks the door and holds it open, then says he'll be right back.

As he heads towards the main house, sugar in hand, I enter the bungalow. This is where Ben lives – a separate guesthouse on his parents' property. Unsurprisingly, it has made him both enormously popular and *un*popular at college. Anyone who knows him thinks it's the greatest thing going, everyone else thinks it makes him a pretentious little rich boy.

The front door opens into a combined living room and kitchen, with a breakfast bar separating the two. There is a bowl of fresh fruit on the counter and I open the cupboards to find shelves stocked with tinned and packaged food. The fridge is chocked with soft-drink cans, salad items, cheese – and all sorts of other things that look like they've been put there by Ben's mum. It certainly doesn't shout that the place is occupied by a teenager.

I sit on one of the high stools next to the counter and wait for Ben to return. When he does, he throws me a towel and then disappears once more, saying he'll be back in a moment.

There's a mirror on the wall, so I untie my hair and rub it hard, then comb it with my fingers, trying to get the knots out. I take off my shoes and towel my feet, then I rub underneath my layers, trying to dry off as best I can. None of it stops me feeling cold.

Five minutes later and Ben hasn't returned, so I do a lap of the living room, looking at the pictures and paintings until I arrive at a window that overlooks acres of fields at the back of the farm. On the sill are three photographs in identical frames.

The first shows Ben and Naomi, dressed up ahead of our school's formal dance. Ben's in a kilt with black tails; Naomi is wearing an emerald dress that stretches to the floor. They somehow manage to look both young and old at the same time, the flawless skin and optimistic gazes mixed with outfits that no one under the age of about fifty should have to wear.

The next photo has Ben, Robbie, Naomi and myself on a beach. It was the first trip we went on after Robbie passed his driving test. I remember sitting in the back seat with Naomi, singing at the top of our voices with the windows down and music up.

The last is the four of us with our cheeks smushed together. It was taken at Langham's Party In The Park a year ago, the weekend before Sarah died. It was a glorious day and we spent the afternoon listening to bands and then having a picnic on the edge of the lake. Naomi took the photo on her phone, stretching her arm as far as she could, but still managing to crop out the right side of her face.

'Can you believe that was only a year ago?'

Ben's voice makes me jump so badly that I almost drop the picture. He is only a few steps behind me, apparently moving with the silent stealth of a ninja.

I glance to the photo once more and then back up.

'It seems like it was ages ago.'

He nods and takes the photo from me, looking at it with a gentle smile and then returning it to the windowsill and lining the three pictures up.

'Do you remember that girl in the pink wellies? She didn't want to get them dirty and every time we saw her, she was wiping them down.'

I'd forgotten until he mentioned it but now the stranger burns brightly. She was all blonde extensions, long nails and pink, pink, pink. Mud was not her thing and we spent the day following her around and trying to take photos without her noticing.

Ben grins, taking a step towards me. He's close enough that I can see the peppering of stubble on his chin as his eyes burn through me.

It feels as if I'm unable to move my feet, unable to escape his gaze. It is blue and bright, fixed only on me.

'What?' I say.

'Sorry for not texting. I didn't know if I should.'

I have no idea what he's talking about, so shrug. 'It's okay.'

'Really?'

'Of course.'

He moves so quickly that I don't have time to step away. His hand is cupping my chin and cheek, lips pressing hard into mine. It takes me a second to realise what is happening and then I pull away.

'What are you doing?' I gasp.

'Huh?'

'You're going out with Naomi. I'm with Robbie…'

He raises a single eyebrow. 'Yeah, but after last night, I thought…'

Ben tails off and I can't stop myself from blurting out a 'what?'.

His features fold into a frown, forehead creasing. 'We were in Helen's parents' bedroom. It was late and—'

I hold a hand up to stop him because the memory is suddenly as vivid as if it was happening now.

Oh, no.

Chapter Nine

Ben's fingers cup my chin as he delicately lifts my face until our lips are pressing together. His other hand is in my hair, tracing a path that leads to the base of my neck, which makes me shiver. I'm not pulling away, not trying to stop him. Instead, I'm pushing back into him, one hand on the bottom of his back, other on his side. He kisses me… no, we kiss each other. It feels good, gentler than it is with Robbie. His lips trace their way down to my neck and then I'm clutching him tighter, chin resting on his shoulder. The digital clock reads 10:42.

I blink myself back into Ben's cottage, memory brimming with guilt from the previous evening. We were upstairs in Helen's house, in her parents' bedroom having blocked the door with a clothes hamper. In the background, the house party was ongoing with the undercurrent of music and teenage chatter, plus the wafting smell of barbecue. Naomi was slumped in the swing chair that hangs from a tree in Helen's garden, having had too much to drink. We left her there and headed inside.

Ben is staring at me, waiting for me to say something. I can only manage a weak: 'We kissed.' Fact, not a question.

His eyes narrow and he takes half a step away from me. 'You don't regret it, do you? I mean, I don't think it's the time to tell Naomi, but…'

'We didn't…?'

His eyes narrow and for the tiniest fraction of a second I want to run. We couldn't have done…

'You know we didn't,' he says. 'You *do* remember last night, don't you? I didn't think you were drinking...?'

I nod quickly. Too quickly. 'What about Robbie?'

It's more something I'm saying to myself – 'how could I do this to him' – but Ben nods slowly, misunderstanding the meaning. He thinks I'm saying we should tell Robbie about the kiss. Robbie is a year older than us all, taller with a thicker build. I know precisely what Ben's thinking – that if the conversation with Robbie ever happens, he doesn't want any part of it.

'Robbie will be off to uni in September,' Ben says. 'We both know that. He knows it, too. He only needs three Bs and he'll get that easily.'

'That'll still leave you me and Naomi.'

Ben turns away, staring out the window towards the fields. 'You didn't tell him, did you?' he asks.

'Tell who?'

'Robbie. When you left in his car last night, I thought, just for a minute, that...' He stops, clucking his tongue and then starts again. 'I know it was a big rush because we heard those police sirens at half-eleven. Everyone left outside was being noisy and we assumed one of the neighbours must've called. Someone said that the Old Bill were coming in from Langham and we all scattered. The last I saw, you were rushing down the path towards Robbie's car. You looked at me and you were, well... *scared*.' He whispers the final word, still not looking at me.

'I was scared?'

'That's what it looked like.'

'Scared of Robbie?'

He shrugs. 'I don't know. Perhaps it was the sirens? Your mum's bloke is the only police in Westby, so I thought maybe you were worried about him being one of the cops. Later, when I was home, I couldn't stop thinking about how wide your eyes were when you were heading to Robbie's car. Then I had the thought that you were going to tell him on the ride home.'

'Tell him about me and you?'

Another shrug: 'I suppose.' A pause. 'Did you?'

I try to think but there's nothing after being in the bedroom with Ben. I don't remember the sirens, nor leaving the party. I have no memory of being in Robbie's car, let alone knowing what we talked about. It's like knowing the word for something but not being able to say it. The information sits on the edge of my memory but I can't get to it.

'I didn't tell him,' I say. I'm not sure why I lie, or, I suppose, it might not be a lie at all. Perhaps I did – and that's why Robbie was acting so strangely at the Deck.

Ben sighs and nods. He's relieved – but I'm more confused than ever. Is this the person I am? A cheat? Someone who betrays my friends? I've been going out with Robbie for eighteen months or so and all the memories burn brightly. We've been happy together and I've grown up so much since we started seeing one another. Naomi's been my friend forever and yet I've broken both their trusts. And for what? Ben's nice enough – but I only know him as Naomi's boyfriend. We get on, we laugh and joke, we give the piss to people, we go places as a foursome – but that's it. Kissing him last night was a terrible, awful mistake compounded by the fact that I have no idea why I did it.

Then it dawns on me that I've been thinking about *who* held me under the water and not *why* they might have done it. The act by itself is brutal – yet he or she must have had a reason. Now I'm discovering that there are lists of people who could have reason to despise me.

It's not a nice feeling.

Ben must see a change in me because he reaches out. I step away, shaking my head.

'Not today.'

He stares, arm dangling between us until he rests it by his side. 'Probably for the best, I suppose.' He pauses, biting his lip. 'How are we going to do this?'

'Do what?'

'Tell Naomi and Robbie? I know yesterday was the first time and it was just a kiss but if we're going to take things further—'

'Further?'

'We've both felt it between us. We can't carry on behind their backs.'

I cross back to the breakfast bar and sit on the stool, re-tying my shoes. 'I've got to go. We'll talk about this another time.'

'Right…' He takes a deep breath and then adds: 'I suppose I'll see you at college tomorrow?'

I turn and head for the door. 'Yeah – see you at college.'

Chapter Ten

When I push through the front door at home, a pair of voices abruptly stops their conversation. Mum is in the kitchen, leaning on the counter sipping a cup of tea. It's a little after seven but still bright outside. I'm not sure where the day's gone. Much of it feels like a dream. On the other side of the kitchen is Jim – *Uncle* Jim.

He's one of those men who is somehow both noticeable and forgettable at the same time. He stands and walks with a seemingly constant crick in his neck because he's so tall. He dresses in a way that's not quite fashionable, yet not granddad-style either. Today, it's baggy navy blue board shorts that he would have been able to pull off if it wasn't for the leather belt he's using to hold them up. He's sitting on a wooden chair with his knees crossed in the way that I'm not sure men should be able to manage. He's lean and sporty, yet he wears cardigans in the winter.

Everything about him is a contradiction that should make him stand out. Despite all that, he has one of those faces that's easy to overlook. If I wasn't looking directly at him, I'm not sure I'd be able to describe what he's like. There's dark hair, a few wrinkles, some glasses that he doesn't always wear… and that's it. He's been Uncle Jim for as long as I can remember.

As I enter the kitchen, I nod at Jim and then turn to Mum. The playful hello from this morning has seemingly been forgotten as she glares at me before carefully placing her mug in the sink.

I know what's coming.

'There you are,' she says.

'Here I am.'

I'm not trying to sound like a smart-arse but that's the way it comes out.

'I thought you were feeling ill?'

'I was.'

'I thought I told you to get some work done, not spend all day out and about. You were out all day yesterday, too.' She's about to launch into something else when she takes a moment to look at me properly. 'Why are you covered in filth? Where have you been?'

The bottoms of my jeans are covered in the mud from the riverbank.

'I was in the village,' I say. 'Nowhere special.'

'But you walked home by yourself? You're seventeen years old, Eleanor...'

Mum carries on, banging on about the Hitcher, the post office break-in, some nonsense about it 'not being safe nowadays' – and the usual lecture. I stand and listen, well, pretend to.

I know roughly how much trouble I'm in by how much of my name she uses. 'Ell' means we're on good, friendly terms. Perhaps it's Christmas and she's full of seasonal spirit, or I've had some sort of brain trauma and cleaned up around the house. Every now and then, I do things like that.

'Ellie' is the next step up, or down depending on a person's point of view. That's for general use when she wants me. I would say that roughly ninety per cent of interactions involve her calling me Ellie.

'Eleanor' means she's quite annoyed. Luckily, me being out all day and not doing anything I was supposed to hasn't taken me beyond the 'Eleanor' stage. It's the midway point of the scale, so I've not done badly.

'Eleanor Louise' means some serious shit has gone down. The last time I got that was when Naomi and I went to a gig in Langham. I told her I was staying at Naomi's; Naomi told her parents she was staying at mine. Everything was going fine until Naomi's mum called our house because Naomi had forgotten her asthma inhaler. Our mothers put two and two together and unfortunately came up with four. Because we were at a gig, I'd not heard my phone going off and it was only at quarter past eleven that I realised I had thirty-three missed calls.

Yes, thirty-three.

That got me the full 'I've not raised you to act like this, Eleanor Louise' treatment.

Beyond all of that, however, is the blow-a-gasket, steam-out-of-ears, coronary-inducing 'Eleanor Louise Parker'. I've only pushed her that far once, when I first got drunk at the fully matured – in my mind – age of fourteen. That obviously sounds bad – and it is – but, in my defence…

Well… okay, I don't have much of a defence.

Naomi and I had gone through the cabinets in her parents' house when they were out, we'd found some bottles of strawberry-flavoured vodka, one thing led to another, and I was given the complete 'Eleanor Louise Parker' dressing down and grounded for three weeks. Mum even told me she 'wasn't annoyed, just disappointed' – which would have had a lot more impact if she hadn't spent fifteen minutes shouting at me, therefore proving she was most definitely annoyed. Since then, I've not eaten a strawberry and, truth be told, I'm pretty sure they're the fruit of the devil.

Anyway, we're at the Eleanor stage and I'm not completely sure how long I've been standing and listening to mum go on.

'… you're still my responsibility, Eleanor, and you still live under my roof. While that's the case, it's down to me to make sure you live up to your responsibilities…'

I need to breathe but I'm afraid it'll seem like I'm in some sort of huff, so I continue to hold my breath. Mum has a hand on her hip and is getting louder.

'… you've got important exams coming up, young lady. You have the rest of your life to go out with friends. The rest of the summer for that matter. I keep you on a very loose leash and—'

'*Leash?*'

My reply is out before I even realise I've given it. It erupts as a shout, more because I'd been holding my breath than anything else.

From nowhere, the frustration and emotion of the day is with me and I'm furious. I step forward, pointing, no longer leaning and listening. 'You keep *dogs* on a leash, Mum. Not people – and not me. I'm your daughter.'

She stares at me, before nodding a fraction. 'You know what I mean, Eleanor. This isn't about a slip of the tongue, this is about—'

'Oh, shut up.'

'Don't you tell me to—'

'I just did.' I turn my back and step towards the stairs.

'We're not done here, Eleanor.' A pause. 'Eleanor!' A shorter pause. '*Ellie!*'

She continues to call my name but I don't turn until I'm on the bottom step. She's out of the kitchen following me, her voice fully raised to a shout now.

'Don't you turn your back on me,' she yells.

'Why? What are you going to do?'

'Don't talk to me like that. I'm your mother and this is my house. You—'

I have no idea what comes over me but I dig down deep and wrench up the one thing I know will hurt her more than anything. I'm burning with shame from my own actions, of what I did with Ben, of the pain

I could cause my best friend and boyfriend, of frustration at not being able to remember what happened last night. It all fires out in a single, hateful sentence.

'Your house? *Yours?!* This is only *your* house because Dad died and the insurance company paid up.'

There's a terrible silence as we stare at each other. It's too late to back down now so I match her gaze. She peers away first, gulping away what is probably a tear but I can't help myself.

'What?' I spit. 'You know it's true.'

Mum takes a step back towards the kitchen and speaks over her shoulder. 'I think you should go to your room.'

'Is that with or without my leash?'

She doesn't reply, leaving me standing on the stairs having won the argument. What a victory, huh? We Are the Champions. We can be heroes.

When I get to my room I slam the door, but it's more in annoyance at myself. I slide down it, sitting with my knees to my chest, and bury my face in my jeans. They smell of mud, of the river. I want to cry but it doesn't feel like there are any tears in me, as if whatever happened in the river last night has washed away the parts that made me who I am.

I should apologise but it'd mean backing down and admitting Mum was right in the first place about me being out for the entire weekend. I know she *is* right – but letting her know that, well… I just can't. I suppose being dead doesn't stop someone from being a complete bitch.

Chapter Eleven

Sometimes, there's nothing quite like having a good cry to make things better. Well, *feel* better at least. It took me a while to realise that messing something up is simply one of those things.

Because of whatever happened, I can't even enjoy that luxury. The more I want to release my upset and anger, the more I *get* upset and angry that I cannot. I have no tears, so I end up slapping the walls hard, then harder still. It doesn't hurt anyway.

When the rational part of my brain finally takes hold, I find myself staring at the bracelet I fished from the river. It is almost certainly handmade, the type of thing found on market stalls and craft fairs all over. I trace my fingers over the slightly rough plaited leather but it stirs no memories of who might own it. It looks like the type of thing somebody around my age would wear. Adults wear silver, gold or nothing at all – unless they're some sort of hippie-type stuck in the 1960s. This is the type of jewellery someone would pick up for a few pounds, or make themselves.

Eventually I put the bracelet into my drawer, hiding it underneath my underwear, before deciding I don't want to part with it. I think about putting it on my wrist but that seems wrong, too – so I return it to my pocket instead.

That's when it occurs to me that Naomi might have given me a clue. She was scanning through last night's photographs on her phone, so perhaps there are hints there? By now, many of my friends, not to mention friends of friends, will have plastered photos of Helen's party all over the Internet. If I'm going to piece together things I've forgotten, it has to be a good place to start.

My proper phone is still dead, along with any photos I took. Although the old one is slower than an arthritic tortoise, I get onto the Internet and start browsing.

I begin by looking at pictures in which I've been tagged. There are selfies that I've taken and uploaded long ago, plus photos taken by other people. Every time I click a new one, a memory springs forward of who it was taken with and where we were. There's Naomi and me in our old school uniform, our white shirts signed by all our classmates on the final day of term. Because she was in my year, I even asked Rebecca the Raven to sign it. She wrote 'from one bitch to another' on mine, while I simply wrote my name on hers. In the photo, Naomi and I have our arms around each other. We're grinning, each holding onto the other tightly as if we're inseparable conjoined twins.

Knowing what I've done, it hurts to look at it.

The next picture has us in fancy dress last Halloween. She's Harley Quinn from *Batman* and I'm a female Robin. It was her idea and Robbie went dressed as cool all-in-black low-talking Batman, while Ben's there as cheesy 1960s Adam West Batman. There are photos of us by ourselves, in couples, and then all together as a foursome. Everyone seems so happy, which only makes me want to cry again because it's a time to which we can't return.

I keep clicking until I reach last New Year's Eve. There was a large college party that had miraculously been given the go-ahead to happen on campus. In various pictures, I'm sticking my tongue out at the camera, grinning, giving a thumbs up, frowning, pretending I'm not looking even though I know my photo's being taken, hiding behind a glass – which doesn't work because it's transparent. I'm surrounded by faces I recognise. Friends and acquaintances – people in my year and the one above. I zoom in as far as I can, trying to look at people's wrists, wondering if anyone will be wearing the bracelet. There's either nothing to see, or the photos are too blurry to tell.

Once I'm done looking at pictures with me, I move onto Robbie. I can't get past the way he looked at me from the car park of Tape Deck – the confusion and surprise that I was there. He said he wasn't feeling well, which was perhaps true, but what's going to make a person feel worse than drowning someone one night and then finding them at lunch to following day?

Could it really be him?

Did he snap after I told him about what happened between Ben and me?

There are so many photos of us together that it starts to become overwhelming. In almost every one, our arms are around each other, or we're holding hands.

In one, we're feeding each other a forkful of cake that we bought at a little bakery on the seafront last summer. It was snapped a fraction of a second after he lifted his fork deliberately too high and smeared cream across my nose. He's laughing and so am I. I'm entranced by it because it seems surreal, like something that happened to somebody else. A dream.

Another has us sitting underneath a tree staring at one another and talking. Naomi took it when neither of us knew she was there. There's no posing, no playing it up. It's as natural a picture as could have been taken and – even though I know I'm biased – it's a beautiful photo. Two people holding hands under a tree, staring into each other's eyes and simply talking. That's love, isn't it? I love him and he loves me.

I have to click past it because it's starting to upset me. Soon I'm bashing the screen of my phone, trying to move as quickly as I can from picture to picture. There are hundreds of Robbie to get through, but he's wearing a leather bracelet in none of them. Before long, I'm ashamed for even suspecting he could have done something to hurt me.

When I'm finished with his pictures, I search specifically for albums from last night. There are hundreds of pictures, uploaded and tagged by names and faces I recognise. It seems like a typical night: sixteen-, seventeen- and eighteen-year-olds taking over a house and garden: eating, drinking and having fun. People are pulling faces, grinning, laughing, flicking Vs, giving the piss, downing bottles of beer, huddling around the barbecue and arguing over who's cooking what. At one point, someone set up a game of Twister on the back lawn and half a dozen people from my year are busy winding themselves around one another.

Every now and then, there's a photo containing me. In one, I'm sitting on Robbie's lap in the corner of the garden, my arms wrapped round his neck. He's saying something to me and I'm smiling. We have eyes only for each other.

There are at least a dozen with Naomi and me lounging in the garden, then more when the skies are dimmer of us dancing while people cheer us on in the background. In the last one, she has a bottle of Bud and I'm drinking a can of Diet Coke. I'm in the red skirt and strappy top I was wearing when I woke up in the river.

Some of the memories are clear – like being with Robbie in the garden – others feel alien, such as dancing with Naomi, as if someone has stolen my body and inserted me into these situations.

Perhaps my biggest surprise about last night is that the Ravens are there. Rebecca and her crew usually only attend parties and events organised by them, or where they don't have to slip down the social scale and end up associating with people like me. They are a fixture at the end-of-season sporting formals, plus things like the Christmas Ball. Anything that allows them to dress up and thrust their youthful femininity – sometimes literally – into grown-ups' faces. Rebecca, Rachel and Rochelle are in only a handful of photos, all taken inside Helen's house. They're in the living room, leaning close and whispering about whomever it is they have it in for at that particular time. With their designer gear and expensive tastes, I can't imagine any of them wearing something as simple as a cheap leather bracelet.

I continue through the hundreds of photos but there's little to see other than standard pictures of people enjoying themselves.

Click-click-click.

It is only when I reach a photo of someone about to jump into Helen's pool when I spot something. In the foreground is one of the college's rugby team, belly bared, gorilla-esque chest hair on show. I swipe past it at first, before returning because, in the background, largely out of focus, is me in my red skirt. I'm standing next to the back door, leaning in slightly, single finger pointing angrily. The other person is largely hidden behind the rugby player but it looks like it's a man in a blue top with jeans. I have no memory of the event but it's clear I'm angry. It might even be that, instead of pointing, I'm snatching my hand away. There is a clock clearly visible through the open door and it reads 21:31 – so this happened before I ended up in a bedroom with Ben.

I flick back through the photos, looking for someone wearing a blue top with jeans. It's easy to discount people, including both Ben and Robbie, because they're in shorts. Almost everyone has bare arms and legs exposed to the point that after flicking through at least a couple of hundred photos, I've not found the person with whom I was arguing. I move faster and faster until, finally, there's an image of a couple sitting on the living room sofa, entwined in one another. It's a mass of arms and legs but, off to the side, almost out of shot, is the young man in the blue top and jeans.

I recognise him instantly. I've seen him today, spoken to him, and yet he never hinted at the fact we'd argued the previous night.

I download both photos and then swipe between them, the first showing him next to the couple, the second showing me angrily pulling away from him. It's unquestionably the same person: the weird-looking server from Tape Deck.

Ash.

Chapter Twelve

I've always been something of a list person. I don't think it's even the making of the list that's so satisfying, it's the ticking off that comes when something's done. When I was younger, I'd write down all the homework I had to do and then cross everything off bit by bit as I did it.

Needless to say, that got old pretty quickly.

I still made lists, though – like which clothes to wear on certain days. It feels a bit weird now. Insignificant.

Despite that, no matter what's happened to me, there's always time for a good list. I have a purple Moleskine journal hidden under my mattress that Naomi gave me a couple of Christmases ago. At first, I wanted to use it as a diary but then I started to forget and, before long, it was hopelessly outdated. Ever since, I've used it for writing my lists and the odd doodle. On the cover, I've written my name with a Sharpie in balloon-like letters, with a large exclamation mark at the end.

The first list I write pieces together where I was on Saturday.

3.30pm: Langham Fete with Naomi
?: Westby. Helen's party
9.30: Argue(?) with Ash
10.42: Helen's parents' bedroom
11:30(ish): Police sirens
?: Robbie giving a lift home

4.30(ish): River
5:12am: Home

I can't bring myself to write 'with Ben' after the 10.42 entry. The second list is more brutal – a list of people who might have held me under the water. Some have bigger reasons than others.

Robbie, Naomi, Ben, Ollie, Ash.

It's my boyfriend, best friend, best friend's boyfriend, brother – everyone I'm close to – then some weird guy from the diner.

What a list.

Even though I'm not sure he exists, I write 'Hitcher' as the final entry. I really want to start crossing off names but don't feel as if I can rule anyone out yet.

As I'm trying to think if there's anyone else who could be added – Rebecca the Raven? – there is a knock on my door. I push the journal back under my mattress and then sit on my bed cross-legged and grab a random book from the shelf. It's some nonsense about a girl trying to escape a castle.

'Who is it?' I call.

'It's Jim. Can I come in?'

'Free country.'

The door clicks open and Jim ducks under the frame before turning to me. His glasses are on top of his head and his shorts too high. His legs are peppered with spindly grey hairs, knees knobbly and jutting at odd angles. When he folds his arms across his chest, his elbows stick out too. He's like a grasshopper whose limbs elongate back on themselves. I know it sounds harsh because he's always been there for Ollie and me, especially since Dad died. There for Mum, too, of course.

I do like him, I just find him odd.

Before he can say anything, I get in first. 'I'm not saying sorry.'

Jim waits at the end of my bed. 'Is that why you think I'm here?'

'Isn't it?'

For a moment, I think he's going to perch on the edge of my bed but he's simply stretching his legs. 'I'm not your father, Ellie. I never will be and I'm not trying to be. But I was his friend and I knew him since we were nippers. After your father... *passed*, well... I know Zoe... your mother and I have been, um, hanging out for a while now and—'

I can't hold back any longer and snort in laughter. He stops talking, forehead creasing as he peers down at me. 'Sorry,' I say, stifling myself. 'It's the way you said "hanging out". It sounds like you've been *hanging out* by the swings, with a sneaky bottle of cider.'

He smiles a little, unfolding his arms. 'I suppose I didn't know how to put it. Much of this is new to me. I've never had children myself.'

I shrug. 'I'm seventeen, not seven. You don't need to treat me like a kid.'

He nods. 'A fair point. Can we forget I said it?'

I give a non-committal nod of my own. In truth, I spent years believing Jim was gay. He was my dad's friend but never had a girlfriend or wife. I suppose he never had a boyfriend, either. I'd made assumptions. When Mum told Ollie and me that she and Jim had starting 'seeing each other', we were both surprised.

Jim motions to sit again but still doesn't. He rests on the bedpost at the bottom of my bed, re-folding his arms. 'I guess the reason I'm here is that I want to make sure everything is all right with you. I know what happened downstairs was out of character. Yes, your mother and I, er, "hang out"' – he makes bunny ears – 'but I'm also the village's sole police officer. If anything's going on, whatever you tell me is confidential. I don't have to share anything with your mother if that's what you want.'

Before I realise I'm doing it, I'm biting my bottom lip. What am I supposed to say? *I'm pretty sure I died last night and I think someone close to me is responsible?* I could tell him that I woke up in the river, but, by itself, that doesn't mean a crime has been committed – it just makes me look careless.

'Why do you think something's going on?' I ask.

He stares at me and it feels like he's a police officer, not a family friend. His eyes are grey and unflinching. It only takes a moment and I have to look away, knowing that, if he stared at me much longer, I'd blurt it out.

'You tell me,' he replies. 'Your mother says you were ill this morning, yet you've been out all day and come back looking like you slept in a ditch. It's all a bit—'

'Do I look that bad?'

He stops and finally looks away. 'Those aren't my words.'

I tug at my hair self-consciously. When I got into the house, Mum was probably as much worried by the state of me as she was annoyed that I'd been out all day.

'I'm okay,' I say softly.

'Are you sure?'

'Yes.'

'Well, if you ever want to have a chat, we can do that. There's a lot going on at the moment with this so-called Hitcher around the village, plus the post office break-in. You know how things get in a place like this. The locals lose their minds when kids play music a bit too loudly.'

He's watching me again and I think of the fact the police were called to Helen's house on Saturday evening. She lives on the edge of the village with only a handful of houses in the surrounding area. Jim likely knows I was there, because why wouldn't I have been?

'The reports this week,' he adds. 'Strange men hanging around is like Armageddon to some people, especially after what happened last year to young Sarah.'

There's a slight croak as he speaks her name and I feel a twinge of sorrow for him. He's a one-man band policing a small village and surrounding area that doesn't really need policing. He works by himself in a tiny 'station' in the village centre. When Sarah's body turned up, CID cops piled in from the wider area. They spent weeks poking around and interviewing everyone – especially my brother – yet arrested nobody. When they departed, Jim was left by himself trying to answer unanswerable questions about who killed Sarah. He's spent a year walking around with 'failure' written all over him.

'Do you think there's some dangerous bloke hanging around?' I ask.

Jim puffs out a large breath. 'I don't know. The village is surrounded by woods and remote farms. With the decent weather, someone could be living in the open – and popping into the village to get up to whatever – but it's just as likely our friend at the pharmacy saw someone she didn't know and got the wrong end of the stick. Once one person speaks out about this sort of thing, there's always someone else who might or might not have spotted someone similar. Then it's on the front page of the paper, so more people start racking their brains, wondering if they've seen anything untoward. It's certainly bad timing seeing as all this coincides with someone breaking into the post office. You know the way people think around here – when something bad happens, they'd rather blame it on an outsider than believe trouble can come from within.'

He takes a small step back towards the door. 'I don't mean to impose, I just wanted to say that I'm around if you need to talk. You should be able to find me.'

'Okay.'

Jim hovers awkwardly, stepping between the bed and the door, not quite sure what to do next. When I don't add anything, he almost trips over himself, then heads for the door. Once he's closed it behind him, I wait until his footsteps have retreated down the stairs and then put my book to one side and retrieve the journal.

I reread the list of where I was yesterday. From the moment I left Helen's party with Robbie to the time I woke up in the river, there are five hours in which I have no idea what happened. I need to ask Robbie what went on – but the niggling feeling persists that, if he did have anything to do with me ending up in the river, he'd have no reason to tell the truth.

MONDAY

Chapter Thirteen

I don't leave my room for the rest of the evening and spend much of it reading my pair of lists over and over, hoping something will trigger a memory of Saturday night.

Nothing does.

As it gets past eleven o'clock, there is shuffling on the landing as Mum heads to bed. I can only hear one set of footsteps and it doesn't sound as if Jim is staying the night. Sometimes I've heard him whispering a goodbye in the early hours of the morning before slipping away – but it's not the sort of thing I'd ask Mum about, nor something she'd likely want to talk over. I'm not even sure I want to know. She's never gone off on one about Robbie being my boyfriend, so no particular double standards. There was the one time when she wanted to have a sit-down conversation about 'protection' and the like but, well… let's just say that in a list of people with whom I'd want to have that talk, she wouldn't make the top five.

Actually, perhaps I *should* write that list.

Or not.

By half eleven, I'm expecting to feel tired. The last time I know I slept was on Friday evening… or Saturday morning to be precise. I stayed up WhatsApping Naomi until two in the morning, then dozed off, before getting up to meet her. That's a full day and a half or so since I was asleep. I should be shattered and, in some ways, I am. My mind feels sluggish and the bedroom light stings my eyes. It's more weariness than something that'd send me to sleep – like hitting snooze for the fourth time.

After midnight passes, I figure I have to do something, so lie on my side and close my eyes. That lasts for approximately five seconds before it feels as if I'm drowning again. There's one hand on my chest, another on my forehead. I'm grabbing at the person's wrist and then… I'm back on my bed, sitting rigidly upright and gasping.

I spend the next few hours trying to amuse myself. I read some of my book but can't get into it; then I skim my journal and check to see if Naomi has read her messages. Every hour or so, I'll close my eyes again – but the outcome is always the same: water, hands, coughing, fear. Whenever I find myself scrambling for breath, I'm riddled by panic. I'm actually scared, which is a strange feeling.

Watching horror movies can be frightening, so can the dark, or the noises the old pipes in this house make at night. They used to keep me awake when I didn't realise what the sounds were. I was convinced there were monsters coming for me. This is a different type of fear – I'm not scared of something that *could* happen, I'm terrified of what already *has* happened.

Eventually, I resolve that sleeping isn't a good idea. I hug my knees to my chest and wedge myself into the corner of the room, wrapping the duvet around me. It feels like the most basic parts of what it is to be normal have been taken from me. I can't sleep, can't cry, can't eat… I've not even been to the toilet since waking in the river. These are the tiny things most people wouldn't even think twice about, yet they're so easy to notice now I'm no longer capable of doing them.

Feeling sorry for myself, I drop the duvet and stand in front of the mirror. I try to examine my hairline and look at the marks on my chest – but the light isn't strong enough. Creeping around lightly isn't necessary given the way Ollie's snoring echoes around the landing but I tiptoe to the bathroom anyway.

In the mirror, my face looks paler than before. Perhaps more worryingly, I am able to pinch the skin underneath my chin. It feels rubbery and loose, plus it takes a second or two to spring back into place.

When I remove my various tops, the marks on my chest are still there, still shaped like fingers. They've neither darkened, nor faded. They're simply there. I'm shivering but strip to my underwear, crouching to smooth the skin on my legs. They're starting to peel, with long strips of snake-like crust crisping away from the rest of me. I sit in horror next to the bath as I pick and prod at the flaking skin, continuing until I can find no more flaps to pull. There are a few scraps on my arms but they're nowhere near as rough as my legs. The small pile of skin on the floor looks like a baking experiment gone badly wrong, a thought that makes me smile momentarily until I remember it's come from me.

The cabinet next to the mirror is littered with various medicines and lotions. I try rubbing a small dollop of moisturiser into my leg but all it does is mix with the dry skin to create a gritty, grim paste. My skin seemingly will not absorb it. I soon give up and dab it away with toilet roll.

I am literally falling apart.

Is this what death is? Am I in some sort of weird afterlife where everything continues as normal, except for me?

For a minute or so, I sit on the floor wondering what I should do. When the answer comes to me, it feels so obvious. There's little point in sitting and moping over the things I can no longer do, I should embrace what I can for however long I have left. It doesn't seem real that I can live with neither food nor sleep, but then waking up with a lungful of water and still being alive isn't normal either. If I can find out what happened, perhaps I will discover a way to cure whatever's wrong with me.

I unlock and head through the bathroom door – then clatter straight into my Mum. She wobbles and bounces off the wall before straightening herself, while I almost fall down the stairs in an attempt to steady myself. She's wearing a thin dressing gown, the cord drawn tightly across her waist. Her hair is down but it looks like she's undergone electroshock therapy.

She says my name as she steps around me and then reaches out her arms. Before I know it, I'm resting my cheek on her shoulder as she cups my head. I can't feel her touch but it's still reassuring to be close to another person whom I trust implicitly. She pulls me to her, whispering something I can't make out as I press back. Perhaps it's because I want it – *really* want it – or maybe it's my imagination, but I even feel her warmth.

When she releases me, she smiles softly.

'I'm sorry I was such a cow,' I say.

Mum shrugs. 'I'm sorry as well. I know you're under a lot of pressure. Having time off is as important as doing the work.' She steps closer to the bathroom, creasing at the knees. 'Sorry, I really need a wee,' she adds. 'Are you sure you're okay?'

I nod and so does she – then she turns and hurries into the bathroom. When she clicks the lock closed, I stand and watch for a few seconds, wondering if I should've added anything else. If I'm going to tell anyone, it should surely be her?

For now, I don't feel ready.

Back in my room, I wrap myself in my duvet again but this time don't bother trying to sleep. I search the Internet for 'how to remember things', 'amnesia', 'memory loss' and the like – but can't find anything useful. It's either tips for old people, hypnotism, or dodgy movies.

When I realise that's a waste, I pick the girl-in-a-castle book from my shelf and start reading. If I've only got a limited time left, I might as well spend my free moments doing something I enjoy.

I only realise the night has passed when the wisps of early sunshine start to creep around the curtains. It's a little after half past four in the morning – but it's the longest day of the year and the sun seems determined to make sure everybody knows. My bedroom is at the back of the house and overlooks our garden and the trees beyond. A collage of red, orange and yellow is bleeding from the horizon, creating spindly silhouettes of the woods.

It's worth being alive for.

When the clock ticks through to seven o'clock, I hear Mum up and about. The bathroom door opens and closes, then her bedroom door. There's rushing up and down the stairs before I hear her talking to Ollie. Eventually the front door slams and she's gone.

Even though it feels strange, I can't think of anything else to be doing, so I get a bag ready for college. I throw my journal inside just in case.

Ollie is sitting at the dining table downstairs, thumbing his phone with one hand, shovelling through a bowl of Coco Pops with the other. He looks up as I enter the living room and raises his eyebrows, muttering something that sounds a bit like, 'all right?'

I nod at his breakfast. 'How many bowls of those have you had?'

'Three. You missed Mum, by the way.'

'I know – I heard her leave.'

Ollie scoops one more mouthful of chocolate milk and mush, before tipping the bowl upside-down and emptying the final remnants into his mouth.

'Do you need a lift somewhere?'

'I'm all right. I'll get the bus.'

He takes his bowl and spoon into the kitchen, then leaves it unwashed in the sink. With a grin, he tosses his car keys from one hand to the other in front of me.

'You know that car is half mine when I learn to drive,' I remind him. It doesn't shift his smile.

'*When* you learn to drive,' he winks back. Ollie fumbles in his pockets – phone, wallet, keys – then he heads for the door. 'You on a late start?' he asks.

'Yep.'

He opens his mouth to say something but stops himself, before muttering 'see ya' and heading outside.

I watch from the living room window as he gets in his car… *our* car. Mum bought it when he turned seventeen, making it absolutely clear that, when I passed my test, it would be half mine. He's been using it for a year now, while I've never got around to having driving lessons. More to the point, I've not had the money for lessons. It's only a small once-red Ford with a spluttering, booming exhaust that – unlike with some boy racers – isn't deliberate. It'd still be nice if it were really half mine.

Ollie wheelspins his way off the drive – something he'd never do if Mum were home – and then disappears around the corner. We go to the same college and, though I could have got a lift with him, it'd give the Ravens more ammunition with which to give the piss.

I waste an hour watching television and messaging back and forth with Naomi, who is asking what I want to do later. Robbie hasn't contacted me since I saw him at the Deck, but I suppose I haven't messaged him either. Ben's not sent anything, either – though that's probably for the best.

It's warm but I'm wearing layers again, trying to stop myself shivering. As I potter around the house, it dawns on me that, despite everything that's happened, I'm still stuck going to college. At the absolute least, shouldn't being dead get a person out of classes?

There really is no justice.

I'm about to leave the house when I pass the stove on my way through the kitchen. This time there's nobody around, no one to stop me. I know I should leave but there's another part of me saying that I need to know. The gas hisses, the fire flares and I'm entranced by the dancing flames. I hold my hand close to the heat but it doesn't feel hot.

Closer.

Closer still.

The tips of my fingers are millimetres from the blue of the gas flame. It should be hurting, yet I feel nothing.

Closer.

Closer again.

Chapter Fourteen

Mr Hawkins is our history teacher and a person who can only be described as eccentric. On our first day in his class last September, he told us he was a Domesday Book 'enthusiast', with 'more than a passing interest' in the Pre-Raphaelite Brotherhood. A month later, he came to college dressed in some sort of bizarre onesie–armour hybrid, saying his outfit was based on the eleventh-century and that he was wearing it to celebrate William the Conqueror killing Harold at the Battle of Hastings. He has long hair and often turns up wearing a disturbing amount of cord, yet I can't bring myself to dislike him.

As I read through the past exam paper from which we're supposed to be practising, it dawns on me that his antics aren't simply the actions of a maniac. He knows what he's doing. For instance, question five is about why Britain repealed the Stamp Act in 1766 – something to which I know the answer because Mr Hawkins set up some sort of science show that created static electricity which made his hair stand on end. Still looking like a fried clown, he told us about Benjamin Franklin and his experiments with electricity. That isn't directly relevant – except Franklin came to Britain to protest the Stamp Act. I associate that with Mr Hawkins' crazy hair and know the answer. At the time, I – like everyone else – thought he was a nutter.

As I scratch away the answer, my phone, which is on the desk, momentarily flashes. Mr Hawkins has said we're not using full exam conditions and that he trusts us not to cheat, which of course means everyone is checking their phones every few minutes.

It's a message from Naomi:

Whats up wit ur thumb?

I turn to glance at her, two desks away. She meets my gaze and then flicks her eyes at my hand, where the tip of my thumb and fingers are scorched black. I shrug at her and then focus back on my paper. I can feel more eyes on me and glance up to see Rachel the Raven turning back to look at me. She scowls but says nothing and then faces the front again. Rachel and Rochelle are both in my history class, yet they're empty shells without their führer to guide them. Whatever might be said about Rebecca – and I've said plenty – she's the one with the smart mouth and mind for vindictive insults. Her sidekicks are good for sneering and sucking their stomachs in to appear slimmer.

I continue working through the paper, pretending it matters and that I didn't wake up in a river, and then Mr Hawkins tells us we have five more minutes. Soon enough, the bell is ringing and class is over.

Lunch.

I trail Naomi out of class and then we pass through the swarm of students massing in the hallways. It's hard to be heard over the noise, so we say nothing until we reach the canteen on the far side of the building.

When the college announced they were opening a new canteen at the start of the year, there was a competition for naming rights. Somehow, out of all the suggestions from students, somebody somewhere settled on 'The Hangout'. I suppose he or she decided it was what they considered to be 'cool' – but a mixture of derision, confusion and complete apathy met the naming announcement. Some graffiti artist was even commissioned to paint the word 'Hangout' across the top of the doorway leading inside. Of course, nobody in their right mind bothers to call it anything other than 'the canteen'.

Naomi and I pass under the Hangout sign and get into the line that sweeps around the perimeter of the canteen. The air smells of burnt cheese and chips and there is a steady clatter of cutlery on plate. Everyone in line ambles forward slowly until we're eventually at the front. Naomi buys a sandwich and Coke while I get a bottle of water – and then we head through the double doors onto the field.

The college football team play in something close to a man-made amphitheatre, with the pitch sitting in a bowl, grass banks surrounding it on three of the four sides. On the other is an ugly chain-link fence. We find a spot on the bank and then spread out, dumping our stuff next to us and lying back to enjoy the sun.

Well, sort of.

I'm still covered up and can't feel the heat but Naomi rolls down her knee-high socks, which is as close to sunbathing as she really gets. She's still wearing a beanie hat with Miss Piggy ears.

We have a spot to ourselves, though the banks are covered with students finding somewhere to eat in the sun. Down below, there are lads in football kits getting ready to start a game.

'You not eating?' Naomi asks.

'Not hungry.'

She nods towards the pitch. 'What's going on down there?'

'Year Twelve are playing Year Thirteen. I think it's some practice thing.'

'How'd you know that?'

'Ollie and Robbie are both hoping to get into the overall college team for some tournament next month.'

Naomi squints down towards the pitch and then returns to her sandwich.

'Where's Ben?' I ask.

She narrows her eyes at me for a moment. 'It's Monday – he doesn't have classes, remember?'

'Right…'

Here was I thinking he was deliberately avoiding both Naomi and me.

'You okay?' she adds, staring directly at me. I've used a little make-up to try to stop my skin looking so grey, but there's little I can do. I've been getting sideways glances all day – and that was before anyone noticed my scorched fingertips.

'I'm fine.'

Naomi continues to watch me for a second or two and then turns back to the pitch and continues eating. The two teams have kicked off now, with the older team – including Ollie and Robbie – running around with no tops on and the younger lot wearing blue shirts. We watch the game in silence for a minute or two. I'm not particularly bothered about the match itself, more by whether my brother or boyfriend are getting kicked around. My knowledge is admittedly limited but, from what I can see, there seems to be a lot of shouting and not much kicking the ball into the goal. Someone keeps shouting 'line it', which makes it all the more confusing.

'How much do you remember of Helen's party?' I ask, trying to sound casual.

Naomi remains focused on the pitch. 'Most of it. It was only late on that it got a bit messy.'

'Do you remember that server guy from the Deck being there?'

'Ash?'

'Right.'

'Vaguely. It's not like we had a conversation or anything.'

'Who do you reckon invited him?'

'Dunno – it's not as if there was some bouncer on the door. He probably heard it was going on and invited himself. Y'know the type – they finish school but can't let it go. They spend all their time trying to pretend they're teenagers. He was at that Christmas recital thing in the sports hall last year, remember? That Ophelia girl was doing her solo and he was taking loads of photos. It was creepy with a capital C.'

Now she mentions it, I do remember. It was a sort of hybrid talent show/concert, with students from our year and the one above singing, playing instruments and putting on a series of short plays. It was, as expected, awful – with the performing arts lot treating it as if they were getting their big break. The event was open to the public and Ash had bought a ticket. I remember nudging Naomi and nodding towards him as he stood to the side and snapped photos whenever there were young women on stage.

'You hear about his ex-girlfriend?' Naomi asks.

If I have, then I can't remember, so I tell her I haven't.

'It happened around five years ago when they were both about our age,' she says. 'They didn't go to our school, they went to Saint Joseph's in Langham. They went out for a few weeks or something like that, then she broke up with him because he's a creepy weirdo. Anyway, he stalked her big-time after that. Followed her home from school, trailed her round the shops at the weekend – that sort of thing. She'd go to the cinema and he'd be there. This one time, he turned up in her back garden but her dad was in and he went proper mental. Threatened him and said that if he ever saw Ash again that he'd give him a kicking or whatever. That's what I heard anyway.'

She turns to me and winks. 'Now he's got a thing for you.'

'He really doesn't.'

'He's always looking at you when we're at the Deck.'

'He looks at everyone a bit… funny. It's just his way.'

Naomi turns back to the pitch, grinning. 'You keep telling yourself that. Ellie and Ash, sitting in a tree, eff-you-see-kay-aye-en-gee.' She collapses into giggles and I leave her to it.

It sounds suspiciously embellished, the type of story that has a kernel of truth at its core but which has been expanded over time.

She's only teasing but it's a little too close to home. I offer a weak smile and gaze past her towards the game. Rebecca is holding court on the metal bleachers close to the pitch, her Ravens one rung below. A few levels below them are another half dozen girls staring up adoringly at their leader. They're too far away for me to hear what's being said but it's unlikely to be anything pleasant. I watch them for a few moments but then, almost as if she has eyes in the back of her head, Rebecca turns and focuses directly on me. She mouths something and then her cronies burst out laughing while she gives me the finger.

I turn back to Naomi, who's calmed down. 'Who was the girl?' I ask.

'What girl?'

'Ash's ex-girlfriend.'

Naomi hums to herself in thought. 'I don't know,' she concludes, before sitting up taller. She raises her voice to wave at someone behind me. I spin to see Helen walking towards us with a yoghurt in either hand. I've known Naomi all my life but Helen's been in our classes throughout school and now college. We walk that line between acquaintances and friends. In an alternative timeline, if I'd ended up sitting next to her in primary school instead of Naomi, we could have ended up best mates.

Helen has long, wavy red hair – the type that would see her bullied relentlessly as a young girl. Now, it's strikingly, enviously beautiful.

The cow.

I don't really mean that... even though I sort of do.

The cow.

'What's up?' Helen asks.

'Did you get the house cleared before your folks got home from hols?' Naomi asks.

'Just – but Mum stalks me online anyway, so she'll see the pictures eventually.'

'Did you invite that Ash guy?'

Helen shrugs. 'Who?'

'The one who works at the Deck who has the weird side parting.'

Helen shakes her head. 'Was he there? I didn't see him, else I would've got someone to kick him out. Didn't you hear what happened to his ex-girlfriend? I heard he hid in her wardrobe one time.'

That's a new one.

'What was her name?' Naomi asks.

Helen pouts her lips together and makes a clicking sound with her mouth. 'Tina-something, I think. She went to uni, then dropped out and ended up working at the chippy in the village. Quite a comedown, huh?'

We agree and then Helen flips her hair and walks on to wherever she was going.

'I told you he was creepy,' Naomi concludes.

We continue half watching the football until the players stop. They huddle in small groups, drinking water and eating energy bars – all except Robbie, who climbs the bank towards us. The Ravens turn and watch him and I feel a wonderful pang of warm pride that he doesn't pay any of them the slightest bit of attention. He's topless, sweat dripping from his face and torso and he's panting slightly as he stands in front of us.

He nods at me. 'You got a minute?'

Before I can say anything, Naomi is on her feet, grinning a *you're welcome* towards me. She heads off in the direction Helen went, saying she'll see me after lunch.

As Robbie plops himself next to me, it's clear there's no way of getting out of it – now's the time for a conversation with the person who might well have killed me.

Chapter Fifteen

Robbie sips from a bottle of garishly coloured liquid as he wipes the perspiration from his taut belly and then dries his hand on the ground.

'Sorry about yesterday at the Deck,' he says. 'I wasn't feeling well. I probably ate something dodgy at Helen's party. You know what it's like at barbecues with undercooked food and the like.'

'It's fine.'

He reaches out and puts his hand on top of mine. I'm sitting up but leaning back, palms on the ground to support myself. Because of that, we don't interlock fingers but it still makes my stomach tingle when he's rubbing the back of my hand.

It's so good to feel *something*.

He wants me to look at him properly but I'm not ready for that. Unsure what to say, I remain quiet until he pulls his hand away.

'C'mon, Ell – don't be like that. I'm sorry I didn't call you last night, or text this morning, but I knew I'd see you here. I had some work to do this morning and Mum was giving me a hard time. You know what she's like.'

I don't actually mind – we've never been a clingy couple who spend every waking moment with one another. If anything, I am with Naomi more of the time. For whatever reason, I still feel like giving him a hard time.

'You found time for football,' I say, nodding towards the pitch.

'You know I'm trying to make the team for the all-counties tournament. The final's at Wembley, Ell. We talked about this and you said it was fine.'

'Sometimes I say things because I want you to read between the lines.'

I finally turn to look at him, but I remain defiant and daring. It's hard not to soften when I see how utterly beautiful he is. His long legs are stretched in front of him; his chunky, muscled calves tensing and untensing. His hair is spiky and brown, glistening with sweat. He has a square, solid jaw peppered with the thinnest of dark stubble and his shoulders are broad and muscled. Now that I'm looking at him properly in the sunshine, it's hard to believe he's anything other than the guy with whom I'm in love.

'I'll make it up to you,' he replies – but now he's looking at the floor, worried that I'm genuinely upset at the way he ran off yesterday.

Robbie sighs but then quickly glances up, leaning in and kissing me on the lips before I have a chance to realise what he's doing. There's the tiniest moment where I think I can feel the warmth emanating from his lips but then he pulls away and stares at me.

'What's wrong?' he asks.

'Nothing.'

He continues to stare unflinchingly but I can't read him and am now self-consciously touching my lip.

'It felt…'

'What?' I say.

From below, there's a blast of a whistle and then Robbie's leaping to his feet. 'Sorry, I've got to go,' he says. 'Your brother is a proper slave driver now he's captain. I'll message you later and call you tonight if I can – then I'll see you tomorrow. Sorry I'm so busy.'

He leans over and pecks me on top of the head, then races down the bank towards where the game is restarting. It's hard not to feel sad as I watch him go and I wonder how he was going to finish the sentence. It felt… what? It felt good to me – more or less the only thing I've felt since waking in the river. It's hard to imagine that he could be capable of harming me and yet I've still not asked him what happened on the night he drove me home from Helen's. There's a large part of me that doesn't want to know. It's hard to view my friends, my family, my boyfriend as people who might have harmed me. How am I supposed to treat them as both?

As the football kicks off again, I stand and brush a few strands of dried grass from my palms. Naomi has found a spot on the bank not too far away and is sitting by herself, reading something on her phone. When I sit down next to her, she gasps in surprise and then puts her device away.

'You two all sorted?'

'I suppose.'

'I didn't know you'd fallen out.'

'We haven't.'

She shrugs. 'Right.' Naomi stretches her arms high until something clicks. She makes a satisfied groaning sound and then lies back, staring up at the blue above. 'It's *such* a nice day. The longest day, too. Did you think about doing something for Sarah? Or ask your brother?'

'Sorry, after Mum went mental last night, I ended up forgetting. I didn't even see Ollie until this morning. What were you thinking?'

'I don't know… but it'll be light until late tonight.'

'Mum's not going to let me out so late tonight. She's already on one.'

'She doesn't need to know, does she…?'

Naomi looks at me with a sideways smirk before she starts to laugh. I don't join in, smiling instead – at least until I notice that Rebecca has turned around on the bleachers below and is staring directly at us again. She mouths something I can't make out and then turns back to her fellow Ravens, top lip curled into a sneer.

Chapter Sixteen

When they named the Westby village chip shop, someone really pushed the boat out on the creative side. They could've gone for something like 'The Plaice to Eat', or 'Codfellas'. 'The Codfather' is an obvious one, as is 'Chips Ahoy'. My personal favourite would have been 'Frying Nemo' – but the owners went for the creatively bereft 'Westby Fish & Chips', which must have taken them all of three or four seconds to come up with. The only debate must have been between the word 'and' or the ampersand.

Name-wise, the shop-owners might not have a clue – but fish-and-chip-wise, they certainly know what they're doing.

By the time I'm back in Westby, it is half past five and there's a queue of people out the chip-shop door, winding its way along the street and then neatly paperclipping around so as not to block a side alley where nobody's going to drive anyway. The village's inhabitants are nothing if not overwhelmingly polite to people's faces.

I walk along the line, nodding at the odd person as I go. One of my old primary school teachers is there and gives a small wave as I pass. I mumble 'hello' and smile but keep moving. Mrs Patchett – she of the horrendous fashion sense with a shop to match – is wearing something that looks like a faded lampshade. She nods politely but keeps her lips clamped together in pure 'I-don't-want-to-talk-to-you' style. That's fine – I'd have nothing to say to her anyway.

Mrs McKeith is there, too, fresh from spying long-haired interlopers who might or might not be out to bring down all of civilisation by trying to hitch a lift through our village. She glances at me quickly and then instantly turns away.

I slot in at the back of the line, trying to keep my head down so that I don't actually have to talk to anyone. Just in case anyone tries, I take out my phone and focus intently on the screen as if I'm doing something important. I'm not entirely sure why the line is so long but figure it's something to do with the longest day.

I have a theory – unproven by anything remotely scientific – that people get loopier about the weather the older they get. When a person is young, heading outside without a coat when it's either a) cold; b) raining; or c) both, is a normal everyday thing. Ending up a bit wet or cold is all well and good because it doesn't take much to warm up again. I think the age at which you're officially old is when you start heading back *inside* to grab a coat because, to quote Mum, 'it looks a bit peaky out'.

Because of this, I'm assuming the extended sunlight has driven the locals slightly bonkers with a craving for chips. We bob forward at regular intervals as a few people get into line behind me.

As I near the shop itself, I begin to sense the merest hints of salt and boiling oil. It's faint – but I've leapt from nothing to something, like going from a cool air-conditioned building into blazing heat. It's almost overwhelming and I have to lean on the outside glass to steady myself.

When I get into the shop, I manage to focus on what's around me instead of my returning sense of smell. There's a wide illuminated board high at the back, listing everything for sale. The waiting area is small, with a chest-high counter that has a see-through cabinet. It is speckled with browning-yellow grease, with rows of battered fish and sausages on the other side. There are two people behind the counter. A young lad, face blotched by pocked acne, is taking money, while a woman a little older than me is at the other end of the counter slapping food into trays. Both are wearing white smocks, with triangular hats that look like napkins.

At the front, I order a small portion of chips and hand the lad some change before shuffling to the other end. The woman who's serving is the only female behind the counter.

'Are you Tina?' I ask.

She peers up at me, surprised. There are hints of greasy black hair poking out from under her hat and her face is beaded with sweat.

She dumps a small shovel's worth of chips into a cone. 'Do I know you?' she replies.

'Not really – someone told me you were the person to talk to.'

'About what?'

'Ash.'

She frowns as she holds the salt shaker in mid-air over the chips I won't be eating. 'Who told you to come to me?'

'Someone at college.'

The person behind me in line sidles across, fumbling with his wallet. Tina looks to him, then me. 'Salt?'

'Just plain.'

She puts down the shaker and then passes me the cone while nodding at the line. 'You'll have to wait.'

'Where?'

Tina points towards the small green opposite. 'I don't know when I'll be free – but if you're out there when I am, then we can talk.'

I thank her and head outside, crossing the street and taking a seat on the wooden bench next to the path. When I hold the chips close to my nose, my stomach churns angrily, so I dump them in the adjacent bin. This is probably the most un-British thing I've ever done. If I chucked a bunch of PG Tips in after it, I'd be arrested for treason.

Forty-five minutes pass and nothing happens, except that a pair of seagulls swoop in and begin fighting over my discarded chips. They squawk and snap at each other until eventually deciding – sort of – to share and share alike. They're on the grass still nipping at each other when Tina sits down next to me with a sigh of exhaustion. She's no longer wearing her hat and her bobbed hair is greasy and flat. She tugs a packet of cigarettes from her trouser pocket and lights one before offering me the box.

'You smoke?' she asks.

'Not really.'

She returns the packet to her pocket and inhales deeply. 'What does that mean?'

'I've tried it a few times.'

'And…?'

I shrug. 'I don't think it's for me.'

Tina breathes a long, thin plume into the air and nods at the seagulls. 'Are the chips that bad?'

'I couldn't finish them all.'

She has another puff and then leans back onto the bench. 'So, you seeing Ash or something?'

'No, I just—'

'What?'

'My friend reckons he has a thing for me.'

'Oh… you're one of those girls who go to Tape Deck all the time.'

'What do you mean?'

She laughs slightly. 'You'll grow out of it – when you're old enough to go to actual pubs.'

'Right, um…'

Tina turns to me but she's no longer laughing, not even smiling. 'What have you heard about Ash and me?'

I gulp, unsure if I should repeat Naomi's story, but she raises her eyebrows, not in the mood for messing around.

'Someone told me that you went out but, after you broke up, he followed you around and ended up in the same shops or the same cinema as you. Then he was in your garden and your dad scared him off.'

Tina sucks deeply, deliberately on the cigarette, thinking over what I've said. She nods ever so slightly when she turns away. The seagulls have now finished fighting and flown off, presumably to look for the actual sea.

'How old are you?' she asks.

'Seventeen.'

'He's the same age as me, more or less – so he'll be twenty-two or maybe twenty-three. I can't remember his birthday. What's your name?'

'Eleanor... Ellie.'

'Right, I've seen you around. You live in the village?'

'Yeah.'

'Look, Ellie – when you're twenty-odd, probably thirty-odd, five years isn't a big gap in ages. Nobody cares and everyone ends up working or socialising together or whatever. It's different when you're a teenager, especially your age when you don't know what someone else's motives might be. If you're—'

'We're not going out. I have a boyfriend who is my age.'

Tina turns to look at me again, not seeming convinced. 'So why did you come to see me?'

'I told you, my friend says Ash has a thing for me.'

'So what? You've got a boyfriend, right? Other friends? If all he's doing is looking across the diner at you, tell him to get lost.'

I feel awful as I say my next words. It's a lie, a complete fabrication, and yet I don't know a better way to get the information from her. She thinks I'm a silly girl.

'I think Ash might be following me.'

Tina takes the final suck from her cigarette and then scuffs it out on the ground. She examines me closer than ever, frowning. 'You sure?'

'Not completely, but that's why I wanted to hear what happened to you.'

She sighs again and rolls her eyes. There's a moment in which I think she's going to stomp back to the shop. 'You know this was ages ago, don't you?' she says wearily. 'I was only a little older than you.'

'I don't know any proper details – it's why I came.'

'You want the truth? Fine.' She sounds annoyed. 'Look, I was in my final year, ready to go to university. I was still… well…' She looks over her shoulder and then lowers her voice. 'This is between us, right? I'm telling you because I've seen you around and it sounds like you've got something going on.'

'I'm not going to tell anyone else.'

'I was still a *virgin*.' She glances over her shoulder again but there's no one there. 'I didn't want to go to university like that, so I had this whole plan about what I was going to do in my final year before I went away. Anyway, somehow I ended up going out with Ash. I know he's a bit weird but he was in my year and I got talking to him in the library one time and he seemed all right. He was quiet and into all sorts of sci-fi stuff that I wasn't but I figured quiet and sci-fi was better than loud and knob-like. He was bloody desperate, mind, and I figured it'd be nice to have someone hanging on my every word. Y'know, at my beck and call and all that.'

She stops to fumble for another cigarette, sparking it and taking two quick drags. 'Look, I'm not proud of this but, if I'm honest, I mucked him around a bit. We went on a few proper dates, if you want to call them that. I'd get him to buy me stuff and then listen to him saying he was in love with me and everything. It was all a bit crazy, so I said we weren't going anywhere. I was off to uni and he'd end up doing whatever he was doing. It was just a bit of fun. Anyway, he didn't take it too well. What you've heard, well, it's not far from the truth. I went shopping with my friends one Saturday and he kept turning up in the shops we were in. He'd hide behind the shelves and pretend to be looking at something when he was really looking at us. In the first shop, I thought it was a coincidence and nodded a sort-of "hi", but then he kept showing up everywhere. We went to the cinema afterwards and, about halfway through, I realised he was sitting two rows behind me.'

Tina has devoured the cigarette and mashes it on the ground next to the first. She then picks up both butts and lobs them in the bin. 'That summer – in between school and uni when I was still waiting for my A-level results, some of my friends and I went to Tenerife. It was only for a week but it was the first time I'd been abroad without my parents. There were five of us and the youngest had just turned eighteen, so we were all up for a few days of carnage. We flew out and checked in, then went straight out that night. We didn't get in until four or five o'clock in the morning and went to bed. We had two rooms between us but I was the only one who got up for breakfast. It was one of these buffet places where you have to check to see if everything's cooked properly. I was busy stacking up these potato things when I turned around and there he was.'

I gasp involuntarily and she nods in acknowledgement.

'I know, right? He's sitting at this table by himself, not looking up. I was still hungover and thought I was seeing things. Then he looks up, spots me and instantly turns away again. I go and sit opposite him and ask what the hell he thinks he's doing. He can barely speak, mumbling something and claiming that it was all a big coincidence and that he was just staying there. I have no idea how he found out where we were going, let alone which hotel we were staying in. After that, I wouldn't go anywhere without one of the other girls.'

'He followed you on holiday?'

It sounds so over the top, so crazy, that I have to repeat it to believe it.

Tina nods and raises her eyebrows to say, 'I know'. 'That story about my dad finding him in the garden is true as well,' she says. 'It was the week before I went to uni – after the Tenerife thing. He claimed he'd lost a hat or something mad like that. My dad had a few words – well probably more than that, I didn't hear exactly what was said – but then it ended. I've not really seen him since – other than at the Tape Deck. I didn't know he worked there when I went, else I wouldn't have gone.'

It takes me a second or two to take it in. 'I can't believe he followed you.'

She snorts. 'Believe it. Look, I've not spoken to him in years. I've not heard about problems from any other girls in all this time. I assumed it was just a one-off. Sometimes we all do crazy things when we're that age. I don't know what's actually going on – but if you *really* think he's following you, then contact the police. If you don't want to do that, then make sure you're with a mate or something.'

'Is he dangerous?'

'I don't know – with me, it was just… *creepy*.'

That word again.

Tina stands and wipes her hands on her apron. 'I've got to get back but I'm assuming you're here because you're worried. I don't want to get involved – it's all in the past and I'd rather forget it.'

She shivers, mutters the word creepy once more – and then heads back across the road.

Chapter Seventeen

Because I haven't had enough drama for one day, I still don't head home. Instead, I cross through the centre of the village and start to walk up Gold Hill. The road climbs steeply and then zigzags back and forth, narrowing as the hedgerows become more and more overgrown until the daylight has been replaced by descending gloom. I know it eventually winds into the woods before stopping at a dead end, but don't need to go that far.

Westby attracts families with money and when they ran out of large houses in and around the village centre, people started building their own in the surrounding area. Gold Hill is now home to a dozen or so large properties, each a little set back from the road. Some have solid walls to separate them from the rest of civilisation, which, if you ask me, kinda defeats the point of moving to a little village. If a person wants to barricade themselves away from everyone else, that could be done anywhere.

Not all the houses are like that, however. Around half have long driveways, with manicured lawns on either side. Sometimes Naomi and I would walk up here when the places were being built, simply to have a nosy at what was going on. I know for a fact that at least two of the newer houses have indoor swimming pools, while another has horse stables at the back. Westby is that kind of place.

The Lipskis own what is probably the smallest of the properties on Gold Hill. Rather than having something custom built, they bought a house that was owned by an old man I didn't know. There's a brick garage close to the road, with a scrunchy stone path that leads to a large cream house overlooking an overgrown garden. I've been here a couple of times before, on both occasions with Ollie to pick up or drop off Sarah.

The Lipski family were well known in the area, as they owned and ran a deli in the village centre. They imported meats, cheeses, fruits and vegetables from various places around Europe and then sold them on to locals for crazy prices. Mum bought things from there every now and then but I could never tell the difference between that and something from the supermarket.

After Sarah's body was discovered, the deli was closed and it hasn't opened since. Aside from one time they were in a car passing through the village centre, I've not seen either of her parents since.

I crunch along the Lipski path and the doorbell offers a satisfying ding-dong. Usually, knocking on a door or ringing the bell brings the sound of shuffling from the inside but I hear nothing. I think about trying again, or perhaps walking away and then, with no warning, the door swings inwards.

Mrs Lipski looks so much like her daughter that I have to stop myself from gasping as she stares at me. She has a rounded face with naturally tanned skin, greying blonde hair tied into a loose ponytail. It's only the hint of wrinkles that stops her looking too much like Sarah.

'Hello,' she croaks.

'Hi, I don't know if you remember me. I'm… um—'

'I know who you are.'

'Right, er…'

She turns towards the inside. 'Do you want to come in?'

'Um… Oh… kay.'

I wasn't exactly expecting that but she turns and pads along the hallway, then stops and waits for me to get inside and close the door.

I follow her through a kitchen into a living room that has me open-mouthed, unsure what to say.

It is a shrine to Sarah, the walls patterned by photographs of the dead girl. There are ones of a young blonde playing with a doll; another being pushed on a bike. The photos go through her lifetime, showing her in school uniform, playing hockey, growing into her teens until… there are no more pictures to show. Perhaps it's accidental but there is a thin strip of bare wall close to the front window where Sarah's life has nowhere left to go.

'Do you want something to drink?' Mrs Lipski asks.

It takes me a moment to answer. 'Water, if that's all right.' I'm not sure if it comes out clearly but she seemingly understands, offering a weak smile and then passing me to head back into the kitchen. For a few moments, I'm alone with the wall that shows picture after picture of a ghost. It's hard to look but even harder to look away. There are so many sets of smiling eyes following me around the room.

I jump as Mrs Lipski returns with a beaker of water. She offers it to me and then sits in the corner of a creaky leather sofa. It's awkward to continue standing, so I perch on the matching armchair.

'We don't get many visitors nowadays,' Mrs Lipski says. 'When we ran the shop, we'd have people coming by the house and the shop every day – sometimes for deliveries, sometimes locals wanting us to order things in for them. Now… not so much.'

'I'm sorry.'

She shakes her head. 'My husband's pottering in the shed at the back if you wanted him.'

'I'm not sure who I wanted.'

Mrs Lipski eyes me for a moment and then sips from a mug of tea. We sit silently for a moment and I find myself struggling to remember why I came.

'It might not mean anything now,' she says, 'not after so long has passed – but, for the record, my husband and I never believed your brother was involved in anything that happened to Sarah.'

I gulp and it feels like I want to cry, even though I know I can't. I sip my water, forcing it back. She sounds so sad but so strong at the same time.

'They really did love each other,' she adds. 'I know you're here because it's a year tomorrow. I don't blame you. It's nice to see someone.'

At least I don't have to explain why I'm here, even if that's not entirely the reason.

'It's hard to make sense of it all,' I say and she nods. 'Did the police ever…?'

'What?' she replies when I tail off.

'I don't know… I suppose I'm wondering if they ever mentioned suspects.'

'*Suspects?*' She looks at me as if I've brought up something she's never thought of. I've been too forward, too direct, but it's a little late now. I sip the water and say nothing, hoping she'll fill the silence.

'Are people still harassing Oliver?' she asks.

'Not so much now.'

Mrs Lipski nods. 'The police never talked to us about things like that. They spoke to Sarah's friends – to Oliver, obviously. They went through her things. If they ever had a feeling for who… did that… then they never said.' He voice cracks and it takes her a moment to find it again. 'Why do you ask?'

I can't meet her stare, instead focusing on the bare patch of wall. 'I suppose I've been thinking about Sarah a lot this weekend.'

It's not a lie…

'People talked,' she adds as if I haven't spoken. 'People from the village, neighbours, customers. You've lived here longer than me – you know how it gets. A lot of them mentioned your brother, of course.'

She stops to drink her tea but hasn't mentioned Ollie in an accusing way, more matter of fact. People *were* talking about him when Sarah was found in the river.

'It wasn't Ollie,' I say. It blurts out like a reflex. I've spent month after month saying or thinking the same thing.

Mrs Lipski smiles with her mouth but not her eyes. She looks like she needs a good, long sleep. 'There was only ever one other name but it took me and my husband a while to realise it. They'd asked us if Sarah ever ate at that diner place on the way to Langham.'

'Tape Deck?'

'That's the one. We didn't know – but then they came back with a photo someone had taken.' She pushes herself to her feet and mutters something I don't catch before disappearing through the door.

I'm alone again, not knowing where to look, but I can feel something tingling, too. If the police were talking about the Deck, who else could it be but Ash?

Mrs Lipski returns moments later and pushes a piece of paper towards me. The quality isn't great as a cheap printer has inked the photo on basic paper but the figures are clear enough. Ollie is slurping a chocolate milkshake, Sarah a strawberry. Both are grinning as they press their cheeks to one another and behind them is the wall of cassettes from Tape Deck. Off to the side, either sneaking into or out of shot, is Ash, who is staring directly at the camera. It could be a coincidence – it probably is seeing as he works there – yet his narrow-eyed expression reeks of fury and hatred.

'They asked about the boy at the back,' Mrs Lipski says. 'I don't know him but apparently his name came up.'

'Came up how?'

'I don't know – as far as I could tell it was just gossip. It's a strange photo, a moment in time. He looks so angry but then he could've just dealt with a bad customer, or had to clean a really dirty table – that sort of thing. Still images can tell many lies…'

She tails off once more and then takes the photo back to stare at it herself. 'At first, my husband and I – probably me more than him – were looking for a person to blame. We wanted justice. Vengeance, perhaps. We clung onto every tiny detail, hoping it would lead somewhere. It took a while before it sank in that these other people – including Oliver – had families, too. It's easy to throw a name out there, to spread rumours, to insinuate, and so on – but when you do that, unless you know for sure what you're talking about, all you're doing is creating another victim.'

I'm not sure how to reply at first. It's a lot to take in and seems so… grown up. That makes it even stranger because she *is* grown up – but not everyone acts like that. I'm not sure that I could or would.

'Why that photo in particular?' I ask eventually.

The cadence of her words has slowed, like she's got a lot off her mind with her speech. 'I'm not sure. They asked if my husband or I had ever seen the young man at the back of the picture. Had he been hanging around the house? I'd never seen him then and I've not seen him since. I don't eat at that diner.'

As she speaks, I begin to answer my own question. If Naomi had heard the rumours about Ash and Tina, there's a good chance someone told the police a year before. They'd have realised Sarah had eaten at the place where Ash worked and started asking questions. In the end, they likely led nowhere. It's still a link from Sarah to me, though.

Before I can get too far ahead of myself, Mrs Lipski continues talking. 'Do you ever find it hard living here?'

'Westby?'

'We came to your country from a big city, then we lived in an even bigger city for many years. We wanted to come here to give Sarah a chance to get away from that. We never realised how hard it is to escape in a small village.'

She looks up to me and I know exactly what she's thinking. 'Everyone knows everyone,' I reply.

'Community is nice but sometimes…'

She tails off but she's said enough. Sometimes, it's nice to be in a place where nobody knows, or cares, who you are. Where visiting the shops doesn't have to be planned in advance in case there's a chance Mr or Mrs So-and-So might be there at the same time. Where sitting on the swings by yourself is peaceful and relaxing, without Mr or Mrs So-and-So coming over to check how you are, how your mum is, and so on. I feel that resentment, too – and it can only be worse for the Lipskis given what happened to Sarah. Even well-wishers will end up being an inadvertent nuisance.

'I'm not sure why you came but it's nice that you did,' Mrs Lipski says.

'I don't know why I came either.'

She puts down her mug of tea and uncurls her legs from the sofa, perching forward and peering more closely at me. I wonder if she's thinking about why I'm wearing so many clothes, or if she's noticed how grey my skin is looking.

'Do you mind if I give you some advice?' she asks.

'Not at all.'

'There are always rumours, always some bogeyman. Look at the news this week with this "Hitcher" fellow. When you're young, it's monsters under the bed. Nothing changes when you grow up. It's terrorists wanting to blow up your plane, foreigners stealing your job or giving you exotic diseases. It's burglars, rapists, murderers. There's always – *always* – someone to be scared of. After my daughter…' She gulps. '… after *Sarah*, I should be scared of everything. I was for a while. Noises in the night, the crunch of someone on our path, knocks at the door. It's easy to be scared – but now…' She turns to face the wall of photos and gulps deeply. 'I miss her so much, but *now* I can't be scared of any of that. The moment you allow yourself to be frightened of everything is the moment you stop living your life.'

She turns back to me, stares into me with teary, round eyes. 'You understand, don't you?'

I don't even need to think. 'Yes.'

Chapter Eighteen

Mrs Lipski's words rattle around my head on my way home. After everything she's been through, it astounds me that she can be so calm. It's great to say don't be scared, but not that easy when it comes down to it. She has me wondering about what I'm scared of, especially now, but it's hard to think past those hands in the water – one on my chest, one on my head, holding me under. Every time I close my eyes, I see it, *feel* it – and I *am* frightened. It's impossible not to be.

When I'm in my room I take out my journal and stare at the list of names. There's Robbie, the last person to see me on the night I died. I don't know if I told him about kissing Ben but, if I did, is it arrogant to assume he was so consumed by anger that he attacked me? There's Ash, whom I don't really know but who has an apparent history of stalking young women. Or perhaps he was in the wrong place at the wrong time? There's the Hitcher, who might not exist; Ollie, whose girlfriend was killed a year ago; Naomi, whose trust I might have destroyed; not to mention Ben himself, who could have been consumed by unrequited love or something stupid. None of them have a really strong reason to have held me under the water and yet I'm coming up with suggestions anyway.

Being dead gives a person a real ego.

I've told Mum I'm revising, which at least gives me an excuse for shutting myself in my room. Over the evening, I hear her and Ollie making their way up to bed and the house gradually goes quiet. I want to feel tired and, in many ways, I do. My thoughts are cluttered and confused. When I get a message from Naomi asking how I am, I can't think how to reply. Robbie texts me something similar and then I get a lone message from Ben that simply reads 'hi'. I tap out responses over and over, then delete each one, unsure how I feel about them and myself.

Are they friends or foes?

Somebody over the past two days has been lying to my face but I don't know who. I silence my phone and spend the evening reading.

The sky has dimmed to a deep mauve when my phone starts to flash at a few minutes to eleven. The screen pulses with Naomi's name. I think about ignoring it but it's nice to remember the late nights we'd spend lying on our respective beds, talking into our phones to one another about whatever was going on in our lives.

'Hey,' I answer.

'Ell?'

'Who else would it be?'

'Oh, you sound… different. Never mind – we're parked outside number twenty.'

'Number twenty where?'

'On your street. Didn't you get my messages?'

I um and er, not quite sure what she's talking about. 'I think there's a problem with my phone,' I say.

She sounds excited: 'Whatever – we're down the street waiting for you. Come on.'

'Where are we going?'

'We're going on an adventure.'

I remove the phone from my ear for a moment and stare at the screen. Naomi's name is still there but it feels like I've missed something. I have, of course, having left my phone on silent all evening.

'Who's going on an adventure?' I ask.

'We are!'

'Who's we?'

Naomi sighs. 'Who'd you think, Ell? Check your phone. You, me, Ben and Robs. Hurry up!'

'I can't – Mum's not going to let me leave the house, not after having a go yesterday. She keeps going on about exams and revising. Plus, we're supposed to be at college tomorrow and—'

'Ell!'

'What?'

'Forget all that. We're outside number twenty. Hurry up. YOLO, remember?'

I start to reply but the screen has gone blank and the phone is silent. Then I realise what Naomi said and it's hard not to laugh. *She* might only live once, but me...

There's little chance of me getting out the front door without being heard by someone. Mum's a deep sleeper but it's not quite eleven o'clock and she's probably in bed reading or playing games on her phone. Ollie will definitely still be up. If I'm going out – which I've decided I am – there's only one way to go.

I pile on the layers and then open my bedroom window. Below is a drop of a metre or two to the roof of the shed, and then a second plunge of a similar height to the ground. After that, it's over the back gate, follow the lane around the rear of the houses, and then onto the main street. It won't be the first time I've made this journey...

Carefully, I lift myself onto the windowsill and then spin so that I'm sitting with my legs dangling out the window. I shuffle forward slowly until I'm balancing on the ledge outside, back pressed against the glass, and then remember that I should probably make sure nobody else is watching. Although our house doesn't back onto anyone else's, if any of our neighbours were in their gardens, they'd be able to look up and see me performing my daredevil act. Luckily, with the light dimming rapidly, the evening is silent and there's nobody in sight.

The window pushes closed, though I don't latch it, and then I shift sideways until the shed roof is directly below. It takes some twisting but I'm soon hanging from the ledge and then I drop comfortably onto the roof, landing both feet and gently bending my knees in near-perfect gymnast style. It might not be a ten but it's got to be worth something in the nines.

The next drop should be easier as there's no window to close. I walk to the edge of the shed roof, double check there's nobody in the kitchen that overlooks the garden, and then hang once more. It should be simple but it's not. As I slide along the roof so that I can drop onto the grass instead of the path, my fingers glide through a thin layer of mulched twigs that's coating the rim of the roof. When I try to get a better grip, my fingers slip sideways and, before I can do anything, I'm hanging one-handed. I try to push upwards but I'm off-balance and not expecting it. It's already too late and when my shoulder clicks, I know I'm falling before I actually am.

The drop is probably less than a second but I still manage to twist in the air, somehow ending up on my side as my entire weight crunches down. My hand is sandwiched between my body and the concrete path and it's hard not to yelp, to cry out – especially when the vicious crack of a bone echoes around the garden.

Chapter Nineteen

I bite my lip to stop myself howling in pain, except... there is no pain. When I unfold my limbs, the ring finger on my left hand is jutting at a near right angle. It should hurt, should be agony, but I feel nothing. The urge to shout and cry is from the expectation of falling and the pain, not the reality.

Although it doesn't hurt, there's surely no question that my finger is dislocated, perhaps broken. I grasp the tip of the shattered finger with the thumb and forefinger of my other hand and then let it go, watching it flop uselessly. Still it doesn't hurt. I squeeze it but there's nothing, almost like it's somebody else's finger.

A glimmer of light flashes from my pocket – probably Naomi calling, wondering where I am – so I wrap the fingers on my other hand around the drooping digit, close my eyes, and then yank it back into place in one, swift movement. I catch myself grimacing even though it doesn't hurt and, when I reopen my eyes, everything looks as it should. I try wiggling the finger and it moves more or less as normal.

It's all a bit surreal but then everything that's happened recently has been like that. I rush to the back gate, lift myself over and then race around the back lane until I emerge on the street. Robbie's Vauxhall is idling with the headlights off outside number twenty and when I wrench open the back door, Naomi shrieks in alarm.

She's in the passenger seat and spins to look at me, then gasps. 'You scared the crap out of me.'

Ben's alone on the back seat and there's nowhere else to sit except next to him. I close the door, strap the belt across myself and then Robbie pulls away. When he reaches the end of my road, he flips the headlights on.

'Didn't you get my messages?' he asks, eyeing me in the rear-view mirror.

'My proper phone died, so I'm using my old one. It's all over the place.' I hold it up but Robbie's looking ahead and Naomi's directly in front of me. Only Ben notices and he offers an awkward, watery smile.

'Naomi called shotgun,' he says.

'Shotgun!' she shouts from the front seat.

'What *is* shotgun?' I ask.

'It's where you get the front seat,' she replies.

'Well, obviously. But why's it called "shotgun"? Why wouldn't you just yell "front seat"?'

Naomi twists to peep through the gap between the seat and the headrest. 'You think too much,' she says.

Ben clears his throat dramatically. 'It's to do with the Wild West and old stagecoaches,' he says. 'The driver would be the bloke holding the reins of the horses, the guy next to him has the shotgun to stop them being robbed.'

There's a short silence in which I can read the thoughts of both Robbie and Naomi. *There's always a smart arse.*

Robbie catches my eye again in the mirror. With no words and only the movement of our eyes, he asks if I'm all right and I tell him I am. For the first time since waking in the river, I feel normal. There's the pulsing fire of adrenaline flowing because this is exciting.

Naomi passes back a brown plastic bottle of cider but I hand it off to Ben. I can barely manage water and haven't eaten in two days, so who knows how booze will affect me.

'Where are we going?' I ask.

Naomi is back facing the front, the light from her phone reflecting off the side window. She's playing a tap-tap game badly. 'It's a surprise,' she says.

Robbie is driving away from the village and the lanes are getting narrower and darker. There are no streetlamps, with the light coming from a mixture of his headlamps, the moon and the red of the horizon.

'She won't tell me either,' Ben says. I can feel him trying to catch my eye but ignore him. Naomi giggles and then reaches for the cable dangling from the radio. She plugs in her phone, twists the volume dial and then moments later, 'Here Comes the Sun' by The Beatles is tinkling from the speaker behind my ear. Long live Tape Deck, hey? We must be the most music literate kids in the country.

Naomi turns and grins at the irony as the sun has almost entirely disappeared. She shouts the 'do-do-do-do' bit and then we're all joining in.

We get through three more songs about summer and then Robbie turns off the main road. Ben and I are bumped up and down by the rough, gravelly track as the car rattles in and out of potholes before we finally roll to a stop.

'This it?' Robbie says, turning to Naomi.

'You're the one driving.'

'I'm only going where you said.'

'Then it's probably right.'

We all pile out of the vehicle to find ourselves in a gravel car park. When Robbie remembers to switch off the headlights, it leaves us in near darkness. Around the rim of the parking area are lines of tall trees, slightly swaying in a cool tickle of wind. The glittering white of the moon peeps through the forest, leaving the night a shimmering silver. There's a large board ahead of the car, welcoming us to some country park, but the rest of the car park is deserted.

Robbie opens the boot and Naomi grabs two large bottles of cider, passing one to me. Ben has the opened one and she hands him a supermarket bag for life that's filled with something I can't see.

'What are we doing?' I ask.

Naomi doesn't answer, instead illuminating the flashlight on her phone and heading towards the trees. She's wearing muddied Doc Martens, her trademark over-the-knee socks, shorts and the denim jacket we decorated together a few years ago. It's covered in sparkly stars and painted swirls. It would look ridiculous on me but has always suited her. She's also sporting a Kermit the Frog beanie, his long legs dangling down her back.

Ben scuttles off to catch her but Robbie slides in alongside me and takes the cider bottle. He's in a hoody and loose basketball-style shorts. 'I'm glad you came,' he says.

'Came to what? Where are we going?'

'No idea. Naomi told me to drive here. You know what she's like when she gets an idea. She said it was an adventure.'

We follow Naomi further through the woods. There's a mossy path with low-lying bracken on either side, plus the odd cluster of twigs and stones that are there presumably to trip up people walking through the woods in the dead of night. Naomi seems to know where we're going and doesn't look back, so there's little option other than to follow.

Eventually, we arrive at a clearing that doubles as a picnic area. There are half a dozen wooden tables and benches around the rim, with red-lettered signs telling people to use the bins and not litter. That's fair enough, obviously, but it always astonishes me how obsessed people seem to be with bins and, specifically, emptying them.

Last year, our bin day fell on 25 December, meaning that week's collection was postponed. Fair enough, huh? No one wants to work on Christmas Day. Except the locals almost rioted. There were talks about people driving their junk to the council building in Langham and dumping everything on the pavement – which seemed a lot more work than simply bagging it up and waiting a week. Here, there are more signs than bins – and there are almost more bins than benches. Whoever wrote the messages on the signs is a big fan of exclamation marks. 'Warning! Use the bins provided! Do not dump your rubbish! Litterers will be prosecuted!'

There is, predictably, a Mars bar wrapper flitting around the clearing.

Naomi sits on one of the benches and takes the bag from Ben. She looks inside and then stares up at him. 'I thought I said, "bring food"?'

'That *is* food,' he protests.

She pulls out a large paper bag and removes an uncut loaf of bread. 'It *is* food,' she says. 'But what are we supposed to do with this? I meant chocolate, crisps, cold pizza – not a crusty loaf from the village bakery.'

He shrugs and sinks onto the bench next to her. Naomi pulls out three tins of tuna – no tin-opener – and a tub of margarine – no knife. 'Twiglets,' she says. 'You could've brought Twiglets.'

'You said "bring food". If you'd said "bring Twiglets", I'd have brought Twiglets.'

Robbie stands over them. 'Can everyone stop saying "Twiglets"?'

He pulls out a utility Swiss-army style knife from his shorts pocket and finds some tool that soon has him slicing into the can. After that, he slides open a serrated blade and cuts the loaf into slices. 'Tuna sandwiches it is,' he says.

Naomi looks between the boys and then to me. She shrugs and then lies back on the bench, staring up at the sky. She lets out a long, breathy gasp and then I look up too.

It is wonderful.

The pinprick dots of stars stretch far across the breadth of the near-black sky, winking and blinking. It goes on and on, elongating in all directions, only interrupted by the height of the trees.

'Wow,' Robbie says. I look to him quickly and he and Ben are both staring up. He offers me his arm and it feels right, so I cuddle into his side and together we both gaze at the beauty of what's above. It's only when he holds me tighter that I realise I'm no longer feeling cold. For the first time in almost two days, I'm comfortable.

'Y'know,' Naomi says, 'with Robbie playing football all summer, then going off to uni, this is one of the last times we'll be together as a foursome.'

Robbie's fingers clench on my side as he tenses, though he says nothing. None of us do. Forgetting everything that's happened – as hard as that is – this moment does feel like the end of an era. All the linners, all the giving the piss... we'll soon be going our separate ways.

The crack of a twig and the breathy swearing of an unseen female interrupts our silence. We all turn to the path and then Helen emerges, the moonlight blazing from her green top. She's in a short black skirt with boots and her red hair is loosely tied back. There are more people behind her, too. Students from our year and the one above. More acquaintances: people to nod at and say hello to. Not friends, but close enough.

Naomi leaps up from the bench and bounds across the clearing towards Helen, relieving her of a lager six-pack. 'You made it!' she shouts.

'We did indeed,' Helen grins back.

More people arrive, bringing more food, which thankfully doesn't include a granary loaf with filling. There are cool boxes full of ice and more six-packs. Someone's brought along a pair of speakers and starts bluetoothing music from their phone. Within a few minutes, the clearing is humming to the sound of our impromptu party. There are young people everywhere, standing in small groups and chatting, or bobbing away in the centre of the clearing that is doubling as a dance floor.

It's a while until I find Naomi again. She's ditched her own cheap cider and is swigging from a can of beer.

'Did you plan this?' I ask.

She shrugs. 'I figured we could have a longest day party, mixed with a goodbye thing for Sarah. I told a few people – including you if you'd answered your phone – and we managed to get word around.'

Naomi nods over my shoulder and I turn to see Ollie walking through the crowd by himself, hands in pockets. My brother doesn't notice me, instead plonking a bottle of vodka down on what has become the drinking table and then disappearing into the swarm of people.

'Eh, up,' Naomi says and I spin a second time, this time to where Rebecca and her Ravens are perching on the edge of one of the picnic benches. They look immaculate, utterly out of place in the forest. They are all wearing short black dresses and heels, bare knees crossed provocatively. Within seconds, a pair of lads has descended upon them, asking if they want anything to eat or drink. Rebecca takes a cigarette from one of them and starts puffing away.

'Did you invite them?' I ask.

Naomi snorts. 'Not directly. I wanted it to be a celebration. I suppose if people want to come, they can come.' She still gives a withering frown in the Ravens' direction before dragging me towards the centre of the clearing. 'C'mon – let's dance.'

And we do.

The music plays and we dance, we sing. I don't even know half the words but nobody cares because there's a crowd of us all doing the same. La-la-la is a popular lyric. More people arrive, some I know, others I don't, but it doesn't matter because I'm having fun. Genuinely enjoying myself. It's so good to forget and to be me.

Everything is going great until the party comes to an abrupt halt when the music cuts out. Everyone carries on dancing for a few seconds until we realise and then there's a sullen groan. I'm on tiptoes, trying to peer over the mass, expecting blue flashing lights or some police officers, here to send us all home. Instead, it's an altogether more surprising sight.

Ollie is standing on one of the wooden picnic tables, looking down upon the rest of us. He has his arms out, trying to hush the rippling murmur of voices. My brother clears his throat and then calls 'hi'. There are more mutterings, then people shushing the mutterers, then even more people shushing the shushers. It sounds like a steam train is on the way.

'Hi,' Ollie tries again when it's finally quiet. 'Sorry to interrupt the music. I know we're here to have a good time but I just wanted to say a few words about Sarah. I—'

'Murderer!'

The cry has come from somewhere in the middle of the clearing, the anonymous male voice sheltered by the surrounding horde. Ollie gulps and tries to say something else but he's lost the crowd, his voice drowned out by the back-and-forth braying of people who want to hear him and those who don't. I don't know what to do but Naomi is tugging my sleeve, moving me away from the dance area, closer to the table on which Ollie is standing. He's disappeared from sight but then another figure appears on the table.

'Shut up!' Helen shouts. 'Hey! Shut it.'

Volume is not – and never has been – a problem for Helen. It's like she's swallowed a foghorn and she has her silence in an instant.

'I don't know why you're here,' she says, 'but I'm here to celebrate the life of a person we know, not to mention the end of term. If we can all stop shouting for a couple of minutes we can get back to whatever we want.'

There are more grumblings and then another series of shushes. Helen's red hair is rippling gently and she's giving everyone a shit-stare that's so good, my mum could learn tips. She's bound to end up being a teacher one day.

When she's done, Ollie clambers back onto the table. It is as quiet as it's going to get. He coughs and then tries again. 'Sorry, I know some of you don't want to hear from me and that's fine. I understand – but whatever you might think, I loved Sarah and she loved me.'

He takes a breath and peers slightly upwards, pushing any hint of tears away from view.

This time, nobody interrupts. 'I know she's not coming back but if we're here for any reason, then let's remember who she was. She loved animals – so much so that, even though she was scared of spiders, when she spotted one, she'd make me pick it up carefully and then take it outside so it wasn't harmed. She wanted to travel through South America, to teach in Hong Kong, to sing and write her own music.'

Ollie stops again, taking a larger breath this time. He has his silence. There's no holding back the tears this time. 'She liked rocky road brownies, those ones you can get in the café in Westby; she ate ketchup with everything; she had these Little Miss socks that she loved so much, she kept wearing them even though they were full of holes.' Another breath. 'Those are the things I remember but a lot of you knew her, too. I know we're here to celebrate the summer and the end of term – but if you knew Sarah, then please remember her, too.'

Ollie glances quickly around the crowd and then spots me. He offers the slightest inclination of his head and then ducks down, out of sight.

With him gone, there's a strange atmosphere around the clearing. There's a hint of sympathy but also confusion. Many only knew him as 'that kid who killed his girlfriend' – and now people don't know what to think.

A low ripple of chatter starts and then silences as another person appears atop the picnic bench. Rebecca the Raven straightens her skirt and stands tall. Her hair is so dark, skin so bright, that the white glimmer of the moonlight is making it look like she's glowing. As much as I dislike her, she's utterly breathtaking.

'Hello, everybody,' she says, using a girly, childish voice. 'I know you didn't all know Sarah as well as I did, but she was the kindest, sweetest, most bestest friend…'

I have no desire to hear the rest because it'll only be the same load of made-up look-at-me self-indulgence that she came out with a year ago. For most of the people around me, Rebecca *is* the tearful face of what happened.

As everyone listens in reverence, I slip between the people around me and then make my way through the crowd until I'm on the edge of the woods. It's quiet but not quiet enough – Rebecca's bleatings are still floating on the breeze, so I press on through the trees. It's hard to keep my footing at first as the clingy, thin roots criss-cross the ground, shielded by a blanket of grass and moss. I trip three times before steadying myself until I eventually end up in front of an enormous tree that is three or four times the width of me. It's so big that the trunk has branched into two and then grown back on itself, creating a natural heart shape.

I lean against it and stare up at the sky, listening to the silence. When the stars become too bright, I close my eyes.

The water comes instantly this time. I try to breathe but it's swilling around my mouth, in my nose. I push up towards the surface but there's a hand on my chest, another on my head. I'm thrashing, trying to fight, but the person is stronger than me and the only thing on which I can get a proper grip is the strap around his or her wrist. I pull the bracelet, while pushing up as hard as I can, fighting for air, scrapping, heaving but getting nowhere.

Dislocating my finger did not hurt at all – but this is agony. I'm reliving it all again, gasping, coughing, crying, pleading.

If I can only open my eyes and stare through the water, I should be able to see the shape of my attacker. Even a silhouette would help. Spiky hair, or long? Wide shoulders or narrow?

I don't get a chance to find out because the river evaporates, the hands disappear – and I'm jolted back to the present by somebody grabbing my arm.

Chapter Twenty

'Are you okay?' Robbie is standing over me, gripping my wrist. It takes a second or two for me to get my bearings: the water becoming earth, darkness becoming trees, my attacker becoming... my boyfriend.

'You looked like you were choking,' he adds.

I tug my hand back and brush invisible grit from my face. I feel tired, perhaps even exhausted enough to sleep.

'I'm fine,' I say.

Robbie takes a small step backwards, clouding almost all of his face in shadow. There's nobody behind him, no one anywhere near us. When he reaches for me again, I flash back to the water. My instinct is to get away but the tree trunk is at my back and there's nowhere to go.

'I'm sorry if I upset you,' he says.

'You didn't.'

'I know we've not seen much of each other recently – and I know it's my fault. I've got my exams, plus I've had the uni application forms. Football's picking up, too. Then I was feeling ill on Sunday and my dad's got me that factory job next month to get some money before I go away. I'm not trying to avoid you, I'm just really busy.'

I shrug and he steps towards me, but the thought of the river is still burning into my mind and I slip to the side. Robbie stops, crossing his arms.

'What's up, Ell? Did I do something wrong?'

I stare up at him, wondering if he did… knowing *I* did.

'What happened on Saturday night?' I ask. The question is finally out there.

'When?'

'We left Helen's house in your car. What happened?'

'Don't you remember?'

'I wouldn't be asking if I did.'

I can't escape his gaze but neither can I read it. I have no idea what he's thinking. In this moment, we're two strangers. He stares past me into the darkness and then his chest slumps. 'I drove you home, Ell. Nothing happened.'

'Before that.'

He shrugs. 'We were at Helen's house – at the party – and you disappeared. I asked Naomi where you were but she was out of it on that hammock in the garden. The next time I saw you was when we heard the sirens. You were at the bottom of the stairs saying we should go, so we did.'

As he says the word 'stairs', it's like he's telling me that he knows I kissed Ben up those stairs. There's resignation in his voice, perhaps sadness. Not anger, though.

'I'd probably been upstairs for a wee,' I say. Robbie doesn't react, so I add: 'What happened in the car?'

'Not much – it isn't a long journey back to the village, so you asked if we could drive around for a bit.'

'Did we?'

'You know we did. I took us out through Langham and we did a couple of loops out on the plains.'

'What else?'

Robbie sighs again and starts tugging on his hair. He does this sometimes when he's nervous or frustrated. This time, he catches himself and stops, folding his arms instead. 'We played some music and you were singing along. Then we pulled up in the car park at the back of that Morrison's and we talked.'

I have no memory of anything he's telling me – either the driving around or the stopping to chat.

'What did we talk about?'

'Stuff.'

'Stuff like what?'

Robbie stares straight at me and I know the answer. His big eyes are dark and sad, like a puppy that has lost its favourite toy. 'You really don't remember?'

'Please just tell me.'

'We talked about the same stuff as always. You know what it's been like for the past month or so. Since Easter, really. We both know what's coming. This is the end, isn't it?'

Robbie gulps and turns away. Not just looks away, actually turns so that I'm facing his shoulder. He can't look at me, which is good because I can't face him either. I so want to cry, yet it's stuck in my throat. I have to keep speaking, to continue pushing, because I need to know what happened that night.

'The end?' My voice is a croak, a frog with laryngitis.

He turns away a little more, facing the trees and talking to them: 'We're going our separate ways, Ell. This is the end of an era. Our era. We both know any sort of long-distance relationship isn't going to work. I'm going one way this summer and it'll be your turn next year. Perhaps we'll catch up a year or two down the line? Maybe we'll end up together – but this is the time where we go and do our own things. If that eventually brings us back together, then great. If it doesn't, then we've still had these past couple of years.'

Robbie peeps over his shoulder at me and there are tears in his eyes. He's broken and that only breaks me. I screw my eyes closed, not to stop the tears but to try to summon them. I'm a tin can in a microwave, ready to pop. There's a thump in my chest and then, from nowhere, I'm crying. Tears are running along my cheeks and then I'm sobbing even harder because I'm so relieved this part of me still exists. I squeeze my eyelids into my cheeks, pressing so hard that they hurt.

'Did you drop me at home?' I manage through the sobs.

'You know I did.'

'What time?'

'I don't know. Around half twelve or one o'clock, I suppose...'

He tails off.

'What?' I say.

'I suppose I didn't drop you *home*. I left you at the end of your road. You wanted to walk the last bit.'

'Why?'

'I don't know, Ell. You were upset. *I* was upset. We'd been talking about this stuff and I figured you wanted some air.'

It sounds like me and, if we had been having this conversation, chances are I would've wanted to try to clear my head before going home.

Robbie turns back to face me and his expression is so sad that I'm suddenly riddled with doubt, wondering if he does know about Ben and me. Moments ago, I was certain, now I'm not. I want to ask him if we talked about Ben in our 'end of an era' conversation on Saturday night but he seems so downhearted, so shattered, that I don't know if I want to make it any worse for him.

He reaches towards me but I shake my head and sidestep away. I'm not ready to admit to him what I've done and I'm embarrassed by myself. But there's also that tiny voice in the back of my mind saying he was the last person to see me before I woke up in the river. I find it impossible to separate the two thoughts. I should trust him but I absolutely can't.

'Sorry,' I say, mumbling. 'I'm not in the mood. Sarah and everything.'

He runs his tongue along his top row of teeth and nods. 'Shall we go back?'

'As long as Rebecca's stopped talking.'

Robbie offers me his arm and I link mine through it, walking at his side as much as I can while we negotiate the twigs and branches.

Back at the clearing, the party has picked up again. Rebecca is no longer on top of the table and music is playing. For a moment, I wonder if she's left, having had her time in the spotlight, but then I see her sitting on one of the benches, head in hands. She has a Raven on either shoulder, plus three or four lads crowding near, offering sympathies. There are fewer people dancing but more hanging around the edges of the treeline, drinking and eating.

Robbie says he's off to find some of the football team, so I offer a thin smile and leave him to it. I ask a couple of people if they've seen Naomi but get only shrugs and head shakes. I want to avoid the corner of fake grief surrounding Rebecca so head in the opposite direction – where I walk straight into Ollie. He steps back and straightens his top, looking down upon me.

'Hey,' he smiles.

'Hi.'

'Does Mum know you're here?'

'What do you think? Does she know *you're* here?'

'What do you think?'

We offer sad smiles to one another.

'How did you get out?' he asks.

'Teleport. You?'

'*Mission Impossible*-style. Tunnelled into the attic, up onto the roof, jumped from house to house, then stole a helicopter.'

'Nice. I thought about doing that but didn't want to be a flashy git.'

He nudges my arm playfully. 'I won't tell if you don't tell.'

'I've always been a fan of mutually assured destruction.'

He holds out his little finger towards me. 'Pinky swear?'

I think about it and almost link fingers with him. In the end, I tilt my head and offer my best look of disdain. 'How about you don't tell Mum I snuck out and I won't tell her about that hidden folder of video files you keep on the laptop?'

He gulps and then lets his arm sag to his side. 'You know about that?'

'I do now.'

I give him a wink and then spin on my heels, off to find Naomi.

TUESDAY

Chapter Twenty-One

I'm not sure if it's the right thing to do but figure that by acting completely normally with my friends and family, eventually somebody will crack and ask me what's going on. Someone held me under the water until I went limp – and now that person will be panicking, wondering what's happened. By being myself, I'll be driving him or her crazy. That is unless the so-called Hitcher – or some other stranger – was involved. If that's the case, I'm not sure what I can do.

When I find Naomi, she's dancing with Ben in the middle of the clearing. Actually, not just dancing, they're partaking in what the swimming pool rules board would call 'petting'. That's something else I've never understood. No running, no bombing – fair enough. It's all fun and games until someone gets hurt, then the fun really begins. But no petting? Firstly, why is it called petting *specifically* at the swimming pool and nowhere else; secondly, if people are going to strip down to their barest of essentials, isn't that a place where 'petting' is most likely to take place? Not only that, the rules board is woefully incomplete. The powers that be who run the place are worried about a couple sneaking a quick kiss, but they're not fussed enough to have a 'no weeing' rule? That'd be the first line if I was writing that board – no bodily fluids. After that, take your pick.

My mind-drift to swimming pools is interrupted by Ben. Naomi has her back to me, so he's peering over her shoulder, eyes open, staring directly at me as he clings to his girlfriend. It's far too creepy, so I turn and watch Rebecca the Raven talking about the friend she never knew instead. That's marginally more agreeable.

I'm wondering what I should do when an out-of-breath Naomi appears at my side, tugging my wrist. 'C'mon – let's dance.'

'I'm not—'

'C'mon!'

She's bounding with excitement and it's hard to say no to her in that state. She's like a mini kangaroo, bouncing on her heels. I allow Naomi to drag me away and then I'm laughing again. We're dancing and other people are too. It's normal and it's fun and wonderful.

The party continues and it feels like a final hurrah. Not just a goodbye to Sarah, but a goodbye to the older students who'll be taking exams and then going off to do their own things. After this, it's jobs, university and the rest of life. Even for those of us in the lower year, it's so long to our friends.

There's so much laughter and chatter that it stops feeling like we're in a forest, surrounded by nature and the outdoors. We're cramped onto a sweaty dance floor somewhere, or squeezed into someone's living room. It's claustrophobic with everyone on top of one another but it doesn't matter because, after this, we'll all go our own ways. It's all of those things, yet none of them.

I only notice people have started to drift home when the music stops. The lad who brought the speakers is ready to leave and offers an apologetic wave to those of us remaining as things go silent. The clearing has emptied, but I hadn't noticed. There had been forty or fifty people crowded in but at least half have gone. The Ravens are nowhere to be seen, likely having got some lad – or lads – to give them a lift home. That's what usually happens at college.

Ollie seems to have gone, too, and so has Helen. Robbie's sitting on one of the benches slurping from a can of full-fat, full-sugar, teeth-rotting, we're-all-doomed Coke. He looks exhausted, with sweat clinging to his arms. For some reason, he has taken off his shoes. When he spots me looking at him, he fails to stifle a yawn. Ben is lying on the floor at Robbie's feet, either sleeping or pretending to. Naomi, meanwhile, has stopped bouncing as much as she was. Her hair is poking out at angles from under her Kermit beanie and has matted to her forehead. Her arms and face are drenched with sweat and her eyes are unable to focus properly.

'Let's get you some water,' I say, hooking an arm around her and directing her towards the boys. Robbie understands and unscrews the lid from a bottle of water before passing it over. Naomi sips, then gurgles. She takes off her jacket and then lies on the ground next to Ben, her eyes closed, using the jacket as a blanket.

'I'm sleeping here,' she says.

'Where's everyone gone?' I ask Robbie.

He glances at the watch on his wrist. 'It's just after four in the morning, Ell. Where do you think?'

'*Four?*'

'We've been here for hours.'

I pull his wrist towards me and look at the time because it's hard to believe. It felt like an hour, two at most. Was I really dancing with Naomi for all that time?

'You were really going for it,' Robbie says, confirming my thoughts. I don't reply.

A handful of others say goodbye but most trail back along the path without a word, tired and ready for a kip. Without the music, it's no longer a party – just a small group of people hanging around in the woods. Naomi and Ben are sleeping – sort of – so it's just Robbie and me.

'You want something to eat?' he asks. The table of food looks like it's been in the path of a tornado. There are wrappers and crumbs everywhere. So much for the bin signs. I shake my head and start clearing up – something Mum wouldn't believe if she could see me now (although I'm glad she can't).

It's not long before the four of us are the last ones standing – or lying, in Naomi and Ben's cases. We watched the sun set and now it's beginning to rise again, with the first peeps of red and orange creeping through the trees. Insects are starting to buzz, birds beginning to chirp. I can't feel the warmth but it's lovely nonetheless. It's a year to the day that Sarah was taken and we're all here, all still standing.

'Did you have fun?' Robbie asks.

'I guess.'

'I didn't know her very well.'

'Sarah?'

He nods. 'I know she was your brother's girlfriend and in my year but we didn't have any classes together. I don't think I even knew her name until she was found in the river. She was just the girl at your house every now and then.'

I'm not sure what his point is and have no idea how to reply. Sometimes it's easier to say nothing, to let a statement hang.

'Shall we go?' I ask. Robbie shrugs, so I nudge Naomi gently with my foot. She grumbles, rolling into a defensive ball, so I flick her once more.

'I'm sleeping,' she says.

'We're going,' I reply. 'You can come if you want, or we can leave you for the bears.'

'There are no bears in England.'

'The squirrels then.'

Naomi pops an eye open, then two. She sits up cross-legged and stretches her arms high, before aiming a kick at Ben. He squeals and rolls over.

'It's the morning,' Naomi yawns.

'Very observant,' I reply.

'We stayed up all night.'

'Also observant.'

Naomi scratches her head and yawns again. 'We are such badasses.'

'I'm pretty sure there are far more badass things out there.'

She straightens her hat and tugs up her socks. 'Let's go then.'

The four of us trudge back to Robbie's car and then he drives us back to Westby. We pass a milk float on the way, at which gets Naomi excited for an unknown reason. She loses interest almost immediately and then needs to be woken up when Robbie pulls up close to her house. She twists in the seat, kisses Ben on the lips and then wraps her arms around me. She slurs goodbye to Robbie and then stumbles her way up the path.

Ben is dispatched next, though he is half asleep too, then it's just Robbie and me. I clamber into the front seat when it's just us, squeezing between the gap in the seats and then plopping down, all elbows and knees.

'Aren't you tired?' Robbie asks with a yawn.

'I don't even know any more.'

He drives the short distance until we're on my street and then he parks outside number twenty. It's almost daylight, though early enough that people are unlikely to be out of bed.

'Are you going to be at college in, er' – Robbie looks at his watch – 'five hours?' he asks.

'I don't know.'

'I'll see you one way or the other. I know your phone's on the blink.'

'Right. See you later.'

I don't give him a chance to kiss me – I can't face that – so open the car door quickly. In trying to get out so fast, I stumble and only stop myself from falling by grabbing onto the passenger seat.

'You all right?' Robbie asks.

Because of the way I tripped, my head is level with the seat. I struggle to keep myself level but have a clear view underneath. There's a moment in which it feels like everything has stopped.

Under the seat, directly below where I've been sitting, are the silver, strappy pair of flat shoes I was wearing on the night I ended up in the river.

Chapter Twenty-Two

'I need to tie my lace,' I say.

Robbie nods and turns back to the front as I crouch down and pull my flat shoes out from underneath the passenger seat without him noticing. I drop them on the ground next to me, out of his vision, and then untie and retie the shoes I'm wearing.

'Done,' I tell him. 'See you soon.'

He nods as I close the door and then he pulls away, leaving me alone on the street. I spend a few moments looking at the shoes. They're definitely mine because one of the two criss-cross straps on the left one has a small tear in the fabric. I somehow managed to cause that within a week of Mum buying them for me.

After the evening we've had together, where it's been fun and normal, it's hard to believe that Robbie could be the person who attacked me and yet I simply don't know. He says he dropped me off at the bottom of my road in the early hours of Sunday morning but if that were true, wouldn't one of us have noticed I'd left my shoes in his car? As soon as I'd climbed out of the car, I'd have surely asked where my shoes were. If for some reason I hadn't, wouldn't my boyfriend have queried it?

Unless that's not where he dropped me off.

Unless something else happened on the journey home from Helen's house.

There's little I can do for now, so I head along the lane at the back of the houses. I clamber over our rear gate and then find the key that's hidden in the hanging basket next to the back door. I close it very quietly and the sneak into the kitchen… which is where Mum is sitting at the table, steaming cup of tea in hand.

I open my mouth to protest my innocence – I'd heard a noise in the garden and gone out to investigate – but she doesn't seem angry, simply tired. She nods at the seat opposite her, though I don't sit.

'Want a brew?' she asks.

I put my shoes down on the floor but she doesn't mention them. 'No thank you,' I say.

She yawns and I wish it was infectious. Yawns are supposed to be. One person starts and then everyone in a half-mile radius is doing the same. It's not working on me, though. I've been awake for two full days but can't sleep.

'I wondered when you'd get home,' she says.

'How long have you been up?'

She fires back straight away: 'How long have you been out?'

'I've been out for precisely one minute longer than you've been up.'

She smiles and then laughs, which is so surreal I'm not sure how to act. When I saw her sitting at the table, I was expecting another 'my house, my rules' lecture. I wonder if I should ask if she was awake when Ollie got in but then realise he might not have made it home yet. If he has, I'd only be dropping him in it, too.

'Soooo…' I begin. 'How are we going to deal with this?'

'How do *you* think we should deal with it?'

'Honestly? I think you should return to bed and get a couple more hours' sleep. Perhaps this will seem like a dream when you wake up.'

She laughs. 'Oh, Eleanor… you really are my daughter.'

'Does that mean I'm not in trouble?'

'You could at least say sorry.'

I finally take the seat. 'If you want me to *say* sorry, then I will – but if you want me to *be* sorry...'

She sighs and drinks some more of her tea. 'Where were you?'

'Honestly?'

'Honestly.'

'No throwing cups or that sort of thing?'

'When have I ever thrown cups?'

'When Ollie locked himself out and woke you up at three in the morning, trying to get in.'

Her eye twitches and half a smile forms. 'It slipped,' she says.

'That's not how he tells it.'

'Do you believe your brother or your mother?'

'A little from column A...'

She laughs again. 'There will be no cup-throwing, nor hurling, flinging or chucking of any kind.'

'Lobbing?'

'No lobbing either.'

I'm not entirely sure what's going on but it really does seem as if I'm not in trouble. It might be a trick to lure me in but I figure she'll probably find out sooner or later.

'There was a party,' I say. 'It's hard to explain. It was sort of a one-year anniversary thing for Sarah. People talked about her and what they remember. Then it's almost the end of the school year and people wanted a final blowout before exams. Plus, it was the longest day and everything. It all happened together.'

She looks at me and, for a few moments, I'm not sure what she's going to say. It's like she's reading my mind, scanning to see if I've left anything incriminating out. Wondering if I've really been doing drugs in some sex dungeon.

'Was Ollie there?' she asks.

'Um…'

She shakes her head. 'No matter – I was young once, y'know…'

'In the 1800s, yeah?'

I get a stony look.

'So, I'm not in trouble?' I add hastily.

She sighs. 'You really should be. I know I go on about this stuff – but you're at an awkward age. I don't want to say your whole life hinges on the next couple of years because it doesn't. That's what adults tell you when they want to keep you in line. I try not to be like that.'

'I can become an alcoholic crack addict and it'll be fine?'

Her raised eyebrows silence me. 'Know when you're on a winner, Ell. Look, lots of people have amazing, productive lives with few qualifications at all – but plenty of others have appalling lives despite getting amazing exam results when they're teenagers. It's not necessarily what you do, it's who you are. But part of that is discipline – so if you *can* discipline yourself to revise for exams and do well, that's something that'll hold you in good stead for the rest of your life.'

I nod, not because I feel I should but because I really do get it. I think about saying 'it's only one night' – but, hey, as she says, I'm on a winner.

Mum reaches out and I kneel on the floor, allowing her to hug me. I hug her back, too. Twice in two days has to be a record. It's not that we have a bad relationship but touchy-feely isn't our thing. It's more of a noddy-winky thing, which, in all honesty, sounds like a dodgy kids' TV show.

When I pull away, she reaches out and strokes my necklace. My *re-gifted* necklace. Not that I'm still bitter.

'You know this was your grandmother's, don't you? Your great-grandmother's before that, then mine. That's four generations.'

I shuffle further away and sit back on the chair. 'You've mentioned it once or twice.'

Mum gives me the lopsided 'you're on thin ice' stare. 'There's nothing wrong with family, Eleanor.'

'I'm not saying there is.'

I play with the necklace myself. There's an emblem at the front, some sort of circle within a circle.

'Your great-grandmother was some sort of mystic. She used to do tarot readings, those sorts of things.'

'Tarot?'

Mum nods. 'Your grandmother believed in it all, too – but then she was brought up with it.' She points to my necklace. 'That's supposed to keep you safe.'

My first reaction is to snort and then I find myself clutching the circles. '*Safe?* How?'

'I have no idea. That's what she said when she passed it on to me. I think it had been blessed or something like that. Cursed, maybe? I don't know. I wore it for a year or two when I was your age and then put it away.'

'You don't believe the story?'

Mum rolls her eyes and then catches herself. 'I believe in science – but if other people choose to believe the things they do, that's up to them.'

The metal circles of the necklace are smooth but feel cold. I let it drop to my chest. 'Do you know what the circles mean?'

'They're just circles. Your grandmother believed a lot of things. She'd never eat meat on a weekend. She thought aliens built Stonehenge. She was sure her old house was haunted. You name it, she probably believed in it. Some magical protective necklace is just one thing in a long list. I'm not sure why I mentioned it.'

She finishes off her tea and then crosses to the sink. 'You should probably get some sleep. You have college in a few hours.'

I wonder if I should tell her that I've not slept for more than two days and might not need to ever again. It's a fleeting thought, though. She'd start to think I was turning into my grandmother.

I say 'goodnight' instinctively, but my timing makes her snort in what might be amusement, though could also be annoyance. I'm still marginally on a winner, so don't push it. I'm at the bottom of the stairs when I hear her calling after me.

'You're still coming tonight, aren't you?' she asks. 'Ollie would want you there.'

I lean back, making sure she can see me through the kitchen door. 'Of course, I'll be there.'

Chapter Twenty-Three

Even though I don't need to sleep, I'm not in the mood for college. I hide away in my room, waiting for Ollie and Mum to go their separate ways. When they've left, I emerge into the empty house. I don't know Naomi or Robbie's plans for the day – but there will be lots of people sleeping off hangovers this morning and, sooner or later – likely sooner – news of our late-night party will leak.

I'm not sure if I believe much of what Mum told me about my grandmother's theories over the necklace. Actually, I am sure – I *don't* believe it has magic powers that somehow kept me alive – but it would be nice to get a second opinion.

I search the Internet for the intertwining circles of my necklace but it's hard to find anything that matches. Any wider searches for things like 'occult' and 'mysticism' only lead me back to the realm of the barmy, so I quickly give up. Sometimes, as distressing as it is in this digital age, the Internet can only get a person so far – and there's only one thing for it.

Purton-on-Sea is the closest resort to Westby, though 'resort' might be pushing it a little. That stokes up thoughts of long sandy beaches, bright blue skies, crystal-clear waters and, perhaps, sticks of rock.

Purton-on-Sea offers little of that.

It's a small town with a cobbled beach, which, if you ask me, isn't a beach at all. A beach has sand, not a long pile of rocks. People can lie on beaches comfortably, without having solid edges jutting into limbs. Being buried on a sandy beach can be relaxing; being buried on a cobbled beach is grievous bodily harm. What's more, people cannot – nor will they ever be able to – build a rock castle. Piling stones on top on one another does not count.

Although Purton-on-Sea is quite crappy, a description that hasn't made the welcome sign, it is easy to get to. A single bus takes me the hour from Westby to the sea and, by lunchtime, I'm strolling along the path next to the cobbled beach. Because there aren't enough rocks on display, they've built a massive seawall out of cobbles, too. I have to wonder if it's because someone, somewhere, simply liked saying the word 'cobble' and, before anyone knew it, things had got out of hand.

There are a handful of holidaymakers strolling around, likely because Chernobyl was booked up as a holiday destination. A few maniacs are actually sunbathing on the 'beach', towels down and all in case a sudden swarm of a thousand tourists descend.

Other than that, Purton-on-Sea offers little. There are tat shops at either end of the street that face the sea, with an ice cream van parked halfway along.

I head past the van and turn onto one of the streets that head towards the town centre, trying to remember where I'm going. It's been years since I visited here on a day out with school, which I remember largely because Ian Lemon disappeared for two hours and nobody noticed until it was time to catch the coach back. Having that name meant he was, of course, mercilessly bullied anyway, but he certainly made sure he was remembered that day. One of the teachers eventually found him strolling along the broken pier at the far end of town, where he was apparently crab fishing. In fairness to him, he had found something with which to amuse himself among the boredom of Purton-on-Sea.

I find myself weaving in and out of the small alleys that are largely filled with shops displaying closed signs. There's a chippy and a fishmonger, plus a small bakery with rows of brightly iced gingerbread men in the window.

You can judge a lot about a person by how they begin their assault on a gingerbread man. Those who go for the legs first are generally more compassionate. It's a necessary demolition but people can still get around without legs. It's obviously a bit more difficult, but things could be worse. I tend to think that's making the best of a bad situation.

Biscuit-eaters who initially go for the head are a little more worrying. I have to confess that it's funnier to go for the head first, primarily because of the imagery of something blundering around with nothing on top of its shoulders, but it's still a brutal assault. All the more so if the figure is smiling. I feel better about biting off the head of a frowny gingerbread man.

The real psychos, though – the absolute nutters – are those who first go after a gingerbread man's arms. It is a targeted, vicious act. The legs or head are open goals – there for the taking – but the arms are wedged into the middle, so the assailant has to go out of their way to eat the arms first. It requires foresight and planning, both signs of a person not entirely balanced.

Never trust a person who eats a gingerbread man arm-first.

After the bakery, I pass a museum chronicling the history of the town. It is predictably tiny – barely the size of our front room at home.

When I find myself back on the seafront, the seagulls are forming a beaky-looking army close to the ice cream van. If they have their act together they could definitely take the driver, but I haven't got the willpower to wait around and find out.

I finally find what I'm searching for two streets back from the seafront, hidden between a joke shop and a door that offers no clue as to what's behind. I'd already walked past what I was looking for once, but missed the faded stencilling above the door.

'Mystic Martha', it reads – except the first 'S' and final few letters have disintegrated to such a degree that it reads 'Mytic Mart'. There are some swirls spiralling from the top but those are faded, too. I knock on the door and wait… then wait some more. After a second knock, there's another pause and then it swings inwards with a shrill creak that is so pantomime that I half wonder if it's a sound effect.

Standing in the doorway is a woman who wouldn't bother the five-foot mark on a height chart. She has straggly silver hair poking from underneath a dark shawl, with a purple scarf around her neck. Her face is shaded with wrinkles and it's hard to know how old she is – anywhere from forty to ninety.

She ducks her head to the side, peering onto the street, and then finally focuses on me.

'Can I help you?' she asks, voice as creaky as the door.

'Are you Martha?'

'I am… and you're…' She stares at me and, for a moment, I think she's going to pluck my name from the air. Then she adds: '… in need of help.'

'I suppose.'

She wafts her hands around the air in front of me, as if painting an invisible picture with her bare fingers. When I step back, she scowls and follows me, still flapping.

'Your aura is damaged, girl.'

'My aura?'

'Your chakra is in need of repair.'

'My what?'

She stops moving her hands and shuffles back to the door, nodding inside. 'Come.'

I figure I've come this far, so follow her through the door. I end up in a musty hallway, full of dust, hardback books and dreamcatchers that are hanging from the ceiling and pinned to the walls. My sense of smell is still off but hints of bitter incense make my nose twitch.

Martha leads me through the hallway into a small study-type room that is lined with even more dreamcatchers. There are far too many to count, but the spindly twigs and strings are attached to every surface. Across the top of the room is a large purple sheet that blocks the ceiling. Aside from the dreamcatchers, the other major feature of the room is the word 'FAITH' written in spindly calligraphy over the door.

I'm ushered onto a stool that's so short it wouldn't be out of place in a primary school. Martha stands behind me, out of sight, and I get the sense she's waving her hands around again.

'Rarely have I seen an energy field that needs cleansing more than yours, my dear,' she coos.

'I have an energy field?'

I turn but her hands grip my shoulders firmly and she forces me to face the front. 'Not for much longer if this is allowed to continue.'

'Um…'

She suddenly appears in front of me but I'm not completely sure how it happened. One moment she was behind me, a blink later and she was in front. She's bobbing from foot to foot and I'm not sure where to look. I feel dizzy and am left wondering whether she's moving at all, or if it's me. It's all very disorientating.

'It will be incredibly draining to cleanse an aura this damaged,' she says. 'Terribly, terribly draining.'

'I'm not sure if—'

'An act this tiring will require a significant donation…'

'I don't really have that much money.'

She stops bouncing. 'An aura this damaged would generally require at least fifty pounds' worth of donation.'

'I'm not really here for that.'

'My dear, you might not have *intended* to come here for this – but you were likely drawn to me. Our bodies are channels and with an aura so badly affected, nature will have guided you to me.'

'Right… it's just, even if I was led here, I still don't have fifty quid.'

'You cannot put a price on work this essential.'

I stare at her, wondering if she's actually for real. It was her who put a price on the 'work'.

'I'm only really here to ask you a question,' I say. 'I was hoping—'

'Child, I cannot answer questions from a soul whose very essence is so irrevocably damaged.'

We stare at each other, at an impasse for a moment or two.

'Doesn't "irrevocably" mean "irreversibly"? In other words, I can't be fixed…?'

She shakes her head initially and then starts to nod slowly but ends up making a sort of diagonal swish. 'Let us hope it is not irrevocably…'

Martha finishes with a flourish of both her voice and hand.

'I still don't have fifty pounds,' I say, fumbling in my pocket and emerging with a screwed-up fiver. 'This is pretty much all I can manage.'

She eyes me, then the money, then me again. Eventually the money wins and she snatches the note from my hand, immediately dispatching it into her robe.

'Can I ask my question now?' I say.

'Your aura…'

'Maybe we can fix that afterwards?'

She draws herself up onto tiptoes, which makes her tower over me only because I'm on such a low stool. 'What would you like to ask?' she says.

I tug my necklace out from under my top and point the circular pattern upwards. 'Do you know what this is?'

Martha leans in, taking the emblem in her hand. We're so close that her shawl is touching my cheek. Damaged chakra or not, she doesn't seem to have any problem with inappropriate closeness.

'Where did you get it?' she asks.

'It was my great-grandmother's.'

She steps away and narrows her eyes, creating even more wrinkles on her forehead. She looks like a shrivelled potato.

'It's very old,' she says – which, in all honesty, isn't exactly going out on a limb.

'Right… does it mean anything in particular?'

'Symbols mean many things, child.'

'Exactly – so do the circles mean anything *specifically*? They sort of interlink which each other. I wondered if they had a significance…?'

I'm beginning to get the sense that Mystic Martha isn't simply lacking in any sort of mystic powers, but that she's not even particularly smart at concealing the fraud.

From nowhere, she springs forward and presses a hand to each of my temples. I have no time to stop her, then, before I can react, she recoils as if I've electrocuted her. She shrieks and blows on her fingers, backing towards the door.

'What?' I ask.

'You must go.'

'Huh?'

She scrounges into her robe and withdraws the five-pound note I gave her, dropping it on the shelf next to the door. 'You can take your money but you have to go.'

'Why?'

Martha is shaking her head so viciously from side to side that her features are a blur. She opens the door and backs through it, not taking her eyes from me.

'You're nothing,' she whispers.

'I'm what?'

'Go!'

She shouts with such venom, such fear, that I leap to my feet. As I approach the door, she continues to back through it until she's in the hall. When she reaches the far corner, she screeches again, holding her arms defensively across herself.

I leave the money and try not to get too close to the woman, instead holding my palms up to show I mean no harm.

'I don't know what I've done,' I say.

'Leave.'

'What happened when you touched me?'

She shrinks even further, cowering from me. I stride to the front door, leaving me at one end of the hall, her at the other.

'I'm not trying to hurt you,' I say.

'So black, so empty.'

'Me? *I'm* black and empty?'

'Black,' she repeats, still holding her arms in front of herself. I stare at her for a few more moments, wondering if she's going to add anything. She peeps through the gaps between her fingers and then shrieks once more. There's little else for me to do, so I open the door and head outside, wondering what on earth has just happened.

Chapter Twenty-Four

I find myself sitting on the seafront wall close to the bus stop, staring out across the grey-brown swill of water. Suddenly the militant seagulls, rubbish cobbles and everything else about this horrible place doesn't seem so funny.

I don't believe in things such as mystics, psychics, mind readers and the like but if my necklace really does mean 'protected', as my grandmother claimed, I figured a second opinion would do no harm. If someone independent had confirmed the circles have some sort of significance, then I'm still not sure I would have believed that's what brought me back to life in the river.

It at least would have been an explanation, however. It might have been a mad-sounding theory but it's better than anything I had before. With Mystic Martha, it was easy to be superior and smug and then... I don't know what happened.

She wasn't acting, she was *actually* terrified of me. '*Black*'? '*Empty*'? What does that mean? *I'm* black and empty?

If she is a fraud, she's a good one... or an awful one considering she offered my money back.

Buses only go once an hour and I've narrowly missed one. With little desire to explore the rest of the town, I'm left watching the tide slowly flow in. It covers the slick of mud and starts to lick at the edge of the cobbles.

Black and empty.

When she was younger, Mystic Martha must've been a right laugh on a date.

When I check my phone, half an hour has passed. I've got four texts from Naomi, each asking where I am and wondering if I'm going to college. There's another from Robbie, who wants to know if I'm okay. I'm not in the mood to reply, not yet, so simply sit and watch.

Black and empty.

What an absolute cow.

The bus eventually arrives but it's almost four o'clock by the time I'm back in Westby. The village is quiet but that's only because everyone's gearing up for what's going to happen this evening. All the locally owned shops are starting to shut, with sandwich boards being carried inside and open/closed signs being turned. I get a couple of nodded acknowledgements as I head along the high street, then I cut into one of the shortcuts that will take me home. I follow the wall that spans the cemetery until reaching the front of the church and the green ahead.

None of my family are religious and I've never been brought up to believe in, well, anything, I suppose. Not even Santa. At primary school, my friends and classmates used to talk about what Father Christmas was bringing them and I'd ask – without trying to be mean – why they didn't realise it was their parents giving them gifts. Isn't it odd to tell a child a made-up story until they're a certain age and then admit it was a lie all along? It's a bit rich when parents then teach their children to tell the truth. I've never been sure if I missed out on something growing up, whether I was normal or the weird one.

Whatever I might think of religion, the church is utterly beautiful and unquestionably the sparkling highlight of where I live. The steepling clock tower was refurbished when I was young and can be seen from both ends of the village. Stained-glass Bible scenes surround the walls and there is an enormous, ancient wooden door at the front. A pretty path winds through the cemetery, with a blooming rainbow of flowers on either side. I walk past the church most days, taking it for granted, but on a day like today with the sun high and sky blue, it takes my breath away.

When I get to the main gates, the vicar is busy pinning something on the noticeboard. He notices me, nodding at first and offering a cheery smile. I return the acknowledgement but am already past him when I stop and turn.

'Hi,' I say.

He's a stumpy, round man, wearing dark trousers with a grandpa jumper, even though it's warm. The white of his collar peeks through above the wool. Aside from a few lonely strands of hair threaded across his head, he's bald.

'Beautiful day, isn't it?' he replies.

'It's lovely.'

I continue looking at him, not sure how to phrase things, but he seems to understand, peering over his rimless glasses at me. 'Can I help you with something?'

'I think I have a question.'

He smiles again and it's so reassuring that I wonder why I've always ducked my head and speeded up any time I've seen him. As if I'm scared that saying hello to someone who believes in God might make me suddenly start singing 'Kumbaya' in the shower.

'You *think* you have a question?' he says with a smile.

'Okay – I *actually* have a question.'

'Would you like to ask it?'

I turn to look over my shoulder, suddenly self-conscious that someone could overhear and think I'm losing the plot.

'Do you want to come into the church?' he asks.

He nods towards the open doors and, for a reason of which I'm not sure, it feels like a good idea. He takes a couple of steps up the path and I follow, half a step behind.

'Do I have to call you father or something?' I ask.

'I've never been much of a stickler. Some feel comfortable using my first name – Mark – while some of my other parishioners address me as "Reverend Newby" or "Vicar". I don't really have a preference. It's Eleanor, isn't it?'

I glance sideways at him as we continue to walk, wondering how he knows that.

'Ellie,' I reply.

'Ellie it is.'

He leads me through the front door and my footsteps echo from the hard floor as my eyes struggle to adjust from the bright light of outside to the murky gloom of inside. When I manage to blink into the room, I see a large golden cross at the front, with a beaming stained-glass image of Jesus being crucified behind. Wooden pews line both sides.

'Would you like to sit?'

I rest a hand on one of the pews but continue standing. I'm not trying to be rude, it's just that it feels like the seats should be there for those who believe.

'I… You're going to think I'm a little crazy if I ask you what I want.'

The vicar smiles kindly, the type of *heard-it-all-before* fatherly look. 'How about you tell me what's troubling you, and if it sounds a little "crazy" so be it.'

I face the front. 'Jesus came back from the dead, didn't he? That's what you believe.'

'That is, indeed, where I put my faith.'

'But how did it happen?'

'It was by the grace of God—'

'But how did it *actually* happen? Was it like he was sleeping and then woke up?'

The vicar doesn't reply at first. Though I'm not looking at him, I know he's smiling softly. 'Jesus was sealed in a tomb. There is only one who can know the answer to that.'

Sounds a bit convenient to me. Resurrecting in front of a crowd is quite the trick. Behind closed doors, well, who's to know what's gone on there...

'Do you think anyone else has ever come back from the dead?' I ask.

I feel a hand on my shoulder but don't jump. It's comforting. For a time, neither of us speaks, though I can sense him breathing. 'It's been a hard year for everyone, Ellie. The death of young Miss Lipski is something that hit the village hard, none more so than her friends.'

I open my mouth to say that I wasn't referring to Sarah but stop myself, as there's no point. What should I say? That I think *I'm* back from the dead? Resurrected in the river after being drowned? I shouldn't be here.

'It's tough for anyone,' he continues, 'but especially for the young to find meaning and understanding where it appears there is none.'

He removes his hand and we stand side by side, staring at the light beaming through the glass depicting Jesus tied to a cross, spear jammed into his side, red twinkling glass trailing to the floor.

'Can I ask you one more thing?' I say.

'Of course.'

'Why do you believe Jesus came back from the dead?'

The vicar answers immediately: 'He did so to cleanse our sins.'

'I know... well, I mean I know the story. It's just... why do *you* believe it happened? I'm not saying it didn't—'

'I know what you're asking, Ellie.'

'Sorry.'

His hand is on my shoulder again and I feel better. 'Don't be sorry. These are questions mankind has been asking itself for thousands of years. The reason I believe Jesus died for my sins is because I have faith. Other people believe different things – and that's absolutely fine. It isn't my job to try to persuade everyone else I'm right, it's my job to counsel those who have the faith I do.'

His fingers tense and squeeze my shoulder but I'm not sure whether I can actually feel it, or if it's simply that I can sense it.

He spins and I turn to face him. 'That belief is something that cannot be defined through concrete proof or science,' he adds. 'Someone might offer a thousand reasons why something can or cannot be true – but that does nothing to dispel true, genuine faith.'

I have no idea why, yet I feel teary again. It's ridiculous and I am embarrassed by myself once again. There are, thankfully, no tears but my throat feels raw.

My voice is croaky but I somehow get the words out: 'You believe what you believe regardless of what anyone else thinks?'

'Precisely.'

I don't say it but the thought is there nonetheless. Dead or not dead, drowned or not drowned – perhaps the reason I'm here isn't down to anything I'll ever be able to prove. Perhaps it *is* more about belief.

Chapter Twenty-Five

It feels like the entire village is arranged in two-by-two formation, with one long line stretching far behind me. I'm near the front, Naomi at my side. It's after ten, almost dusk, and everyone's holding a candle as we head solemnly along the high street in near-silent reverence. Someone behind is sobbing but I don't want to turn to see who it is in case the person behind walks into me and creates a chain reaction along the line.

It is eerie to be moving in such silence. The shops on either side of the street are closed and there are no internal bulbs blazing, leaving only our candles and the dying light of the sun to guide us. The vicar leads the line by himself but Mr and Mrs Lipski are directly behind, then it is Ollie alongside Mum. A few of the parish councillors are next, then it's Naomi and me, with Robbie and Ben somewhere behind with their own families.

The procession continues along the high street and then turns to pass the church, before looping around the green and heading to the river. I have tingles as we cross the bridge and then start to line up along the river. We stand in silence until everyone has filed onto the car park by the bank.

I don't know how many people are here but it's definitely in the hundreds and I wonder where all the candles have come from. My back is to the river, which is fine by me. I can still feel the tug of the water.

The vicar whispers something to Mrs Lipski, who nods, though neither of them say anything out loud. Meanwhile, the final few villagers cross the bridge and slot into the mass. Rebecca and her wraith-like Ravens are there, skin pale, hair darker than ever in matching tight buns. Rebecca's head is bowed and her shoulders are bobbing slightly as she sobs into her hands. It's all a bit odd and I'm unsure if I'm annoyed or bemused. One of the older men from the village is wearing a suit and offers her a tissue. Rebecca sniffs as she takes it and then dabs at her eyes. Everyone is watching her. Just the way she likes it.

There's a low wittering as people start to fill the silence. Naomi leans in close to my ear: 'Where have you been all day?'

'Around and about.'

'They cancelled morning classes and laid on counsellors in case anyone wanted to talk. Your mum's bloke was there, too. It was all a bit over the top. Most of us went and sat on the grass instead, getting rid of our hangovers.'

I'm about to ask her how many students turned up but then the vicar clears his throat loudly, getting everyone's attention. Mrs Lipski is standing on a box that's appeared from nowhere, head and shoulders above everyone. Her voice is delicate and quavering, yet the still of the night amplifies it like a bass-heavy speaker.

'Thank you for coming,' she says. 'It's so touching to see your support.'

As she speaks, I spot Ash standing near to the river, closer to the water than anyone. His back is to the crowd but I have a side-on view, allowing me to see his shadowed face. I shiver again as he stares towards the spot where I awoke two and a half days ago. Almost as if *he* has eyes in the back of his head, Ash spins and locks onto me. For a moment I'm frozen, colder than ever, but then he turns away, focusing on his shoes. I look towards Mrs Lipski, who is still speaking, but can feel Ash watching me once more.

'… I know we've withdrawn from the community over the past year,' Mrs Lipski continues, 'but we have really appreciated the way people have tried to reach out to us. It's been heartening to see how many of you genuinely cared for and loved Sarah in the way we did.'

She reaches out her hand and, unprompted, Ollie emerges through the crowd and takes it. There's a gasp so deep that it feels as if everyone has inhaled at the same time.

Mrs Lipski smiles and she releases Ollie's hand. He turns to face the crowd but is struggling to peer up from ground level.

'Many of you know Oliver,' she says. 'I want you to know that it is my choice to stand alongside him. I've heard the same rumours as you – but Oliver and Sarah were in love. It might have been what you call teenage love, it might have been more – but when you love another person, that isn't a feeling that goes away. In a few months, Oliver will have the chance that Sarah did not. He'll be going to university with the rest of his life ahead of him and, with all my heart, I wish him well.'

Her voice cracks and Ollie looks up, clasping her hand briefly and then letting her go. She nods in acknowledgement but is determined to continue. Meanwhile, Mr Lipski is brooding. He's older than his wife, or looks it. He is wearing a suit with a flat cap, watching his wife speak, face blank.

'I'm tired of the innuendo,' Mrs Lipski adds. 'I don't want to listen to the blame game any longer. Sarah wouldn't want it and neither do I.'

There's a chastening silence, filled with the tapping toes and fidgeting discomfort of gossiping busybodies who didn't expect to be told off. I almost want to punch the air – this has been a year in coming. Sarah's mother has used the moment most special to her to slap down all those who have spent the past twelve months whispering conspiracies. Mum is standing a little to the side of Ollie, lips tight but eyes beaming with thanks.

'What about the Hitcher?'

The female voice comes from somewhere near the back of the crowd but it is immediately supported by flurried mutterings. People either genuinely scared, or desperate for something else to gossip about. I'm never sure how cynical I should be.

Mrs Lipski, who has remained so strong, now seems out of her depth. She turns in a semicircle until Uncle Jim steps forward. He helps her down from the box and then stands himself, shushing the assorted murmurs and waiting until he can be heard. He's so tall to begin with that he's now a couple of heads taller than anyone, a pillar illuminated by candlelight.

'Hello,' he says. Although he still doesn't have the silent respect Mrs Lipski had, he continues anyway: 'Thank you all for coming out tonight. Believe me, I do feel the responsibility that whoever attacked Sarah Lipski is still at large. It's not something I take lightly. It's been some time but that doesn't mean it's something myself or my colleagues in the wider area have forgotten about.'

The whispers are becoming louder around me and it's clear Jim hasn't simply lost the audience, he never had them.

He clears his throat loudly and shouts this time: 'If this so-called Hitcher is out there—'

'He is!'

I don't need to turn to know it is Rebecca who is shouting. At her interruption, another three or four people call out to insist they've seen this 'Hitcher' as well.

'*If* this so-called Hitcher is out there – and he poses any sort of danger to the community, then I will of course do all I can to keep people safe. As yet, nobody has been able to give me any concrete directions as to who he might be, where he could be staying, or if he had anything to do with the break-in at the post office.'

'Rubbish!'

Another voice – male this time – chimes from the back.

Jim is becoming frustrated. Perhaps unwittingly, he rolls his eyes, which is a big mistake as the catcalls begin. People are shouting for him to resign, to 'do his job' and more. To counter it, he pushes himself onto tiptoes, getting himself even higher and then starts shouting. I'm not sure I've ever seen him angry but this is pretty close.

'It's not rubbish! I'm here to protect this village and the surrounding area but I can only do that if you trust me as a community. There's no evidence that this person – this so-called Hitcher – has done anything wrong. That doesn't mean I'm not looking into it, it simply means I have to prioritise *actual* crimes.'

Nobody sounds convinced because it isn't what they want to hear. Couple a break-in to a village institution with a possible mysterious stranger and they want SWAT squads, helicopters, the SAS, MI5 and whoever else to investigate. Having one poor bloke who looks after a handful of villages say he's not sure what's going on would be bad enough, even without it being on the anniversary of a murder.

'Please!' Jim shouts. 'If you see anything, if you have any concerns, come to me. Or call 999 if it's an emergency. So far, people have spoken to the newspaper before me.'

It's a naughty rebuke that'll make him few friends but perhaps it needed to be said. The overwhelming grumbles of the crowd doesn't make it feel like a good idea.

Jim is about to step down from the platform when a woman emerges through the front of the crowd. She has long red hair and is wearing a dark jacket with her bare legs showing. People clear a path for her and she's so frantic that she almost trips over an errant leg. She steadies herself but her face is a mess of streaky tears.

'I've not seen my daughter all day,' she says.

Jim's barely restrained mask of calm slips with a grimace and a nervous glance up to those who are around him. The last thing he wants at this moment is for something like this to happen in front of everyone.

'Perhaps we should do this elsewhere, Mrs James?' he says quietly.

There are tears in her eyes as I realise who the woman is. I don't know how I missed it – they look so alike.

'Has anyone seen my daughter, Helen?' she shouts, turning to the crowd, before looking back to Jim. 'I assumed she was sleeping in this morning. It's only when I got back this evening, when I saw I'd had no messages from her, that I realised I've not seen her since early yesterday evening. She's been gone for twenty-four hours at least.'

I turn to Naomi – we know that's not entirely true, as we saw Helen in the early hours of the morning. Apparently, no one has seen her since then.

When Helen's mum spots us, she turns to Naomi and me and leaps forward. 'You're her friends, aren't you? Have you seen her? Was she in college?'

I don't know because I wasn't there either – but Naomi shakes her head slowly. Mrs James turns back to the crowd, pushing herself onto tiptoes. She shouts to ask if anyone's seen Helen but is met by a series of bemused looks and head shakes. She looks around hopefully and then her chin begins to wobble, before she covers her face with her hands and dissolves into a throat-bobbing flurry of tears.

WEDNESDAY

Chapter Twenty-Six

It is a cool morning in the countryside, with wispy trails of mist billowing across the fields, engulfing the trees. Dew clings to the grass and the bushes, making it look like the area has been doused by rainfall that hasn't been seen in weeks.

'Halt!'

The shout comes from somewhere off to my right and the long line of people stops as one, everybody turning towards the voice. My shoes are sodden from the dew, not that it's a major ongoing concern. The village has turned out again – this time as an organised search team.

Jim and some of his police colleagues from Langham are at Helen's house doing whatever it is they do. The other handful of officers has sorted the village volunteers into long lines to pick through the fields and woods by which we are surrounded. It feels as if the entire village has joined in to help the search. Perhaps they have.

'Continue!'

As the second call comes, we continue to march ahead one steady step at a time. I'm in one of the large fields outside the village, part way towards Langham. The grass is yellowed and crisp, despite the dew. Underneath, the soil is tough and bobbly, with unexpected ridges crusted along the surface. It feels as if everyone already knows what's happened to Helen given it's a year since Sarah's body was discovered in the river. I've spent the night wondering what I should do. Three days without sleep now, without food. Has Helen been taken because I survived? Because whoever drowned me saw me walking around and believed they'd bodged the job? If that's true, what can I do? Tell people I think I was drowned? That I'm actually dead, even though I'm not. It'd be the ramblings of a lunatic.

I can't escape the guilt that Helen's gone because I'm here. Perhaps the reason I was given a second chance is because I was meant to stop this by finding out the identity of my attacker. I failed and, by doing so, I've allowed this to happen.

'Halt.'

Everyone stops once more as the call comes from the left this time. A man who lives along the road from me is half a dozen people along the line and he points towards a spot on the ground. One of the uniformed policemen steps forward with an evidence bag and picks up a few threads of cotton that look like they've disentangled themselves from a pair of socks. It could be something, could be nothing. Who knows?

'Continue.'

Naomi is walking next to me, dressed in jeans with a sombre-looking black beanie. It's not the day for a muppet hat. She's barely spoken since we assembled at the meeting place this morning. The Ravens are here, too. The trio are walking in a line near the hedge on the far right, wearing matching jeans with wellington boots, ever conscious of who might be watching.

Even I can't begrudge them being here, though. Everyone knew Helen. She drifted effortlessly between the school castes, friends with people like Naomi and me, civil with the Ravens and their adorers, and offering a flirty smile or two to enchant the computer crowd. She went out with one of our high school's rugby team last year, too, so even they are accepting and friendly with her. Somehow, among the most entrenched class system ever devised – teenagers at school – she got on with everyone. When the media get here, people will say they don't understand why anyone would want to hurt her.

They'll be right, too.

I'm so engrossed in my thoughts that I almost trip over an exposed root. I catch myself just in time to spot something dark in among the grass in front of me. I hold my hand up and there's an instant 'halt' from the nearby officer, which brings the line to a stop.

When the policeman nears me, I point him towards what I've seen. I can feel the tension, including from Naomi, wondering if it's something or nothing. So far, every time we've stopped, it's been nothing. The officer crouches with a bag and reaches into a small clump of overgrown grass. When he pulls his gloved hand away, I gasp. It looks like a soft leather bracelet, the same as the one I found in the river. It matches, it's just like the one that's buried in my drawer at home, it's…

Not a bracelet at all.

The officer twists the small circle of twigs in his hand and then places it into a bag anyway before standing again. 'Was that it?' he asks me. He's not trying to sound accusing or harsh, but it's hard not to feel that way.

'Yes,' I say.

He nods. 'Continue.'

Everyone does, step by gradual step.

When we reach the edge of the field, the search party stops for a few minutes as the officers consult one another. As far as I can tell, the only things we've uncovered are crisp packets, chocolate wrappers, string and twigs. Nobody is talking in anything other than short sentences. Robbie, Ben, Ash and Ollie are all part of the line – all suspects, I suppose, if only in my mind. I really don't know what I'm doing.

Among the hush there are still whispers about the Hitcher. He's become the prime suspect among the village, even if there's no proof he actually exists.

Better to look for a devil without than a devil within.

I know Jim spent part of last night speaking to some of the residents who'd apparently seen the Hitcher, but I don't know if he got any more from them than what was in the paper. When Mum, Ollie and I left to return home, he was still hanging on and giving the impression that he wouldn't be sleeping any time soon.

'It's my fault.'

Naomi speaks so unexpectedly that I jump. She doesn't notice, tucking her hands into her armpits and tightening her arms around herself.

'How is it your fault?' I ask.

'I should've made a bigger deal when I didn't see her at college yesterday. We're in the same classes. I knew she was off.'

'So was I – so was half the college.'

Naomi shakes her head, unconvinced. 'We weren't great friends but I should have said something.'

'What else could you have done? The teachers must've known she was off.'

'Have you heard what everyone's saying about her?'

I shake my head, not sure if I want to hear the theories. I've seen how gossip affects people.

'Her phone's either off or destroyed,' Naomi adds. 'Nobody's been able to get an answer and no one's seen her since our party in the woods. They're saying she left in a car with some of the upper-sixth lads.'

'Who?'

'Don't know – that's just what I heard. Apparently, the police are going to want to talk to us all at some point. They know about the party. The only reason we've not been questioned yet is because they're so busy.' She stops for breath. 'Did you see her leave?'

'No, I didn't really notice anyone leaving. We were dancing most of the night.'

She nods. 'I know.'

I wonder how much she actually does know. These rumours are already spreading, so how long will it be before people from the party are saying they saw Helen leave with those upper-sixth lads just because that's what they've heard?

It's not malicious lies, it's people wanting to help. If five of their friends say they saw something, it's natural to want to be included. It's why everyone's talking about the Hitcher. One person sees someone they don't recognise and suddenly everyone is seeing the same person.

It's why people turned on Ollie.

He's standing on his own a little away from the hedge, scuffing his shoes into the ground while staring downwards. He'll feel the eyes on him, people wondering if he's somehow conned Sarah's parents, all the while focusing on a new target.

Then a flitting, chilling thought tickles across me. What if it *is* him? I've told myself it's not but do I truly share the faith of which the vicar spoke? Do I *really* believe he's innocent, despite the rumours, despite all that's happened? Despite the fact he's my brother?

I'd love to say I was confident but Helen's disappearance has left me confused to an even greater degree than I was before.

I have no idea how to prove, or disprove, any theory. If I was home alone, I might be able to search Ollie's room. I'm not sure what I'd be looking for, but perhaps it would go some way to help dislodge the niggling doubt.

Another person by himself is Ash. He's standing rigidly a few metres from the hedge, arms behind his back as he watches the officers. For a moment, I think he'll pull the eyes in the back of his head routine but he doesn't turn to look at me. Instead, I realise someone else is eyeing him, too. Tina from the chippy – Ash's ex and, perhaps, only girlfriend – is focused on him. She notices me watching her and turns away, saying something to one of the people near her.

Before I can start deciding anyone else is the killer, the officers call us to attention, saying we're going to start on the adjacent field. Everyone troops across and lines up, before we begin the slow march back the way we came.

We find more rubbish, more twigs, more nothing. Definitely not Helen or any sign of her. When we arrive back at the car park near the river to discover that the other search parties have found nothing either, the atmosphere starts to become disheartened. Someone from the local café is pouring teas from a large urn into polystyrene cups but the crowd is already split. Some are saying they're off to the woods to conduct their own search. Others are arguing, saying we should listen to the police because they know what they're doing. That only brings the expected 'if they know what they're doing, then who killed Sarah Lipski?'

For that there is no answer.

Naomi nods towards the dissenting group who are off to the woods, saying she's going with them. 'Are you coming?' she asks.

I feel like I should be doing something more, sharing my story, trying to figure this all out – but I'm not brave enough. No one will believe me because I'm not convinced I believe it myself.

I nod as I follow Naomi towards the other side of the bridge, stopping to take one more look towards the water below. Sarah died there. I died there. And now I can't help but wonder if poor Helen has drowned somewhere in the waters around this village.

Chapter Twenty-Seven

The day comes and goes with no sign of Helen. After ridiculing villagers for always finding something to complain about, for being uppity about chain stores and for being ludicrously insular, I now find myself feeling under attack, too. It feels like this community, this way of life with which I've grown up, is under threat. One girl dead a year ago, another missing now – and, unknown to anyone else, someone attacked me as well. This is the type of thing from which a group of people never recover.

I've been to the village police station a few times before. Once or twice it was to see my dad, who was hanging around with Jim. Before that, it was for a primary school trip – if it can be called that – when I was six or seven. There were three officers who worked there at the time, though I have no idea now what they all did. Westby and the surrounding villages have never been crime hotspots, not until now anyway.

As a child, it was frightening to be taken down echoing stone stairs into the station's basement and shown the single jail cell. The bars at the front and freezing walls terrified me then and would probably still do now. The upper floor was more like an office, with a front counter, more desks behind, and then an interview room. I remember being fascinated by the cassette machine built into the wall of the interview room, thinking it was the coolest thing I'd ever seen. I guess I was easily pleased at that age.

The station isn't what it was. As far as I know, the cell is still in the basement but the upper floor has halved in size, with the front desk removed entirely and a false wall inserted. I have no idea what's on the other side but Jim's desk was overflowing with papers when I passed it.

A decade after my first visit, I'm sitting in the interview room, eyeing the video camera in the top corner and its blinking red light.

'Are you all right, Ellie?' Jim asks.

It's just me and him in the room and it's cold. Or perhaps it's not cold and it's me. I don't know any longer. Either way, there are large pools of patchy black and brown damp clinging to the ceiling in both the corners I can see.

'I'm okay.'

'Just so that you know, other officers are in Westby interviewing people. They're at various potential witnesses' houses, plus we've commandeered one of the smaller classrooms at the primary school. The reason I suggested we do this here is because I wanted to make sure anything you said would be recorded.'

'Why me?'

'Because, from what I understand, it's likely you're one of the final people to have seen Helen.'

So he does know about the party in the woods. Hardly surprising.

I must have a terrible poker face – probably because I've never played. He moves swiftly on, as if he knows exactly where I was. 'I figured you might be more comfortable talking to me than one of the other officers,' he adds.

'Okay.'

'Can you tell me, in your own words, about the last time you saw Helen James.'

In your own words? What is it with police officers?

'There was a party at the country park between here and Langham,' I say.

Jim is on the other side of a table, nodding as he writes something on a pad.

'What sort of party?'

'There were a bunch of us there to celebrate the end of term – and because it's been a year since Sarah…' I stop because I'm muddling my words. 'Not celebrate. Talk about and remember her. You know…?'

He doesn't acknowledge what I've said, moving on efficiently: 'How many of you were there?'

'Around fifty? Maybe more? I'm not sure. A few.'

'Were they all people you know?'

'Sort of. People from the college, I suppose. I don't know all the names but recognised most of the faces. It's not like I went and talked to everyone.'

'Who did you talk to?'

'My friends – Naomi, Robbie, Ben.'

He repeats back what I've said along with their last names. He obviously knows the details already. 'And you saw Helen James at this party?' he adds.

'She was there. We didn't really talk.'

'What do you mean by "really"?'

I take a second to think: 'I suppose we didn't talk at all. Not one to one. Ollie was giving a speech to everyone about Sarah but people were interrupting. Helen stood up and told everyone to shut up.'

Jim writes something else on his pad and looks up. The areas under his eyes are a murky grey and it doesn't seem as if he can keep them all the way open. I wonder when he last slept. Whenever it is, I can definitely win if that's what we're comparing.

'Did it feel like what she said went down well with everyone?' he asks.

'How do you mean?'

'If people were interrupting Ollie, did they interrupt her? Or shout anything else?'

'No. She has that effect on people when she wants something.'

'What effect?'

I find myself swirling my hand, searching for the right words. 'I don't know how to put it. She's a nice person. She told everyone to be quiet and they were. It's like a respect thing.'

Jim nods but doesn't write anything down. I'm starting to anticipate the movement of his pen, wondering what he already knows and what he doesn't. Wondering if he's writing anything at all. Perhaps he's scribbling up and down for some reason?

'To change tack slightly,' he says, 'how well did you know Sarah Lipski?'

'Sarah…?'

Jim doesn't look up but his pen is pressed to the pad. He's never once asked me about Sarah. This time last year, it was someone from Langham who interviewed me.

'She was your brother's girlfriend…?'

'I don't understand why you're asking about her now.'

'Two girls are taken from this village a year apart. One turns up dead in the river and the other's missing. Don't you think there could be a connection?'

He's looking at me now and I feel tiny. This isn't Uncle Jim, nor is it Mum's boyfriend. This is Jim the police officer.

'Sorry,' I say, stumbling. 'I only really knew her through Ollie. I didn't know her before they started going out. After they did, I saw her around the house a few times, plus I was in the car once or twice when he dropped her home and picked her up.'

'Did you ever have any conversations where it was just you and her?'

'Not really.'

The pen darts across the pad and then Jim peers up again. 'Is that yes or no, Ellie?'

'Both, I suppose. It depends what you count as a conversation. We'd say hello when we saw each other in the village. She borrowed a book off me once and lent me some shoes. We were planning to go shopping one weekend but… well, we never got to it.'

I stop speaking, remembering the conversation in the hallway back at the house where she had excitedly told me about the stores we'd go to together. I've never been a big clothes shopper and Naomi's only ever interested in a handful of places in which she can buy T-shirts, beanies and patterned jeans. The way Sarah explained it sounded fun and I was looking forward to an afternoon out with her. Barely a fortnight later and she was gone.

'I knew her but I didn't,' I say.

'What about Helen?' he asks.

It takes me a few seconds to think because it's hard to define the sort of relationship we had.

'Sort of the same,' I say. 'I wouldn't say we were friends as such – maybe we were – we just knew each other. I liked her and I think she liked me. We've been at school together since we were kids. We did a lot of classes together and used to play hockey in the same team a few years ago.'

It's only after I've finished speaking that I realise I've used the past tense. I already think of her as gone.

Jim either doesn't pick up on it or, more likely, keeps it to himself. 'Did you socialise with her often?' he asks.

'Not really.'

'But you did on Monday night at the country park?'

'I suppose. We were in the same place and we know the same people.'

'Did you notice anything untoward about how she was behaving in the woods?'

I rock back in the chair, forcing my brain, desperately trying to think. 'I don't know,' I say. 'I don't think so.'

Jim taps his pen on the pad. 'Was she drinking?'

'I don't know.'

He looks up, fixing me with an extremely non-uncle-like stare. It feels like a proper inquisition.

'Some people were,' I add, before realising that he's used some policeman mind trick on me.

'Drugs?'

'No.'

'Is that a definite "no", or an "I don't know"?'

I bite my lip and remember the man who knocked on my bedroom door a couple of days ago, telling me so politely that I could confide in him if I needed to. That it would be between us and not something he'd automatically share with Mum. I remember Naomi's wild, wide eyes from when we were dancing, and her energy.

'I don't know if there were drugs,' I say, being careful with each word and hoping he moves on.

He does: 'Whose idea was it to have a party in the woods on Monday night?'

'I'm not sure.'

'How did you find out?'

'My friend Naomi called me. She'd texted earlier in the day but I broke my proper phone and the old one doesn't work as well. I didn't see the messages until after she'd called.'

Jim sifts through his notes and then flicks back to where he was. 'This is Naomi Grant, correct?'

'Right.'

'What time did she call you?'

'About eleven.'

'At night?'

For a moment, I think there's a hint of a smile creeping around his lips but, if there was, it's gone instantly.

'Yes.'

'And what did she say?'

'Just that they were going on an adventure.'

'Who's they?'

'Her, her boyfriend, Ben, and my boyfriend, Robbie. We hang around as a foursome a lot.'

'You left the house and then Naomi drove—'

'Robbie drove.'

'… and then Robbie drove you out to the country park, which is where many of your friends were gathering?'

'Exactly.'

He pauses for a moment, still going through his notes. 'And there were around fifty people there?'

'That's a guess. Something like that. I didn't go around and talk to everyone. I spent most of the night dancing with Naomi.'

Jim is in the middle of writing a long sentence and finishes with a flourish. When he's done, he looks up again, smiling slightly this time. 'Tell me about the party.'

'What do you want to know?'

'What happened there?'

I snort and shrug, squirming in the seat. It feels like I'm being interrogated by Mum. 'It was a party. People danced, sang, ate, drank. What do you think?'

'You're not going to be in trouble for anything you tell me.'

'There's not really anything to tell. I spent most of the night dancing.'

He nods and presses a full stop hard into his pad with his pen.

'You told me you didn't talk to Helen much on Monday – but did you see her much?'

I'm rocking back and forth in the chair and the seat is becoming more and more uncomfortable. It has metal legs and a plastic back, like the ones at school that do nothing except create kids with back problems.

'She was dancing for a while,' I say, 'but that's more or less the only time I saw her. I think she might have waved at Naomi and me.'

'Was she dancing with anyone in particular?'

'It wasn't that sort of thing. Everyone was together in this clearing, so we were all dancing with everyone else. It was mainly girls. Most of the boys were eating and drinking, or sitting around the sides watching.'

He chuckles slightly and, for the first time in a few minutes, it relaxes me. 'The boys you know aren't ones for dancing, huh?'

'I don't think it's just the boys *I* know. I think it's all boys.'

His smile spreads. 'Fair enough. Can you remember what Helen was wearing?'

It only takes me a moment: 'I think it was a green top with a black skirt.'

'Do you know when she left?'

I shake my head. 'She was gone by half four.'

'But you can't be more precise than that?'

'I didn't see her go. I didn't see many people leave. Naomi and I were still dancing.'

'That's a long time to be on your feet…?'

He leaves the question hanging but this time I don't blurt my way into the silence. There's little I could add, anyway.

'When did you leave?' he asks.

'Maybe five? Naomi, Ben, Robbie and I were the last ones there. First in, last out.'

He nods. 'Was Oliver there?'

'My brother?'

Another nod. 'Unless you know another Oliver…?'

'It's just you called him Ollie before. It kinda threw me.'

Jim says nothing and there's a long, awkward silence in which he does nothing but stare at me.

'Why are you asking about Ollie?' I add.

'Because I'm trying to compile a list of who was at the party and who wasn't.'

'But why him *specifically*? You could throw any names at me and ask if they were there.'

'Perhaps I will?'

There's another silence but neither of us seems ready to break it. Jim starts to tap the pen on the pad, but he is relaxed in the chair, no longer seeming so tired.

I crack first again: 'Ollie was at the party.'

'Did you see him leave?'

More silence. I stare at him and he stares back. It feels like a battle of wills. From the corner of my eye, I can see the light underneath the camera blinking at me, presumably recording everything I'm saying. It feels like I'm stitching my brother up, even though I'm telling the truth.

'I didn't see him go,' I say.

'But you're sure Helen and Ollie had both left before half past four…?'

'I guess.'

He nods and makes a squiggle on his pad, then flips the lid closed. 'Is there anything else you'd like to tell me, Ellie?'

I wonder if he's going to use his superpower mind trick on me to extract the information that could either help him, or have me dragged off to some insane asylum. I bite my lip, thinking about it. If it wasn't for the camera and the flickering light, perhaps I would tell him that I awoke in the river. I'd tell him that I daydream of a person's hand on my chest and forehead, dunking me under the water until I stop breathing.

I take a breath, thinking it over.

'No,' I whisper.

His chair scrapes backwards and he stands, motioning for the door. 'That's that, then,' he says cheerily. 'You've been very helpful, Ellie. Thank you.'

Chapter Twenty-Eight

Mum is drinking tea in the living room when I get home. Without a word from either of us, she stands, meets me in the middle of the room, and wraps her arms around me. She holds me so tight that it feels like it should hurt. It doesn't, obviously, because nothing does.

'I'm so glad you're safe,' she says when I pull away. She looks tired, with sagging eyebrows and dark rims around her cheeks, as if exhaustion is a disease that's catching around the village.

I think about sitting down but I'm not sure I can take an evening of Mum's sideways glances of concern. She looks at me and thinks I could've been Sarah or Helen. She's right but I already know that and don't need the added burden from her.

'It's been a long day,' she says.

'Yes.'

We're dreadful at small talk.

'I'm glad you're home safe.'

'Jim dropped me off.'

'Oh.'

See? Woeful at small talk.

Mum hasn't finished, adding: 'Has he…?'

'He's gone back to work.'

'Oh. Do you know where your brother is?'

'He was on the search but I've not seen him since. I think one of the Langham police were talking to him.'

Mum sits again, leaving me standing. It's silent and awkward, which sums up large parts of our relationship.

'I kinda have something to tell you,' I say.

She looks up expectantly, perhaps thinking I have a clue as to where Helen's gone. Her eyes are wide and I know I'm twisting awkwardly on one leg, suddenly self-conscious. I think about telling her of waking in the river. I *really* want to. I was close to telling Jim but something stopped me. It's a secret I must keep. Every time I come close, my stomach knots as a reminder to shut up.

'What?' she asks.

'It's um…'

I can't tell her.

'… I saw Helen on the night she disappeared. I don't know what happened afterwards, though.'

Her face falls. 'Oh… did you tell Jim?'

'Yes.'

She seems puzzled, expecting more.

I tell her I'm going upstairs and then mooch my way to my room. Mum says it's been a long day and she's not wrong. I woke up in the early hours of Sunday morning, it's now Wednesday night and I haven't slept in between.

I have one hand on the door handle when I stop, turning to see Ollie's closed bedroom door. He's not home and Mum has settled in downstairs for the next few hours at least. I stand next to the stairs, peering over the banister to the hallway below, where there is no movement and only the dimmed sound of a television.

With a couple of sidesteps, I'm back to his door and knock quietly, just in case he is home and Mum has somehow missed him. We do come and go somewhat.

'Ollie,' I hiss.

No answer.

I ease the handle down carefully and push his bedroom door open. I've been in before, sometimes to do things like drop off washing, or ask him to borrow something. It's rare, though. Not even Mum crosses the sanctity of our bedroom doors without knocking and asking. We've argued over many things through the years but personal space isn't one of them – even if she does bang on a bit about keeping my room tidy.

My sense of smell may be damaged but I still get hints of deodorant as I enter Ollie's room. If I can sense it, then it must really be strong for other people. I've never understood why boys spray so much of the damned stuff. It all smells the same, too – like a frozen chicken that's been left in the windowsill to defrost and has partially cooked in the sun, attracting a flock of ants.

For the record, that was an accident.

The rest of Ollie's room is testament to the fact that he still hasn't quite grown up. There's a massive poster opposite the window of a tanned model perching on the bonnet of a flame-red sports car. Her blonde hair is billowing in the breeze and she's wearing heels so high that she could stilt walk in her spare time.

How did he ever get a girlfriend?

The rest of the walls are covered with more posters – a football team who play in red, a couple of movie sheets, plus a black and white one with Muhammad Ali standing over another boxer who is flat on his back. Ollie's duvet is strewn messily across his bed, with one pillow on the floor, another crooked across the bed. There is a small chest next to the bed, with all three drawers hanging open, and socks, underwear and goodness only knows what else piled on the carpet nearby. I'm not sure I want to get too close. It's actually hard to see the carpet, largely because there are so many clothes scattered around. His room is a giant tumble dryer that has thrown his stuff in all directions.

The curtains are nearly drawn, with only a slim gap in the middle. It is silhouetted from the doorway but, as I tiptoe across the floor, the framed photo sitting in the centre of the windowsill becomes clear. It holds a picture of Sarah and Ollie, arms around one another, dressed in sports gear for something I don't remember. It looks like a charity fun run as they each have numbers pinned to their chests. They are both sweaty and dirty but Sarah still manages to stun. Her hair is in a greasy ponytail but it's her smile that envelops the rest of the picture. Ollie is looking ever-so-slightly sideways, towards her rather than the camera. He looked different when he was with her – happier, perhaps. It's hard to tell as, in the time that has passed since last summer, he's changed. He's become more athletic and leaner but it isn't simply physical, it's the sparkle in his eyes. 'Love', as Mrs Lipski said. They were in love.

If Ollie had killed Sarah – and I don't know what I believe any more – why would he have kept this photo and left it in a place where it would be one of the first things he'd see every day?

The picture has thrown me off the reason I'm here, which is to look for anything that could show Ollie was the person who drowned me. Actually, it's more because I *don't* want to find anything, which makes me all the more confused because I'm going through his personal things in an effort to *not* find something. It's also hard to know why he might have wanted to hurt me. We squabble in the way brothers and sisters do, but that's it. The only reason would be if he's a genuine psycho – but he's simply not. I *know* he's not. He has feelings and compassion.

Everything I'm doing is a contradiction but I continue anyway. With my foot, I nudge a few of his clothes to the side and then crouch to look under the bed. The dark makes it hard to see much other than shoes, which have been flung underneath. Under his mattress is something I'd far rather forget, so I move quickly on to the wardrobe. It is about the only part of the room that's actually organised, with tops hanging across the rail and half a dozen pairs of seemingly identical jeans folded on the shelf at the top. At the bottom, there is a pair of football boots, plus a shoebox containing ticket stubs from gigs, sporting events and movies.

Realising I'm not going to be able to go through everything, nor would I really want to, I stand by the slightly open door and take in the room as a whole. If I wanted to hide something so nobody else would find it, where would I conceal it?

As I look around the room, the answer is obvious: I'd hide it with something in which nobody else is interested. If Mum searched Ollie's room for any reason, under the bed and in the wardrobe are the obvious places. He'd have to be stupid to leave something there – and he's definitely not that.

I'm distracted by a low bang from downstairs. I slide around the door until I have one foot in the hallway and strain to listen. At first I think it's a door closing but then I hear one of the kitchen cupboards clinking closed. It's hard to make out the exact noises but the likelihood is that Mum's making another cup of tea for herself. I wait another minute or so, listening for the hint of a stair creak and, when it doesn't come, head back into Ollie's room.

This time I know where I'm going. In the corner is a small television hooked up to a PlayStation. There is a stack of two-dozen games next to the screen, none of which would interest either Mum or myself. The first has a picture of some troll-like dwarf on the front clutching an axe larger than he is. Inside the case is nothing but a disc and instruction manual. The next game is a football one – but that houses only the disc and manual, too. Each of the top ten cases contains nothing but discs and manuals. How very dull.

Then I open the eleventh.

The disc is there, the manual is there – and so is a leather bracelet that has interwoven strands plaited together, with a series of knots along the length.

I drop the game case to the desk, twisting the bracelet in my hand. I want to compare it to the one I found in the river but already know they're identical. My mind swims with possibilities and conspiracies. *How?*

Perhaps it's because of the muffled shuffling of feet, perhaps it's nothing at all – but I suddenly glance up, unable to contain my gasp. Ollie is standing in the bedroom doorway, eyes boggling as he stares at the bracelet in my hand.

Chapter Twenty-Nine

'What are you doing?' Ollie asks.

It is one of those moments in which I wish I had time to come up with something good, something remotely convincing, but my feet are clamped in wet tar and my mouth bobs open uselessly.

Ollie takes a step into the room, blocking my way out. He's wearing shorts and a vest, with a baseball cap. Casual as you like. I think about shouting for Mum, telling her everything – the river, the bracelet, Ollie.

'Ell, what are you doing in my room?' He is angrier this time.

I look at the open game case on his desk. 'I was thinking about playing a game to take my mind off everything.'

Ollie turns to take in his desk and then looks back to me. 'When have you ever played PlayStation?'

'Exactly. I thought I'd try something new.'

He picks up the case and turns it over. The cover shows a man in an army uniform holding an enormous gun as a tank rolls by behind him.

'I was looking for something I might enjoy that wasn't too hard. I'd read a couple of the instruction books inside to see what the games were like.'

Ollie takes another step towards me and I'm almost trapped in the corner furthest from his door. Should I scream? Call for help? If I do, there's no going back. It occurs to me that, given the way my finger popped back into place and how I can apparently feel no pain, perhaps I'm invulnerable. If so, what could he do to me anyway?

He leans forward and plucks the bracelet from my hand, holding it front of his face and eyeing it closely.

'I thought I'd lost this,' he says, more softly. He flicks one of the curtains open with his free hand to allow more light into the room and then slumps onto his bed, staring at the bracelet and running his thumb across the material.

'Where was it?' he asks, not looking up.

'In the game case.'

He glances at the desk and then back to the bracelet.

'Whose is it?' I ask.

If I wanted to rush for the door I could, but the tension has gone.

'It's mine,' he whispers.

'*Yours?*'

I've never seen him wearing it and, aside from his misguided spell of wearing beads a few years back, it doesn't seem like his thing.

He nods and wraps the bracelet around his wrist, tying it underneath and then spinning it around. 'We had one each.'

'You and… Sarah?'

He nods towards the photo in the window and then removes his cap, placing it on the bed next to him. His head needs re-shaving – there's a fluffy stubble of hair on the very top.

'It was the day before she disappeared,' he says. 'We did this fun run in the morning – her idea. It was a 10k, but you had to raise money to enter.'

'I remember you wanting me to sponsor you.'

He shrugs. 'Right – but you didn't because you didn't have any money. Sarah set us up to run for an animal shelter in Langham. She'd taken me out there a week or so before and there were all these abandoned cats and dogs. She sat for about an hour, moving from enclosure to enclosure and talking to them – but the centre relies entirely on donations.'

'How much did you raise?'

'I only managed a couple of hundred quid – but she'd been out knocking on doors and had somehow got two grand out of people.'

'Two thousand?'

He runs a hand over his head and nods. 'You know what she was like when she wanted something.' He pauses. 'Well, maybe you didn't – but there wasn't much she didn't get when she set her mind on it.'

Ollie sighs once more and stares at the photo. 'We did the 10k that morning and she was in this incredible mood because it meant we'd raised so much money for the shelter. We got changed and then went to the Deck to celebrate.'

My mind pictures Ash but I say nothing.

'We ate like you wouldn't believe. I had a triple burger, fries and thickshake. She had the same. Then we ordered more fries. After that, it was still only half one or so, and Sarah was saying she wanted to go on an adventure.'

I shiver. It's unrelated but that was Naomi's word when she wanted me to go to the party in the woods.

'Where did you end up?' I ask.

'We went to Purton, with the cobbled beach.' He looks up and we say in unison: '… which isn't a real beach.'

He grins wider and I smile too. 'Right,' he adds, 'not a real beach – but Sarah liked it anyway. I think because it's so quaint. She enjoyed all that quirky, weird Englishness. Vintage teashops, sticks of rock. She kept going on about visiting a car boot sale on a Sunday morning.'

'Why?'

'Because she'd never been to one – her mum and dad had never gone to one either. I told her, "Look, it's just a load of people selling junk they don't want, plus some maniac selling meat from a van" – but she wasn't having it.'

'Did you ever go?'

He shakes his head, while continuing to stroke the bracelet. 'We were in Purton and it was an amazing day. Sun, blue skies, everything that's amazing about summer. It was just the two of us and we walked along the seafront, then we bought ice cream from a van and had fish and chips.'

'Dessert before main?'

He laughs. 'Sarah always had a thing about dessert before main. Her thinking was that if you got full by eating too much for a main meal, you wouldn't want pudding.'

'Disaster,' I say.

'Disaster! Dessert first and then eat what you can.'

He laughs again and it leaves me with a deep feeling that I wish I'd got to know her better. Lover of animals, dessert-scoffer, thickshake-slurper… what's not to like? She'd have liked Naomi, too.

'So you ate ice cream, then fish and chips…'

'Right, and we walked. We carried on for ages – most of the way to the next town and back again. We passed this lay-by on the way back and there was this woman who'd set up a table-top stall, selling bits and pieces. It was mainly leather goods – wallets, bookmarks, purses, all that. We stopped to look and the woman was laying it on thick, saying how everything was handmade and that we wouldn't find better quality anywhere. That sort of thing. We bought two of these.' He holds up his wrist, showing off the bracelet. 'I say "*we*" – but it was Sarah. I don't really wear jewellery, not since…'

He tails off.

'The year of the beads,' I say.

There is another hint of a smile as he raises his eyes towards me. 'Right,' he says. 'The year of the beads. Let's never call it that again.

Anyway, when we got back to Purton, we were sitting on the seawall and Sarah tied one around her wrist, then put the other on mine. She said they could be eternity bracelets – so that we'd always be with one another.'

Ollie squirms on the bed, shifting his backside but looking at the floor.

'Yeah, I know...' he adds.

'It sounds nice,' I assure him.

He shrugs. 'It felt good at the time. I don't know... like being a proper adult. When you're young and in a relationship, all adults assume it's a first-love thing. Older people can be really patronising, right?'

I think of Robbie and the tainted way I feel about him. Anything we had before has been marred by my confusion over what happened the night of Helen's party. Even with that, I don't think I've ever been in love with him – not in the way that Ollie talks about Sarah. It's hard to know.

'Right,' I reply – wanting Ollie to keep going.

'They think first love, teenage love, whatever you want to call it, they think it's childish and something that won't last. Maybe they're right? Perhaps true love isn't first love? I don't know – but I *do* know the feelings between Sarah and me were real, whatever people think.'

He stops to breathe in deeply and slowly and I'm not sure how to reply. We've never had a conversation like this. It feels like he's finally saying something he's been bottling up for a long time. A minute or two passes and he still doesn't speak, simply looking at the floor instead.

'What happened to her bracelet?' I ask.

'Huh?'

He peers up and I nod at the one on his wrist. 'If that's yours, then where's hers?'

It's a disingenuous question, because I know I have it.

Ollie unties the one on his wrist and holds it in his hand. 'On the night it happened, I dropped her off at the gates to her house and she was wearing it then. It was something that I didn't even think about until later. When the police were questioning me, they showed me pictures of her in the river.' He gulps, glances at the photo in the windowsill. 'You know?'

I know all too well.

'She was already… gone. By then, I knew I was a suspect. The solicitor they gave me was telling me not to say anything but I figured I couldn't get in trouble if I told the truth. I was at the station for a whole day – but it was only later, when I was trying to sleep, that I realised she wasn't wearing her bracelet in the photos they showed.'

'The ones of her in the river?'

He nods.

'So you dropped her off and she was wearing it, then when they found her in the river, she wasn't?'

He nods again.

'Did you tell someone?'

Ollie stands, crosses to the dresser and drops the bracelet back into the game case, which he seals and re-stacks in the pile. He twists so that he's resting on the counter, half standing, half sitting.

'By the time I realised, it was too late. I thought I'd end up in more trouble if I said something. There are photos of her wearing that bracelet, so if they found mine, they could easily assume it was hers. They're exactly the same. Nobody ever asked me about it, so I never mentioned it. I hid mine away and forgot about it until now.'

I think about the one I found in the river – in the exact spot where someone tried to drown me. Sarah's body was also discovered in the water, so perhaps her bracelet came off and ended up there…? Maybe it somehow defied the current and wedged in the silt until I picked it up…?

That doesn't explain why I keep having visions of ripping it from the wrist of my attacker.

Could that person have killed Sarah a year ago, stripped the bracelet from her as some sort of trophy, and then have worn it on the night he or she came after me?

I'm looking for answers and finding more questions.

'I heard the police spoke to you?' I say.

Ollie's voice brings me back into his room.

'Huh?'

'Today. I heard Jim talked to you about Helen.'

'He was asking about being in the woods on Monday night.'

'What did you say?'

'Just that I saw her. I don't know anything – I'm not even sure we spoke directly to each other. He was asking if I saw her leave.'

Ollie's gaze pierces me. 'Did you?'

'No – but you were in the woods, too. Didn't someone talk to you?'

He's still looking at me but I can see in his eyes that there's something he wants to say.

Something bad.

'What?' I say.

He turns away. 'I just hope someone finds her.'

'What happened, Ollie?'

He shakes his head.

'What did you do?'

Ollie spins back, fists balled, nostrils flared, ready to shout. It only lasts a second and then the aggression slips from him and there are tears instead. I'm not sure if they're tears for Sarah, or tears for something else. His Adam's apple bobs as he pinches the top of his nose and bows his head. 'Nothing, Ell. I didn't do anything.'

I watch him for a moment, knowing I've either missed something or that he's holding something back. I don't know if I should comfort him or leave him by himself. I've seen him cry a few times over the past year but never when it was just the pair of us.

In the end, I bottle it, crossing the room and placing a hand momentarily on his shoulder, squeezing gently, and then heading to the door. 'I'm sorry for being in your room. I didn't mean anything by it.'

He doesn't reply, so I close the door behind me, leaving him alone to cry.

Chapter Thirty

In the past two days, I've seen Robbie and Ollie both crying for various reasons. In my disjointed, confused world of suspecting everyone around me, I can't figure out if it is genuine emotion, or something for my benefit so that I let my guard down.

One of my earliest memories is throwing a paddy in a shop when I was young because I wanted a pencil case that Mum wouldn't buy. I was going through a phase of liking pink stuff and there was some sort of fairy princess on the front, with a sparkly pencil inside. Mum said no, so I screamed, shouted and cried, hoping to get my way. Still she said no, so I got louder and then, as I saw her looking around the shop, cringing, she told me to shush and that we'd get it next time *if* I behaved.

Tears can be faked and crying does make people do things they might not usually. Weeping holds so much power, both in the emotional escape and in the softening effect on others. I know this and yet I can't figure out if either Robbie, Ollie or both were faking.

What sort of person does that make me? That my brother and boyfriend can cry in front of me, yet my prime reaction is suspicion?

If I *do* believe them – and neither is responsible for what happened to me – then who is? I open my journal and go through the list:

Robbie, Naomi, Ben, Ollie, Ash, Hitcher

Because I can, I cross off Robbie and Ollie, leaving four names. If Naomi knew about Ben and me, she'd be angry – betrayed – but any more than that? I cross her name off, too. That leaves Ben, Ash and a person I'm not even sure exists.

Ash's name stands out. I think about going to talk to him, concluding that I might as well. At the absolute least, I could show him the picture of us arguing at Helen's party – of me pulling away from him – and ask what was going on. He might tell the truth, he might lie – but whatever he says could stir my memory.

I start to head down the stairs, wondering if he'll be working at Tape Deck this evening, when the hallway is filled by a fleeting blur of spinning blue lights. I dash quickly upstairs, into the bathroom where the wide, slim window is partly open. I have to stand on tiptoes to be able to see properly but there are three police cars parked outside, each with the lights whirling. From the one stopped closest to the house, two men in uniform clamber from the front seats, with a man in a suit emerging from the back.

By the time I get to the bottom of the stairs, Mum already has the front door open, even though the doorbell hasn't sounded. She steps onto the path and I follow. The sky is a mucky grey-blue, a mix of clouds rolling in and dusk approaching. The flashing lights from the police cars spill across the street, with net curtains twitching and faces appearing in windows.

More police officers have emerged from the other parked cars but they're standing next to their vehicles, watching as their colleagues approach my mother. I don't recognise any of them.

The man in the suit speaks first, introducing himself as DCI Somethingoranother. He shows Mum some sort of ID and then stands with his hands behind his back.

'Is Oliver home, Mrs Parker?' he asks.

Mum looks past the DCI towards Jim, whom I hadn't noticed before. He's waiting at the side of one of the police cars by a uniformed officer. He is tight-lipped.

'What's going on?' Mum calls to him.

'I just need to know if Oliver is home,' the first officer repeats.

Mum looks past him again. 'Jim?'

He walks forward slowly, looking from her to the DCI, offering a 'told you so' look to the officer. 'There's nothing I can do,' Jim replies. 'Is Ollie home?'

Mum doesn't need to answer because my brother steps past me onto the path. It looks like he's spent a few moments getting himself ready, as he's changed from his vest and shorts into jeans and a long-sleeved T-shirt with a baseball cap.

Almost as if he knew this was coming.

'I'm here,' he says solemnly, continuing past Mum until he's standing in front of the DCI.

'Oliver Parker?' he asks.

'Yes.'

'I'm arresting you in connection with the disappearance of Helen James…'

The police officer continues to talk but I hear nothing because Mum is shrieking so loudly. She steps towards Ollie but Jim blocks her, holding his arms around her and pressing her back towards the house. Ollie doesn't turn, doesn't say anything, allowing the uniformed officers to lead him towards the police car.

Mum is crying, fighting against Jim and trying to get around him. She shouts: 'Tell them you didn't do it!' but Ollie doesn't turn. He ducks to get into the car and the door slams with a solid clunk.

Moments later, the officers are back inside and the car pulls away in a guff of exhaust fumes, lights no longer spinning. The other two vehicles remain, with officers standing nearby.

Across the road, faces occupy almost every downstairs window in the houses. As Jim tries to get Mum inside the house, I head slowly to the end of the path, turning to look at our next-door neighbours' homes. Curtains ruffle, movement flashes – and whoever was watching on either side disappears. Across the road, faces are vanishing, all except one. Four doors across, Rochelle the Raven is standing in her bedroom window, not watching the road, instead tapping away on her phone. Within seconds, everyone will know what's happened.

As if sensing me, she looks up and we make eye contact across the road. It is only a fleeting moment but she is emotionless: not smiling, nor gloating, simply recording. She turns and disappears, her job done. Rebecca's phone will be buzzing already.

I glance at the police cars and the remaining officers. None of them say anything, nor make any movement, so I head inside, where Mum and Jim are in the hallway. There's a gap between them. Mum's arms are folded and she's squeezed herself into the space between the kitchen door and the wall. Jim is between me and her, his arms at his side, palms open. When I close the front door, he turns and looks between Mum and me.

'Why?' Mum stammers.

Jim shakes his head, still looking between us. The rings around his eyes are so dark that he doesn't simply look tired, he looks ill. His skin's pale. Haunted.

'Zoe...' he says, my mother's name. She backs away into the kitchen, putting the table between her and him. I follow them, cramping the space with three of us in the enclosed area.

'*Why?*' she repeats. She growls. There is red around her eyes, an accusing snarl to her top lip.

'It wasn't me,' he says.

'I asked you *why* – not who.'

He shakes his head, ruffling his already well-ruffled hair. 'You know I can't talk about things like this away from work.'

'He's my son.'

'I know, which makes it all the more inappropriate were I to talk to you about things.'

'Do they think he killed her?'

His tongue is resting on his top lip. 'There's new evidence.'

'New? *New?!* What does that mean?'

'I can't tell you.'

Mum flicks the kettle on but it happens so quickly that it seems more of an instinctive act than anything she thought about.

They stare at each other as if I'm not there. Perhaps I shouldn't be. The air is crackling.

'Where have they taken him?' she demands.

'Langham police station.'

'When can I see him?'

'I don't know if they'll keep him in. If they do, probably tomorrow morning.'

'I thought you're supposed to be police yourself.'

She spits the words with disdain but Jim remains calm. 'I am, but this is a different jurisdiction. A girl is missing and it's gone above me. For want of a better phrase, I'm hired help at the moment.'

The kettle reaches boiling point, fizzing and hissing, then spitting a small spray from the spout before it clicks off. Nobody moves.

'What's the new evidence?' Mum asks.

Jim shakes his head.

In a flash, she lunges for him, whites of her eyes blazing. 'He didn't *do* anything!'

Jim has his hands up defensively but Mum has him pressed against the kitchen counter, forearm across his chest, shoving him hard.

'Get him out!'

He's trying to push her away while using as little force as he can and I'm worried at what Mum might do. I've seen her grieve for my father, seen her struggle to come to terms with Sarah's death and Ollie's questioning a year ago – but I've never seen such white-hot anger. She has a hand raised, possibly to slap him, possibly for balance, but I don't wait to find out. I dive forward and yank her arm away and then pull her hard by the shoulder. I don't release her until she goes limp.

'Mum,' I say. She's still staring past me, boring holes into Jim, who's standing by the kitchen door. I force her to sit on the other side of the table, where she takes a deep breath through her nose. Her eyes haven't once left Jim.

'You're supposed to be family,' she says.

'I'm really sorry.'

Jim's phone starts to buzz and he removes it from his pocket, scowling at the screen and pressing a button to make it stop.

'You should probably go,' I tell Jim, trying to sound sensible as opposed to being mean. It's ridiculous that, of the three of us, I'm being the grown-up.

Jim doesn't move but coughs gently to clear his throat. He glances quickly towards the door twice and fidgets on the spot.

'There's something else,' he says. I don't know if it's deliberate but the pause feels like a surge of energy. I can feel my mother's rage and incomprehension boiling volcanically.

I move until I am standing directly in front of my mother, on the other side of the table, facing Jim. 'What?' I ask.

'There are officers outside who need to search the house. Someone will escort you upstairs to get a change of clothes and any other essentials, but then you'll have to leave. You can probably return tomorrow.'

He lets it hang, which isn't wise given the state of my mother.

'Where can we go?' I ask.

Jim stumbles over his words. 'I'd let you stay at mine but I have to distance myself for reasons I hope you understand. I didn't know if—'

A knocking on the door interrupts him. Jim looks at me and we both know what's coming. Without another word, he heads along the hall and opens the front door, where the other officers are standing, staring at him earnestly.

Mum is on her feet so quickly that she sends the kitchen chair spinning across the room. Her voice is low, bridling with controlled, stifled fury. 'Are you telling me that I need to be escorted around my own house?'

Jim nods and a female officer steps around him, smiling awkwardly. Mum turns to me, says she'll sort something out, and heads for the stairs, stomping up them as if she's trying to crush the very ground beneath her. The officer is two steps behind, still smiling clumsily. What else is there to do?

Chapter Thirty-One

I'm left in the hallway with Jim as Mum shuffles around upstairs. Neither of us speak, although he mutters something I don't quite catch to one of the other officers. There's an eerie, uncomfortable silence, eventually broken by something slamming above. After a second loud bang, Mum bustles downstairs carrying a holdall. The officer trails her, waiting a few paces behind as Mum makes a point of ignoring Jim, before turning to me.

'You all right?' she asks.

'Fine,' I say, knowing she's the one who is really losing it.

She turns to the woman on the stairs. 'This officer is going to take you upstairs, okay?'

'I get it, Mum.'

Perhaps she catches the edge to my voice, perhaps not. I'm not sure she's listening. For whatever reason, this is a show. She nods and walks me past. The officer lets me by and then follows as I head upstairs. I momentarily pause next to Ollie's door, wondering what the police will pull from his room when they get the chance. Was there something I missed? He seemed so passive when they arrived for him, as if he knew they were coming. I push into my bedroom, waiting for the officer to stand in the doorway.

'What can I take?' I ask.

She's somewhere in her twenties, tall with farmer's shoulders. It's one of the features in the area – there are always a handful of boys and girls in each school year who've been brought up working on their parents' farm. They all share barrel chests and beefy shoulders. For most, that means their life has been mapped out since the day they were born. This young woman has done well to make her escape.

'Whatever you're going to need for the night,' she answers softly.

'Only one night?'

'I believe so.'

I fetch a bag from the bottom of the wardrobe and then open my underwear drawer, reaching to the back and grabbing the bracelet I found in the river. Without taking my hand from the drawer, I bundle it into a pair of knickers and remove both, placing them into the bag. I trail around the rest of the room finding pyjamas, shoes, more layers, jeans and a jacket. Then I go to my bed and remove the journal, holding it up for the officer to see.

'I need to check that,' she says.

I think of the names contained within – my list of suspects for who might have drowned me. They might understand what it is, they might not. Either way, it could lead to awkward questions.

'It's my diary,' I add.

She steps forward, hand in mid-air, but I don't offer it to her.

'There are private things in here. Why would you need to know what's inside?'

We make eye contact and then she drops her arm and nods. I place it in my bag and make for the door.

'Do you need a hairbrush or anything like that?' she adds.

For a moment I wonder if she's having a dig but, after a momentary pause, I conclude she's being nice. There's every chance she's done this before, or gone on some training course. People forget all sorts when they're rushing.

'Thanks,' I say, before rummaging through my drawers again to find one.

Back downstairs, Mum is already waiting outside next to the car. Ollie's is parked on the road but hers is a nearly new Mini that Jim helped her buy a few months ago at auction. Before I can head to the car, Jim stops me while I'm still on the path. He looks close to tears – which is becoming something of a theme for the men I know.

'I'm sorry this is how things have happened, Ellie. I know you'll look after her.'

He places a hand on my shoulder and squeezes gently before stepping away. I want to ask him who's going to look after me – I'm the child here – but his attention is already back on the house.

'Does somebody stay here overnight?' I ask. 'Or does someone lock up for us?'

'Someone will be here all night but Zoe gave me a key, too.'

'What are you looking for?' I ask.

It seems an obvious question but when he turns back to me, his eyebrows are raised as if it's taken him by surprise. 'I'm not sure.'

'Are you saying Ollie did something to Helen? Is that why you were asking about him earlier?'

'I can't talk about this, Ellie. You know that.'

I start to reply and then realise there's no point. If he could say anything, he'd have told Mum when she was screaming at him.

At the car, I drop my bag on the back seat and climb into the front. The engine's already idling and Mum pulls away before I've strapped my seatbelt on.

'Where are we going?' I ask.

She doesn't answer, following the road around, taking two quick turns and then pulling to a stop in a cul de sac. With the engine still running, she sits up straight with renewed focus in her eyes.

'He didn't do anything,' she says firmly, twisting against her seatbelt to face me. She reaches out and takes my hand, squeezing. 'Sorry for before,' she says.

'It wasn't Jim's fault.'

She brushes it off with a small shake of the head. 'When he spoke to you earlier, did he ask about your brother?'

'I didn't know anything to tell him.'

She nods, though I'm not sure she's listening. 'They're trying it again – like last time, with Sarah. People have had it in for him since then.'

'Where are we going to stay, Mum?'

'Give me a minute first.'

She takes out her phone and, though I only get one half of the conversation, it's easy enough to work out she's speaking to a solicitor. She asks whoever it is to visit Ollie at Langham police station and then says she'll see him or her in the morning. I'm actually impressed at how decisive she sounds.

'We're going to that B & B on the edge of town,' she says, putting her phone away. 'They're never booked up and it's only for one night.'

She says nothing else before setting off again, doing a three-point turn and then following the roads out of Westby until we hit the country lanes.

Bentley's Bed and Breakfast is a place I've passed hundreds of times, yet never thought twice about. It's essentially a large house with a larger garden, set back a little from the road. It is surrounded by a white picket fence that is pure Americana. There's a sign at the front that reads 'vacancies'. I've never seen it say anything else.

Speed in Westby is a relative thing. If the shops run out of bread or milk on a given day, that's it until the next delivery arrives. Sometimes the van turns up to empty the post box in the centre, other times it doesn't. When it snows in the winter, it can feel like this little corner of

England is cut off from everywhere else on the planet. No roads in or out, panicky conversations about grit and why the council hasn't ordered enough. School gets cancelled and there are days where it barely gets light. Anyone young spends that time in the fields, building snowmen and having snowball fights. It feels like the world has wound down, that time itself has slowed to village pace.

But while some things around here are so slow they barely move, nothing travels faster than news and gossip. I have no memory of what it might have been like in the days before widespread Internet and mobile phones – but it's like light speed now.

When Mum and I walk through the doors of the bed and breakfast, Mr Bentley is already standing behind the counter as if he's been waiting for us. He's short and round with a permanently red face, like a giant radish.

'Good evening, Mrs Parker,' he says with a tight, knowing smile. His shirt is unbuttoned at the top, allowing a wire brush of hair to sprout forth, a Mediterranean waiter without the tan, charm or physique.

Mum is ruthlessly clear: 'I was hoping you have a room free for me and my daughter.'

He nods and reaches for the computer on the counter, single-finger typing as if his opposable thumbs are yet to evolve. 'I'm sure that will be fine. I hope everything is all right with you…?'

If the fact he was waiting for us hadn't already given him away, then the snide sideways glance certainly does.

'Just a complication at the house,' Mum says, which Mr Bentley brushes off with another smile that really isn't.

'I have a room on the second floor overlooking the garden, or another on the third with a view of both the back and front of the house. They're both twins, both en suite and a full English is included in the morning.' He looks between us, settling back on Mum. 'Which would you prefer?'

She asks about prices but it's more her trying to be polite and not give him the satisfaction of appearing anything other than calm. If she were to crack into tears, the news would hit the rest of the village faster than an aeroplane could drop from the sky. Mum eventually settles for the room on the top floor, pays, and then hefts her holdall up from the floor.

'Is there anything I can help with?' Mr Bentley purrs.

'We're fine.'

'If you need anything during your stay, don't hesitate to ask.' He points towards a blank door close to the counter. 'My wife and I will be just through there. Knock any time you like, day or night.'

Mum smiles sweetly. 'We will.'

We're upstairs in the room with the door locked when Mum finally spits what she really thinks. 'I *hate* that man,' she says.

I remember her telling my young self that 'hate' was a strong word that shouldn't be used idly but it's neither the time nor place to point that out.

Mum takes off her jacket and shoes, then tugs at her top. 'Aren't you hot?' she asks. 'It's sweltering in here.'

I'm still wearing jeans, with three layers of tops. Because I was feeling cold all the time, I've stopped noticing the temperature. 'A little,' I say, not wanting to talk about it.

The room itself is like something out of a costume drama – or would be if it was left to rot for thirty years. There are pretty carvings in the four corners of the ceiling but it's hard to tell what anything is as the whitewash has turned a mucky yellow-brown. The wallpaper is a faded pink and the varnish on the wooden floors is scratched in some areas, washed-out in others. There are two single four-poster beds, each covered with too many pillows to count.

Mum sits on the one closest to the door. 'I can't believe that man's done this to us.'

'Mr Bentley?'

'Jim.'

She says his name as if she's swearing.

'It's not his fault,' I say. 'He had a job to do.'

'So, you're turning on your brother now as well?'

'Of course I'm not.'

Mum continues to face the door, bag at her side, unpacked. The silence echoes around the high ceilings and I'm standing close to the other bed, unsure what to do. When Mum doesn't follow up her anger, I start to move the cushions from the bed to the floor, which at least gives me room to lie down. I check my phone and there are messages from Naomi, Robbie and Ben, all asking what's going on. Given it's been an hour or so since Ollie was arrested, they likely already know.

I'm thinking about how best to reply – or if I should reply at all – when Mum speaks again. 'I've known that man almost my entire life.'

'Who?'

'Jim. He was your father's best friend, his best man.' She counts on her fingers, which would seem funny in other circumstances as it's such a primary school thing to do. 'Thirty-six years – that's how long we've known each other.'

She turns to me but her face is so blank that I want to look away. I don't want to be the grown-up in this situation. It's hard to break her stare.

'I first met him when we were all fifteen – your father, Jim and me. I started seeing your father, and Jim was seeing my friend, Pamela. We'd go to the movies together, eat together, that sort of thing. All your stuff about house parties, late-night trips to the woods… well, been there, done that.'

It's always uncomfortable to hear about Mum being young. Doing fun, rebellious things is always significantly *less* fun and definitely not as rebellious when parents got there first. She doesn't wait for me to reply.

'I don't know what happened to Pamela. Her dad got a job somewhere up north and the last I heard, she had four kids. I married your father; Jim got his job with the police and things carried on.'

'Mum.'

'What?'

'If you think about it, things could've been a lot worse. You see stories where the police make a massive deal of arresting someone. There are news cameras there, plus loads of people. I know there were flashing lights but it was kinda quiet, too. Three cars, only one bloke doing the talking. They never handcuffed Ollie. Perhaps the reason it was like that is because Jim made them go easy…?'

She stares at me for a few moments but doesn't speak. Then she shuffles up the bed, buries herself in the pillows and rolls onto her side to face away from me. I wait, wondering if she's going to say anything, but she doesn't. It's not long before it all slows and her side begins to rise and fall with the deep breaths of sleep.

I wish I could do that.

I cross to the window and sit in the creaking armchair, staring out at the moonlit garden. There's a pond at the far end that's reflecting the light like a mirror and a trail of small fairy lights that dot the rim of the green. Aside from Mum's gentle, soft snoring, everything is eerily silent and I know I have no hope of sleeping. Instead, I plug my phone in and sit flipping through the online photographs of me, my friends, and my brother, wondering when exactly it all went wrong.

THURSDAY

Chapter Thirty-Two

I spend the night in the armchair, occasionally blinking my way back into the river before coming to my senses. When the burnt orange starts to creep through the trees at the back of the garden, I realise I've now gone four entire days without sleep – and that's if being dead in the river counts as sleep. Without that, it's five.

By six in the morning, it's another summer's day. I think about closing the curtains but Mum has barely moved all night anyway. She sleeps in the clothes she was wearing during the day and, aside from the occasional snort, hasn't looked like waking up.

It is after seven when she eventually does. I hear her rolling over and then she croaks my name.

'What are you doing over there?' she asks.

'I watched the sun come up.'

When I stand and turn, she is sitting on her bed, looking at mine, which is still-made and unruffled. She asks how I'm feeling and I lie that I slept well. She yawns and manages a weak smile before stumbling into the bathroom.

I spend the time staring out the window, wondering what the day will bring. In no time at all, everything has fallen apart.

Twenty minutes later and Mum is back out in a new set of clothes. She looks fresher than before but still has something of a slump, as if she has the weight of the world on her shoulders. She's slept all night but it's not obvious from the haggard way she's holding herself.

I change and then we head downstairs to check out. Mr Bentley seems disappointed that we're not staying for breakfast but then, on the other hand, our lack of appetites will provide another update for the village grapevine.

There's silence in the car as Mum drives us back to the house. When we pull up outside, there is a marked police car on the road but Ollie's Ford has gone, leaving a gap on the driveway. Mum pulls in front-first and then clambers out. She seems unsure what to do. There are curtains twitching all around as she approaches the front door. Should we knock on our own front door? Let ourselves in?

Before we have to make a decision, the door opens and the female officer with the farmer shoulders holds it open for us. It feels odd to be welcomed into our own home but we go with it. Inside, she hands us a checklist, saying it lists everything that's been taken for further examination. She adds that Ollie's car has also been removed for searching, and asks Mum to read the notice and sign. She does so without fuss and then the officer asks if we have any questions. It's hard to know where to begin but Mum says no and then, with a click of the front door, we are alone in the house.

Mum drifts into the kitchen, flicking on the kettle with an errant swish of her hand, before heading into the living room.

Both rooms have been ransacked.

It looks like a burglary. The kitchen drawer that is full of receipts and menus has been emptied, the contents left on the side. Items of food that were in the cupboard are now on the side and the knives – certainly the sharp ones – have been removed completely. The living room is a similar story and there are so many small things out of place that it starts to become overwhelming. I straighten a picture frame on the wall, which is the tiniest tip of the Everest-like mountain.

'I'll do it,' Mum says.

I want to say I'll help but she sounds so firm that it is a decision not for negotiation.

I reply that I'm going to check my room and then head upstairs and go into Ollie's. It was messy before but it's even worse now. Two of the posters have been torn – presumably by accident – but the one of the woman with the car has been removed. The picture of Ollie and Sarah from the windowsill is gone. I check his stack of games – but the bracelet still sits in the case, either unnoticed or disregarded. So much for a thorough search, this feels more like a wrecking job.

My room has barely been touched and, though I didn't look at the checklist Mum was given, it doesn't look like anything has been taken. The clothes in my wardrobe have been shunted to one side and someone has definitely gone through my drawers – but that's about it. I return my journal to its hiding place but keep the bracelet in my pocket.

I'm not sure what to do with the day. Technically, college is still open. It is a Thursday, after all.

'Ellie!'

I peer over the banister to where Mum is at the bottom of the stairs, car keys in her hand. 'The solicitor just called, so I'm off to Langham police station to see your brother.' She motions towards the house. 'Leave all this. I'll do it when I get back.'

'Do you want me to come?'

She shakes her head. 'It's no place you want to be. I'll see you later. Call me if you need me.'

She doesn't wait for a reply, striding purposefully towards the door.

After the front door closes, I sit on the stairs and yawn. It takes me so by surprise that I'm still reeling when three more hit me. I rest my head against the wall, finally feeling sleepy, although the moment I close my eyes, I'm back in the river again.

When I try to stand, my knees wobble and I need to hold onto the banister to steady myself. I'm even a little dizzy, with the hallway zooming towards me and then away again. When my eyes are open, my head spins; when they're closed, it feels like I'm drowning once more. I end up sitting on the stairs, one eye open, one closed, trying to trick my body. It takes a few minutes but my vision eventually clears and, though my legs are rickety, I reach the bottom of the stairs without falling.

Naomi answers her phone on the second ring, not waiting for me to say anything before asking if everything's all right. I apologise for not replying to her messages, but she doesn't seem bothered, telling me college has been cancelled and that everyone's still out looking for Helen.

Given the circumstances with Ollie, it is unquestionably a risky thing for me to join in but occasionally I get a kick from annoying some of the villagers just to see how they'll react.

Okay, a *lot* of time, I get a kick from annoying the villagers.

I lock the house, checking it twice, and then walk down to the car park next to the river. There's barely a soul on the streets, with work and school apparently abandoned. The few who are around pay me no attention anyway. It's another moody, misty morning with the clouds ready to give way to brilliant, blinding blue. The village search parties are organising themselves around, perhaps predictably, a tea urn.

Naomi welcomes me with a hug and we stand on the bridge talking. She says that Robbie and Ben have already been drafted onto a team currently combing the densest part of the woods on top of Gold Hill. Everyone else is waiting to find out what the plans for the day are.

As we stand together, it becomes apparent that we're the centre of attention, or – more to the point – *I* am. There is a mixture of bewilderment and outright hostility bristling from those in the car park. Nobody says anything because it's rarely the way of those who live here. Instead, it is more sideways glances and mutterings. A woman I only vaguely recognise is passing through the crowd with a plate of biscuits but she doesn't head in our direction when she reaches the bridge. The only person who offers anything even approaching a smile is the vicar.

'Has anyone found anything?' I ask, keeping my voice low.

Naomi glances towards the crowd and then turns her back to them, lowering her voice. 'Is it true about your brother?'

'That depends on what you've heard.'

'That he was arrested.'

I nod.

'That they searched your house last night?'

'We had to stay at Bentley's B & B.'

'Ugh.'

'I think it was last decorated before I was born.'

Naomi lowers her voice even further. It's barely a whisper. 'What do they think he did?'

'I don't know.'

'If they found anything at your house, they wouldn't still have us searching for anything to do with Helen.'

I shrug, unsure what to say.

'People are saying they found Helen's body in your attic.' I step back a little, raising my eyebrows, but Naomi adds quickly: 'I'm not saying I believe it – that's just what someone was saying.'

'Who?'

She nods towards the crowd. 'You know who. The usual lot.'

'The Ravens?'

'And some of the biddies. You know what they're like. They love this stuff.'

As I glance past Naomi towards the flock of villagers, a dozen eyes turn away, pretending they weren't watching in the first place.

'What else have you heard?' I ask.

Naomi is biting her nails nervously. 'Do you really want to know?'

'Yes.'

'That night we were all in the woods, do you remember when Helen stood up to defend Ollie?'

'Of course.'

'People saw them leaving together in the early hours.'

It takes me a moment to process the information. It would explain why Jim was so insistent on asking me about the times at which Helen and Ollie left.

'*Who* saw them?' I ask.

'I don't know, but someone mentioned Rebecca's name.'

'*Who* mentioned her name?' Naomi doesn't reply, waiting until I've stopped eyeing the crowd and am looking at her instead. 'What?' I add.

'You've gotta stop asking me, Ell. You know what people are like. If I'm telling you what I've heard, can you just take my word for it?'

She bites her lip and seems a little upset.

'Sorry,' I say.

'It's fine, but if Rebecca's saying she saw them leave together, maybe she did.' She holds a finger up to stop me interrupting. 'Look, I know she's a bitch but do you really think she'd lie to the police about that? Imagine if someone else said they'd definitely seen Helen leaving by herself, or with a different person. Or if someone came forward and said *they'd* left with Helen. Rebecca would be in loads of trouble for making something up. If she's saying she saw them leaving together, she probably did.'

I take a breath, wanting to be angry with Rebecca, possibly with Naomi. I don't even know. The problem is that Naomi's right.

'Just because they might have left together,' I say, 'it doesn't mean—'

'I'm not saying it does, Ell. You asked what I'd heard, so I'm telling you.'

Naomi is getting annoyed and I don't necessarily blame her. I wait a moment and then take a small step forwards. She snakes an arm around my hips and I put one across her shoulders. We stand facing the water, holding each other and then I ask as calmly as I can if she's heard anything else.

Naomi breathes deeply through her nose and I know it's going to be bad.

'People are saying they raided your house and found Helen's clothes in his room.'

I shake my head. 'They gave us a checklist of everything they took and there was nothing like that on there.'

'Would they tell you if they had found something?'

I admit I don't know, then ask what else.

'It's all rumours,' Naomi adds. 'Some are saying that Helen and Ollie did it in his car.'

'How would other people know that? They weren't even going out.'

She shrugs. 'I don't know.'

We're interrupted by a loud call from the car park as one of the officers starts to organise people into teams again. There's little chance of me being allowed to help given my brother is apparently prime suspect for Helen's disappearance – but I follow Naomi across the bridge anyway. She squeezes my hand and then releases it. For a second, I feel the warmth of her body and it makes me want to cry because of how I've betrayed her with Ben.

It's not just her. There are so many pairs of accusing eyes on me as the officer calls for everyone assigned as 'group A' to head over to one side of the tarmac.

'What group are you?' I ask Naomi.

'C.'

'What does that mean?'

She shrugs.

Naomi's group is called next, so she smiles and says to stay in contact. I'm left standing by myself, a few metres away from the two dozen people assigned to group B. I know I should go but don't want to simply turn and disappear over the bridge. It would seem like admitting I'd done something wrong – or conceding that Ollie had. I stand awkwardly, gazing towards the river when Rebecca calls my name.

When I turn to face her, she's standing tall in skinny jeans with wellies over the top and a designer jacket.

'The cameras aren't here yet,' I say.

She sneers immediately back. 'Why are you here?'

'What's it to you?'

'Because I can't be the only one who thinks a murderer's sister shouldn't be looking for the victim.'

Her Ravens stand at her side nodding in agreement. I wish I had a devastating comeback but my mind is blank, primarily because she's right. Not about the murderer thing, but the sister. I let her have her triumph, putting my hands in my pockets, turning, and then trudging over the bridge, not bothering to look back.

Chapter Thirty-Three

The Tape Deck car park is empty when I emerge from the path that leads from Westby. The light-up board at the front says that today's special is a 'four-bean burger', though I'm not entirely sure what that is. It clearly involves beans and some bread, though I don't think I could even name four types of bean. Does 'baked' count?

The inside is almost as empty as the outside, with row after row of unoccupied creamy-brown tables. With everyone else my age helping in the search for Helen, it's no wonder the place is deserted. It's a testament to how much time I've spent here that I know the song playing is by Billy Idol. If nothing else, this place gives an education in music that wouldn't have otherwise been heard in my lifetime.

I take a seat next to the wall of tapes and take out my phone. There is a message from Robbie asking if I want to have lunch somewhere and another from Naomi, which says sorry – even though she has nothing to apologise for. I reply to the pair of them – telling Robbie I'm not in the mood – and then realise a shadow is hovering over me.

Ash is leaning to the side again, as if the floor is slanted. His hair is still parted the side, though it occurs to me that perhaps it was on the other side when I last saw him. He's not quite looking at me, more at my shoulder. It's incredibly disconcerting.

Even though people generally order at the counter, he has a small pad in his hand and thrusts it towards me. 'Is there something you'd like?' he asks. 'Today's special is a four-bean burger.'

His speech sounds sloppy, as if there's too much saliva in his mouth. I stare at him as best I can, given he's not returning the gaze.

'You did this, didn't you?' I say.

His eyebrows arch in the middle. 'Uh... did what?'

'You did something to Helen James and then found a way to pin it on my brother.'

He steps backwards, tripping slightly on one of the chairs. 'Uh... was there something you wanted?'

I start to follow him as he backs towards the counter, an accusing finger at the ready. 'I've heard all about you stalking Tina. You've got a thing about teenage girls, haven't you? You went for Sarah Lipski last year, you've been following me, then it was Helen.'

We've moved so quickly that his back is pressed to the counter. I'm on tiptoes and, because he's hunched, I tower over him. There are noises from the kitchen beyond, but no one in sight. A noise escapes from him that I've never heard before, a squawking cross between a howl of alarm and a cry of pain. It is animalistic, so shrill, that I back down instinctively. He has his hands protecting his face, even though there was never a chance of me striking him. It takes me a few moments to realise what's happened.

He's utterly terrified... of me.

He makes a second, quieter, shriek and peeps through his hands as I back away.

'I'm sorry,' I say, ashamed of myself. I've become part of the mob.

Ash slaps himself hard across the face, creating a fleshy thwack that echoes through the empty restaurant.

'Hey!' I say. 'You don't have to do that.'

He smacks himself once more and I step forward, which only makes him cower again. I hold both hands in the air as if the police have told me to. 'Ash, I'm sorry. Please stop.'

Ash pushes himself up on the counter and stares towards me. Not *at* me – towards me. 'No,' he says.

'No what?'

'Not again.'

'I'm sorry, Ash. I shouldn't have said what I did – but I don't know what you mean.'

'P-p-police,' he stutters. 'Not again.'

I move towards one of the booths on the side of the restaurant that has all the tapes. 'Come and sit with me. I'm sorry.'

I slide in on one side and continue watching him. 'I've got to work,' he says.

'There's nobody here.'

Ash glances towards the kitchen behind. There is the sound of voices but still nobody visible. He twists from the kitchen to me three or four times, still not quite focusing, and then he makes up his mind. He heads to the booth and perches on the edge of the bench opposite me, staring at the table.

'What about the police?' I ask.

He gulps, taking ten or fifteen seconds to answer. 'They asked about Sarah last year. Said I killed her.'

That's something I didn't know.

'Why?' I ask.

His shoulders rock slightly, but it's barely a shrug. 'Dunno.'

'They must've given you a reason.'

He rolls his shoulders again and it takes him another ten seconds to reply. 'Said they'd heard my name from people who knew her. People said I'd been following her but I had NOT.'

He shouts the final word, peering up from the table and staring at me properly. There's fire in his eyes.

'I believe you,' I say.

'No, you DON'T – you think I killed her, too. And Helen.'

A sloppy spray of saliva ends up on Ash's chin, which he wipes away. I glance towards the kitchen, wondering if someone might emerge. No one does. I'm not sure if I thought he was involved with either Sarah or Helen, or if he drowned me. As he shakes with a mix of fright and terror, I'm certain that he knows nothing about any of it.

'I'm sorry,' I say. 'I was upset because they've arrested my brother. I shouldn't have taken it out on you.'

He's back to staring at the table. 'You mentioned Tina.'

'Yes.'

'You know her?'

'Not well, but I have talked to her.'

'About me?'

'I suppose. Other things, too.'

His chest rises and falls and I get a whiff of his barbecue breath. 'You ever made a mistake?' he asks. His speech is more coherent now.

'All the time. I've made mistakes today.'

'I thought me and Tina were going to get married and sit on the sofa watching movies every evening.'

There's a pause as I panic at not knowing how to reply. It's a very specific thing he pictured them doing and would certainly sound creepy if it weren't so pathetic.

'Right…'

'Me and Tina was a mistake – but I can't go back now. I know people in the village talk about me. I know she tells people. I want to move away but Mama's got bad cancer.'

I want to reply but don't know him well enough to say anything other than that I'm sorry. Anything more sounds as if I'm patronising.

'You think I'm weird, don't you?' he says.

'No.'

'You do. Everyone does – because I've got one leg shorter than the other. Because I used to stammer when I was a kid. Cos of Tina.'

He spits a little as he talks and then brushes the table in annoyance. I'm left feeling a few centimetres high. I spend all my time complaining about the judgy busybodies from the village and I'm no better.

'Do you watch ro-man-tic com-e-dies?' He pronounces each syllable slowly, deliberately, as if the words are a struggle.

'Do you mean films?'

'Have you ever thought how creepy some of those people are? In *Bridget Jones's Diary*, Colin Firth reads Renee Zellweger's diary, then runs off – then a minute later, they're kissing in the street and she's fine with it. In *Love, Actually*, Andrew Lincoln's best friend is in love with Keira Knightley – but Andrew Lincoln is making their wedding video. He crops his own best mate out of the footage because he's so obsessed with Keira Knightley. Then he turns up at her door pretending to be carol singers and shows her all these cards, saying he's in love with her. In *Twilight*, Robert Pattinson is over a hundred years old and Kristen Stewart is seventeen. He follows her around and watches her sleep, hoping she'll fall for him. In *Sleepless In Seattle*, Meg Ryan writes to Tom Hanks, even though she's never met him, then flies to New York to try to track him down. In *Aladdin*, he sees Princess Jasmine, decides he loves her, then stalks her until she loves him back. In *Ghost*, Patrick Swayze dies but he still won't let Demi Moore out of his sight. In *The Graduate*, Dustin Hoffman follows Katharine Ross to California and interrupts her wedding. In *Pretty Woman*, Richard Gere keeps paying Julia Roberts money until she becomes the woman he wants her to be. In *The Time Traveller's Wife*, Eric Bana goes through time, grooming a six-year-old girl to fall in love with him.'

He pauses and then adds breathlessly: 'I watch a lot of movies.'

It's a lot of information to take in – although I've seen most of the films he mentions.

It takes me a few seconds to muster a weak: 'When you put it like that, it doesn't sound so romantic.'

He huffs a breath, which isn't a surprise considering the way everything else came out in one go. 'Did Tina tell you about Tenerife?' he asks. His stutter has gone.

I nod.

'I grew up watching ro-man-tic com-e-dies,' Ash says. 'Mama used to record them off the telly and then she'd watch them back all day. I thought flying out to see Tina would show I loved her. I thought she'd be pleased I was there. If I'd been Hugh Grant or Channing Tatum, everyone would have thought I was brilliant.'

Again, I'm unsure how to reply. In a weird, warped way, he has a point. Sort of.

If a person had been brought up solely on a diet of rom-coms and things like soap operas, it's no wonder he or she would have a distorted view of how to act around others.

Ash is also right that flying to see his ex-girlfriend on holiday could be viewed as a grand romantic gesture. But it's quite stalker-like depending on how the other person sees it. If it goes down well, it's a story for the grandkids of how Grandpa flew around the world to woo Grandma. If it's not reciprocated, it's a restraining order.

'Did Tina tell you about her garden?' Ash asks.

'Yes.'

'I'd written a poem and was going to read it to her. When she looked out the window, instead of wanting to listen, she called her dad.'

I struggle not to cringe. Everything about it is awful. In a dodgy rom-com, the poem would have been met by initial indifference, then giggles, then some snogging while a power ballad played in the background.

'I know now that's not how it works,' Ash adds.

Considering the way in which he's talking about himself, Ash sounds remarkably self-aware. He must have grown up a fair bit in the past couple of years, though it's all hidden under a cloak of physical twitches, such as the limp and the way he doesn't look people in the eye.

'We saw each other on Saturday night,' I say.

Ash finally peers up but he's blinking rapidly and then bats at the air in front of his face. He grabs a napkin just in time and then a sonic boom of a sneeze erupts. I'm not sure but I think I shriek a little.

'So-wee,' he says, cleaning himself up. It's impossible not to feel sorry for him – everything he does is tinged with clumsiness.

He blows his nose into a second napkin and then apologises again.

'Were we arguing at Helen's house?' I ask.

His eyes are still watering but he shoots into a standing position. 'Did you tell the police I was at her house? They're going to—'

'I didn't mention your name.'

His head spins to the doorway as if expecting an ambush.

'Ash – I didn't say anything. I wanted to ask you about it.'

'I wasn't invited,' he says. 'People here were talking about a party and I figured I could tag along, or at least just turn up. I went after shift and the front door was open.'

'I'm not trying to catch you out – but I saw a picture of us. It looked like we were fighting but I don't remember why.'

He calms slightly, though his breathing is rapid and he's wheezing like an asthmatic. 'I was looking for the toilet but didn't know which door. I *really* needed to go. I pushed open one of the upstairs doors and…'

He tails off but I know what he saw – Ben and me. No wonder we were arguing in the garden. I was likely telling him in a not-so-polite way to forget what he'd seen.

'So-wee,' he adds.

When I stand, he doesn't leap away from me. '*I'm* sorry,' I say. 'I've not handled things well.'

I think about ordering something – the four-bean burger, if only to find out what the beans are – then I remember I can't eat.

'I've got to go,' I add. 'I'll see you around.'

He nods but doesn't reply. He's standing at an angle, hand on his hip, arm bent crookedly.

'See you 'round, Ellie-a-nor,' he says.

He sounds excited, slobbering the mispronounced syllables of my name. I try not to wince but it's impossible not to. Though I'm pretty sure he's not responsible for any of what's happened, Ash's awkwardness is something that invades those around him. I can't bear to spend any more time alone with him. I kinda hate myself for that.

I hurry into the Tape Deck car park and head for the path leading back to Westby, mentally crossing him off my list of suspects and knowing that there aren't many names left.

Chapter Thirty-Four

It's an eerie, lonely walk back to Westby, punctuated by lone, echoing voices from the woods as the search parties scuff their way through the trees. I don't see anyone but I can hear the faint calls of 'halt' and 'continue' that ultimately mean Helen is still missing.

There's little point in spending time in and around Westby centre, and I've had no message from Mum to say Ollie has been released or is being kept in. The only place for me to go is home – but when I get there, Robbie is sitting on the low wall at the front of the house. He's wearing shorts but his bare legs are caked with dirt and a series of red scratches. I'd told him I wasn't in the mood but, now he's here, suddenly I'm glad to see him.

I sit on the wall next to him and, perhaps surprising me as much as him, rest my head on Robbie's shoulder. He puts an arm around me and yawns.

'I tried calling you last night and this morning,' he says.

'It was a tough night with Mum and everything. She's gone to Langham police station to try to see Ollie. What happened to your legs?'

Robbie releases me and looks down at the scrapes. 'Searching in the woods is a dangerous business when you're wearing shorts.' He gulps, then adds: 'Have you heard?'

'Heard what?'

'I tried calling, but—'

'Heard what?'

'The police raided the changing rooms at college earlier. People are saying they found the clothes Helen was wearing at the party in the woods on Monday night – green top and a black skirt.'

As he says that, I remember that outfit. 'People are saying lots of things,' I reply.

'I know, but… I think this is true. Someone took a picture.' He fumbles with his phone and shows me the image that was sent to his WhatsApp. The picture is fuzzy but it looks like a police officer holding something green in a see-through bag.

'I'm not sure what you're saying,' I tell him.

He glances away. 'Ollie…'

'Why would they associate that with Ollie and not one of the other players?'

'Because he's the captain. Some of the players are saying Helen's clothes were found in the kit room at the back of the changing rooms. It's where they keep the balls and nets for the goalposts. Only one player has a key for the kit room – and it's Ollie because he's the captain.'

It takes me a second to take it in. I don't believe it. 'There must be another key – even if it's kept in the office.'

Robbie bows his head. 'I don't know, Ell. Probably – but you'd assume the police would be looking into that.'

As the hours tick by, more and more things are coming out about Ollie. Couple that with the fact he was clearly keeping something from me when we were in his bedroom – and the acceptance when he was arrested – and things are looking bad. There's a natural reluctance for me to believe my brother could do something like this but it seems so clear that whoever killed Sarah is the same person that abducted Helen – and the same person who drowned me.

Do I *really* believe that person is Ollie?

'Anyone could have got access to that kit room,' I say defiantly. 'The old captain could have had a key cut, or someone in the office was careless with it.'

Robbie takes a moment to respond. 'I'm not denying any of that, Ell. You're right – but the police will know that, too.'

'They *won't* because they'll know about Sarah last year and they already had Ollie in their sights. They don't need to look for someone else.'

'People are saying Helen and Ollie left the party together. They were seen.'

Naomi already said this – and perhaps this was what Ollie didn't want to tell me in his bedroom. As soon as Mrs James came through the crowd to say Helen was missing, he'd have known that he was one of – if not *the* – last person to see her. He'd have panicked, unsure whether to tell the police. If no one saw him leaving with Helen, it'd be a secret he could keep; if someone had, they'd be coming for him anyway.

'Does that mean he was the last person to see her?' I ask.

'I guess.'

'It doesn't prove anything, though, does it?'

'I don't know, Ell.'

'Isn't it a massive coincidence that his girlfriend and then a girl he leaves a party with both disappear? He's already guilty, even though he's not.'

'Ell—'

I turn to him. 'Do you think he did it?'

Robbie stares at me, then past me. 'I don't know, Ell.'

'You *know* him. You've seen what he's been like all year. With football, you've probably seen as much of him as I have.'

'I know… but if he didn't do it, then either fate or someone is going out of their way to make it look like he did.'

Neither of us speaks for a while because Robbie's right. Either Ollie did all this – *all* of it, including drowning me – or someone else we know is making it look like he did.

It's a while before either of us are ready to talk again.

'If he did it,' Robbie adds, sounding slightly reluctant, 'why would he keep Helen's clothes somewhere the police would look? Why would he keep them at all?'

I think about the bracelet in my pocket. If Ollie told me the truth, the one I have belonged to Sarah – but he kept his own. Maybe that's his thing? He keeps mementoes? Trinkets? I don't know enough about it. Mum says I'm a hoarder but perhaps it's a family thing.

Robbie is twiddling his thumbs, something I've never noticed him do before. It's all a bit odd. 'I've got something to tell you,' he says.

There's a moment where it feels like the world has frozen. A brief pause in which it feels like he could say anything. Where he might ask why I'm still here, alive and relatively well considering someone drowned me a few days before. Where he might admit to anything.

'I've lost your shoes,' he adds.

'Huh?'

'Your shoes. When we in the car on Saturday night after Helen's party, you said they were giving you blisters so you took them off. I dropped you off but you said you didn't want to be left at your door and you didn't want to carry them either. I didn't want to argue, so you left them in the car. I don't know where they are.'

I blink, jigsaw pieces slotting into place. 'I've got them,' I say. 'I took them the other night.'

He looks at me, obviously wondering why I didn't say something. It *is* strange that I elected to walk barefoot back to the house but I suppose I wasn't quite acting myself that night given what I got up to with Ben. Those silver shoes are nice but, like many of the best shoes, they hurt like hell. I suppose that explains why I woke in the river barefooted and why my shoes were in Robbie's car. If I believe Robbie – and I think I do – something happened to me in between him dropping me off at the end of the road and me getting to the front door.

'I was worried you'd be upset,' he says.

I laugh humourlessly. 'Perhaps at one time. Bigger issues now.'

There's another silence and it feels like we're strangers.

'You're bleeding,' I say, pointing at Robbie's leg.

He looks down to where one of the scratches is deeper. A string of blood that hasn't yet scabbed is slowly dribbling its way down to his sock. Robbie licks his finger and wipes it away.

'Some of the blokes from the village set up their own search team,' he says. 'We've been out in the thicker parts of the woods. It's all thorns and nettles.'

'Find anything?'

'Not really. Rubbish. A dead deer.'

I turn away, facing the house where Rochelle the Raven lives. It doesn't look like anyone's home, but the village itself feels empty.

'Can I tell you something?' I say.

'Of course.'

'It's just there are so many lies and rumours going around at the moment, so I'll just say it…'

I pause and take a breath, then the words are suddenly on the edge of my tongue. In a moment, they're out in the open.

'I kissed Ben on Saturday night,' I say.

There's a rush and it feels as if something's been lifted from me. I feel both better and worse. I wait for the response but Robbie says nothing. I don't want to see the expression on his face but the silence is so long that I'm drawn to look towards him. His head is slightly bowed, hands on his knees. There's a small smudge of dirt around his chin and, though his hair is flat today, he's still striking.

His reply is a whisper. 'I know.'

It's me who's dumbstruck now. 'You know?'

'I didn't know as such but I sensed something when the two of you were on the back seat on the way to the woods on Monday night.'

'Oh…'

He reaches out and takes my hand, squeezing it. I gasp – but only because I can actually feel his warmth. Properly feel it. I'm so used to being cold that anything other than that is a shock.

'I don't blame you,' he says.

'Why?'

'It's a difficult time. We both know we're breaking up.'

He releases my hand but puts an arm around me, pulling me to my feet and then hugging me properly. I can feel the warmth of his body and cling to him, not wanting to let go. I want it to last and last but it isn't long before he pats me on the back and takes a small step away.

'I've got to tell Naomi,' I say.

He nods slightly. 'I can't help you with that, Ell. But if you want to help free Ollie, then I *can* help with that.'

For a moment, I think he means breaking into the police station. I have a flash of going on the run, action-movie style.

'What do you mean?' I ask.

'If Ollie didn't abduct Helen, then someone else did.'

'Who?'

'He's your brother, my friend. If we both believe him, then someone else put Helen's clothes in the kit room.'

'Someone on the football team?'

Robbie shakes his head. 'People have alibis. It's all the players have been talking about. Someone could have swiped a key from the office, or had a duplicate, but we're not going to be able to find that out.'

'What are you suggesting then?'

'Before all this happened, everyone in the village was talking about one thing, one person. Now it's all kinda been forgotten. We need to find that person.'

He sounds firm, decisive, as if it's obvious.

'The Hitcher?' I say.

He nods: 'The Hitcher.'

Chapter Thirty-Five

Setting out to find a person that might not exist is an odd thing to do but it's not as if I have a better idea. It's now the afternoon and I've not heard anything from Mum all day. I call her, but she's not answering, so I send a text asking if everything's okay. I immediately regret it, because everything is clearly *not* okay – it's far from it. She's been at the police station with Ollie since morning. Too late now, though.

Robbie drives us towards Tape Deck but we don't get that far. We stop in at the petrol station that sits in between Westby and Langham. Somehow, in the era of chains and big businesses, Urquhart's Fuel & General Store has remained in operation. There is a pair of petrol pumps on the courtyard, each with old-fashioned displays where a set of plastic numbers flip around to show how much has been spent, as opposed to the digital readers in supermarkets. There is a small glass booth at the front, which would have once housed someone to sell the fuel. It is now empty but there's a sign telling customers to go into the mini-market instead. The yard is dusty and dry, surrounded by rusting metal road signs from the UK and America. The collection is tiled together against the wall of a disused garage, brimming with colour and stories.

We head into the small shop at the side of the station and the air-conditioning immediately makes me shiver. The wall straight ahead is lined with car mats, jump leads, seat covers, plus bottles of car oil and de-icer – which would be an optimistic sell at this time of year. On the other side is row after row of chocolate bars and bags of sweets.

A small man with glasses is sitting behind the counter reading a car magazine. He glances up towards us and then peers out towards the empty forecourt.

'Can I help?' he asks.

'Are you Mr Urquhart?' I ask.

He nods and puts the magazine down.

'I was hoping I could ask you about the Hitcher...? The paper said you were one of the people who saw him last week.'

Mr Urquhart removes his glasses and wipes them on his top. He looks from me to Robbie and frowns. 'I'm not sure I understand why you're here.'

'We saw someone, too,' Robbie says quickly, before I can speak. 'We're wondering if it was the same person.'

'Why?'

Robbie and I look at each other but I have nothing. 'Because people in the village are still talking about him,' Robbie says.

'I told them not to print my name, y'know,' the garage owner says. 'Told them it was just some man passing through – that we get them all the time here. If it wasn't for that post office break-in, nobody would've batted an eyelid.'

He sounds grouchy but doesn't tell us to go. After a moment or two he sighs and puts his glasses back on. He points a thumb towards the area at the rear of the garage that backs onto the woods.

'Saw him out there,' he says.

'What did he look like?' Robbie asks.

'Like I told them at the paper, I didn't see much. Just a man in the shadows, looked like he was walking towards the village. Nothing unusual in that – you young folk are always walking through.'

'Was there anything recognisable about him? Anything that made you think it wasn't just someone from the village?'

Mr Urquhart stares at Robbie as if it's a stupid question. 'He was tall, real tall – other than that, just normal. I don't know what the big fuss is about.'

He gives us an are-you-going-to-buy-anything? look and Robbie gets a Snickers bar, possibly out of guilt. We thank him for his time and then start to walk back to Westby along the same path on which the Hitcher was apparently seen. It's well-trodden and Mr Urquhart was right in that it's largely used by the younger people in Westby as a way of getting to either Tape Deck or Langham if the bus or a car isn't an option.

Out next stop is the pharmacy in the village. As we park outside, a handful of people are passing through, walking towards the housing estate on the far side. The search must be over for the day, if not for good. A couple of people look at Robbie and me but nobody says anything.

The pharmacy is family run, owned by a busybody named Mrs McKeith. Her husband died a few years back and there's a portrait of him behind the counter, which I've always found a little creepy – even more so because his picture is directly above the row of condoms. There is no reason to keep condoms behind the counter, of course, other than that Mrs McKeith gets a kick from locals – mainly teenagers, I'd guess – having to ask for them.

She's probably old enough to retire now but Mrs McKeith has run this shop for as long as I can remember. Even when I was young, I never liked her – and that was when she used to crouch and offer me lollies with a pat on the head. Her shop smells weird, a sort of mix between perfume and detergent and I've never been able to separate that from her. She has tight curly grey hair and constantly purses her lips into an O – which shouldn't be annoying, but really is.

The shop is empty and Mrs McKeith eyes Robbie and me suspiciously. It only lasts a moment and then her features soften – but not naturally, more like she's forced herself.

'Oh, my love,' she says, looking to me, 'how awful this must all be for you. How is your mother?'

Her forced enthusiasm has taken me by surprise but it's too late to back down now. 'She's fine,' I say. 'As you'd expect, I guess.'

'Oh, but it's so awful what's happening with your brother... Have you heard anything...?'

She lets it hang breezily and it reminds me of Rochelle the Raven from across the road. They both operate on different grapevines but the outcome is the same and their mutual currency is gossip.

'I don't know what's going on,' I reply.

Her face falls slightly but she reverts to the fake smile almost immediately. 'It must be hard on your mother and you, though. How are you both holding up?'

'We're okay.'

'And then there's the added complication, of course...?'

I know I should ignore her but can't help myself. 'What do you mean?'

'Well, it's so unfortunate – but your mother and policeman Jim. It has to complicate things. It's *you* I feel sorry for. First your father, then everything that happened with that poor girl a year ago, now this.'

My fists are clenched and I can feel my body tensing, ready to explode, but Robbie strokes the side of my arm, reminding me why we're here.

'We were wondering if we could ask you about the Hitcher,' Robbie says.

Mrs McKeith turns to him and shivers. 'Dreadful man. *Dreadful.* Have you seen him, too?'

Robbie nods but doesn't speak. Technically he's not lying, as the nod could've been an involuntary twitch.

She glances towards the door as if he might suddenly burst in. 'Oh, have you told someone?'

'Not yet,' he says.

'Oh, it was awful. I'd gone to the back of the shop to empty my bins and there he was, hanging around in the back alley.'

'What did he look like?' Robbie asks.

She strokes her chin. 'Beard and long hair. Scruffy. Ripped trousers. A proper wrong 'un. You know the type. I'd heard about the post office break-in, of course, and this was the day after.'

'Do people normally hang around in the alley at the back?' Robbie asks.

Mrs McKeith takes her time. She'll have been honing this story ever since she first told it. 'You get kids running up and down there but there's no reason for a grown man to be there unless he's up to no good. I shouted at him, asking what he was doing, and he ran off towards the bridge. You can't help but wonder if this is all connected.' She stops and then adds: 'Is that why you're here?'

She looks to me again but I daren't risk saying anything because it'll be around the village by the time I get out the door. 'We were just curious,' I say.

Mrs McKeith turns to Robbie but he doesn't add anything other than to thank her for her time. She frowns momentarily but quickly hides it again before we leave.

'What do you reckon?' Robbie asks when we're outside.

'The man at the garage said he was tall. That was the main thing he noticed, yet Mrs McKeith didn't mention it.'

'And he didn't talk about the beard or scruffy trousers. They could be different people.'

It feels like a waste of time but at least we're doing something.

'Who else should we visit?' I ask.

Robbie turns to me and doesn't say the name. I can tell what he's thinking because of the way he raises his eyebrows.

'Do we really have to?' I say.

'Have you got another idea?'

I sigh, wishing I did.

We find Rebecca at our first stop – her house. She lives between the village and Mr Urquhart's petrol station in a large place a little away from the road, similar to the ones on top of Gold Hill. I don't know much about Rebecca's background or her parents, but the size of the house makes it clear they have a bit of money about them. Tall metal gates bar the driveway, so Robbie rings the buzzer. There is a pause and then Rebecca's voice comes from the tinny speaker.

'What do you want?'

I look up, but then Robbie points to the camera that is embedded above the speaker box. She can see us but we can only hear her voice.

'Can we talk?' I ask.

'What about?'

'Things… can we do this face to face?'

'Who's with you?'

'Only Robbie.'

'Have you got a car?'

'Robbie's driving.'

'Let's go to the Deck.'

There is a fizz and the speaker goes silent. Robbie and I stand around waiting as five minutes pass. I wonder if she was joking and is now laughing at us, perhaps watching through the camera, wondering how long we'll hang around for. Eventually, there's a clink and then the door next to the gate opens and Rebecca emerges. She's wearing a red dress with matching shoes, bag and lipstick. Her skin is so smooth, so perfect, that she looks like a doll.

She strides past me towards Robbie's car. 'Let's go then. There's no way I'm sitting in the back of this thing. I can't believe it even goes.' She turns to Robbie. 'Couldn't you get a *proper* car?'

She doesn't get a reply as she climbs into the passenger seat and slams the door behind her.

'Your idea,' I tell Robbie.

I get into the back seat, saying nothing as Robbie pulls away.

'Your car smells,' Rebecca says almost instantly.

Robbie doesn't answer.

'Do you have a car?' I ask.

'Daddy's got a special edition Beetle on order for me for when I pass my test. He spoke to someone directly at the factory.'

'Where is your dad?'

'Working.'

'What about your mum?'

'What's it to you?'

'Nothing, just making conversation.'

Rebecca goes quiet and I get the sense that her mum's probably working, too. That it is normal for her to be by herself after college in that big house. That away from the hangers-on, the Ravens are her only real friends and that, rather than being sinister, they simply look out for each other. It's not a nice thought, seeing Rebecca as anything other than the bitch I've long assumed her to be. Or known her to be, I suppose. It's far easier to dislike someone when not having to think of him or her as being an actual person.

The rest of the journey to Tape Deck is spent in silence. There are a handful of cars in the parking area now – and half a dozen of the tables inside are occupied. Rebecca leads the way, slinking into a booth opposite the wall of tapes. In all the times I've visited, I've never sat on this side of the restaurant and everything feels different.

I slide in opposite Rebecca but Robbie doesn't get the chance. 'I'll have a chicken salad,' she tells him before he can sit. 'Make sure they remove the skin. Tell them it's for Rebecca. They'll know what to do.'

Robbie turns to me but I shake my head, indicating I don't want anything, then he heads to the counter. I'm not sure if I can remember the last time I was alone with Rebecca. She's filing one of her already manicured fingernails, avoiding eye contact. Close-up, it's easier to see the amount of make-up she's wearing, which is lots. Less like a doll, more like an actress playing a role.

'What?' she says, not looking up.

'Nothing.'

'I'm surprised you came knocking on *my* door given what's happened to your brother. What do you want?'

I glance to Robbie but there's someone in front of him in line. For now, it's just us.

'You saw the Hitcher.'

She puts down the nail file and looks up. 'I thought you didn't believe me. I thought you said I was making it up…?'

'Did you see someone?'

'What's it to you?'

I count to three in my head. 'Can we be civil to each other?'

'You want to be friends? After all we've said and done to each other over the years? Sorry, but I don't make friends with people whose brothers are psycho killers.'

I count another three again, keeping my lips closed, then say: 'I wasn't *asking* to be friends, I was asking if we could be civil to each other.'

She flicks at her nail. 'Fine.'

'Did you see this Hitcher guy?'

'Why would I lie?'

I almost ask why she'd lie about knowing Sarah so well but I already know the answer – attention. If it's true that her parents are at work so much, then perhaps it explains why she's so desperate for people to notice her.

'Where did you see him?' I ask.

Before she answers, Robbie returns with a tray of food. Tape Deck is a strange place – sometimes an order is instantly ready fast-food style, other times customers have to wait. He takes a burger for himself and then pushes the salad in front of her. Rebecca pokes through it with a fork, making sure the pieces of chicken are indeed skinless.

'This is the Rebecca special,' she says. 'They should put it on the menu board.'

Neither Robbie nor myself say anything, watching as she puts the smallest piece of chicken into her mouth.

'Watching someone eat can give a girl an eating disorder,' she says. I'm not sure if she's joking.

She fishes for another bit of meat and then turns to me before putting it in her mouth. 'Of course I saw him. It's like I told that reporter. He was at the back of the post office the day after it was broken into. When he saw me, he ran off along the alley.'

'Why were you behind the post office?' I ask.

She chews the second piece of chicken, jabbing the empty fork towards me. 'None of your business.'

'What did he look like?'

She pokes her fork into the bowl but doesn't pick anything up. 'The picture was on the front of the paper. He had a beard, ripped jeans. Sort of like a tramp. Tall.'

It matches with what both Mr Urquhart and Mrs McKeith told us. It could be that she heard either of them talking about the person they'd seen and then took the description as her own. In terms of attention-seeking, it's the sort of thing she might do.

'That it?' she asks, looking at me.

'I suppose.'

She lifts another piece of chicken from the bowl. 'Easiest free meal I've ever got. Why do you even care? Trying to find someone to pin everything on who isn't your brother?'

When I don't reply, she laughs to herself. '*Really?* This is the best you can do?'

Robbie takes a bite of his burger, leaving me floundering.

'Is it true you saw my brother and Helen leaving the woods together?' I ask.

Rebecca finishes chewing, although there's the merest hint of a smile in the corner of her lips. 'What do you want me to say, Eleanor?'

She says my name as if it's a put-down.

'Say you made it up,' I reply.

'Why would I have made it up?'

'Because you're a cow.'

She grins widely but still takes the time to eat another bit of chicken. She's not touched the salad. 'I thought you wanted to be civil?' she says sweetly. Annoyingly.

'Old habits.'

Rebecca holds my gaze and I know I've given her what she wanted. Naomi was probably right that we're as bad as each other.

'It's not *my* fault your brother killed his girlfriend last year and now he's done the same again. You're lucky he hasn't come after you.'

'He didn't do it.'

'I don't think that's for you to decide.'

I start to speak but she interrupts by clapping her hand and looking past me towards the door. 'Oh, look who it is. This is convenient.'

Naomi spots us and does a cartoon double-take, unable to believe her eyes that Robbie, Rebecca and I are sitting together. She's changed from earlier and is wearing her Doc Martens with pink-and-white striped knee socks. She walks slowly towards us, hovering by the edge of the table.

She pinches the skin on her wrist. 'Am I in a parallel universe?' she asks.

Rebecca laughs and shifts along, giving Naomi space to sit. She and Robbie are on the outside of the booth, with Rebecca and I opposite each other on the inside.

'I got a lift out with my dad,' Naomi says, looking at me. 'He's in the car park. I'm only here for takeaway. I didn't know you were here.'

'It was spur of the moment,' I reply.

Naomi's eyes shoot sideways towards Rebecca, though she doesn't ask.

'This is lovely and cosy,' Rebecca says.

'What's cosy?' Naomi asks.

'You three here together. I'm surprised you're all still talking.'

Rebecca is staring at me, talking to Naomi. I have no idea how she knows but the glee in her voice is impossible to miss. She's like a giddy child telling a story about going to the funfair.

'Why's that surprising?' Naomi asks.

Robbie has stopped eating and his arms have tensed.

'Because of what happened at Helen's party.'

The three of us are all staring at Rebecca, who calmly lifts another piece of chicken to her mouth and starts to chew. In the silence, Naomi looks to me, asking the question without speaking. I feel frozen, unable to say the words.

'What happened?' Naomi asks, though I'm unsure if she's asking me or Rebecca.

Rebecca takes her time, still watching me with a smirk as she sips from a glass of water.

'Hasn't anyone told you?' Rebecca asks Naomi.

'Told me what?'

She nods at Robbie. 'What about you, Robert? Roberto? Robster? Has your girlfriend told you?'

He doesn't speak but his nose twitches, which makes Rebecca laugh. She points her fork towards him. 'So you *do* know – and yet you're still here trailing around after her.'

Naomi has had enough, slapping her hand on the table. 'What's going on?'

Rebecca nods towards me. 'Go on, Eleanor. Tell her about what you and Benjamin got up to in Helen's parents' bedroom…'

Naomi stares at me, eyes wide. 'What?'

'It's not what you think,' I say, unable to meet my friend's eye.

'What is it?'

I open my mouth to say something but no words come out. It doesn't matter anyway because the croak I do manage is enough of a confession. 'You and Ben?' Naomi whispers

'It was just a kiss. A mistake.'

Naomi's eyes boggle as she shunts backwards into a standing position. She tumbles over a collection of incomplete words, babbling incoherently. Eventually, something meaningful comes out.

'I've been defending you all day,' she says. 'And Ollie. Telling people that you're not who they say you are. Then I find out what you're really like.' She turns and jabs a finger towards Rebecca. 'From *her* – of all people.'

'Don't shoot the messenger,' Rebecca says, waggling the fork, enjoying herself.

Naomi and I call her the same rude word at the same time, but there's no camaraderie between us and Rebecca smiles through it anyway.

Naomi rounds on me, leaning in close. 'I thought you were my *friend* – I thought…' She reels back, gasping, and then skewers her final insult. 'You're supposed to be my friend – but your brother's a murdering scumbag and you're a lying, cheating slag.'

With that, she spins and runs to the door.

Rebecca finishes another mouthful and then dabs her mouth with a napkin.

'Well,' she says, 'that was fun.'

Chapter Thirty-Six

Robbie stands without me saying anything, letting me climb out of the booth.

'Don't leave on my account,' Rebecca says.

I want to scream and swear at her but restrain myself, knowing that it's my fault anyway. Without another word, Robbie and I head outside, just in time to see Naomi's dad's car roaring back towards Westby. Robbie walks towards his car, tossing the keys from one hand to the other. He rests against the driver's side, saying nothing.

'I'm really sorry,' I say.

Robbie's head is bowed slightly. 'How did she find out?'

'I don't know. I'm not sure it matters. You know what it's like. One person tells someone else, who tells someone else. Secrets are never secrets for long around here.'

His lips are tight. 'You want a lift back?'

'I should probably walk.'

He opens the door and then pauses. 'I, um…'

'What?'

He shakes his head. 'Nothing. I'll see you around. Call or text if you need something.'

The engine flares and then a fog of dust flicks up as he heads for the road, leaving me alone in the car park. The day has taken a turn for the worse in more ways than one. The sky is overcast, matching my mood and that of the village in general. A wind has whipped up, sending a collection of small stones and twigs scuttling across the car park. It is probably cold but I'm already chilly enough.

I pinch the scorched end of my finger and then rotate the one that dislocated back and forth. There's still no pain and I'm left wondering what all of this was for. In the days since I awoke in the river, I've achieved little other than alienating my best friend and boyfriend, plus had an argument with my mum for good measure. I would have been as well off remaining under the water.

It's silent and the dark thoughts smudge the edges of my mind, infecting and contaminating. I do my best to blink them away but they're still there, nibbling and whispering.

As I think about my mum, I check my phone and realise I've somehow missed a call from her. She's sent me a message, saying she's still in Langham, still waiting to see Ollie. She tells me to call if there's a problem – but me falling out with Naomi can't really rival the situation she and Ollie are in.

I start walking back towards Westby, willing the clouds to open. It feels like I, perhaps the village as a whole, could do with a cleansing. Before I know it, I'm on the bridge again, staring at the spot where I woke up on Sunday morning. The river's trickling a little faster than usual, likely because it's raining somewhere upstream. The car park that was so crammed with volunteers this morning is now empty. As far as I know, there's no sign of Helen, alive or dead. Ollie's been at the police station all day, yet there's no news from him either.

As I stand and stare at the water, a flicker of movement catches my eye. A man walks out of the toilet block on the car park side of the river. He's tall, wearing ripped jeans, with shoulder-length dark hair and a short beard. He rubs his hands together and then flattens the top of his hair.

He looks exactly how Rebecca described him.

It's so surreal, so unexpected, that I continue to stare, wondering if he's a mirage. I start to walk towards him but he hasn't noticed me. He's heading for the woods at the back of the car park, hands in his pockets. He's even whistling, as if he has no cares.

I think about shouting after him, asking who he is, if he knows the fuss he's caused. Then I realise that, in everybody else's stories, they called after him and he ran for it. I quicken my pace, trying to walk on the tips of my toes to remain quiet but when he reaches the treeline, he turns and looks over his shoulder.

I'm frozen to the spot as if we're playing a game of What's the Time, Mr Wolf. For a few moments, we stare at each other. His eyes are grey and determined.

'Hi,' I say. He continues to stare as I take a step forward. 'I was just wondering if—'

I don't finish the sentence because he turns and bolts into the woods. I only have a moment to think and the next thing I know, I'm running after him.

There might be those who call me something of a tomboy, not because I necessarily am, more because I don't really hang around with too many girls. That might be partly true but one thing I'm definitely not is athletic. I *hated* PE in school, so much so that I used to consistently quote 'female problems' as a reason to get out of stuff. That was until the PE teacher said she was going to write a letter home. I'd missed so many classes that she was certain I must have significant health problems. After that, there was no way out of it. The only thing I really got into was hockey – but that was because a) I was young and didn't know any better; and b) running around with a giant stick is cool. No one can deny that.

I'm almost out of breath by the time I reach the woods. There's no path but I follow the sound of footsteps past a huge tree and then over a trunk that has fallen across the ground. I almost lose my footing by trampling into a dimple in the ground that was hidden by a covering of leaves. I only manage to stay upright by grabbing onto a small tree that's barely bigger than me.

I don't know if it's because I'm nowhere near as fit as someone my age should be, or because of the whole being dead thing, but I'm out of breath after barely a minute of chasing. I stop for a moment, listening to where the sound of the Hitcher is heading, only to realise that I've lost his trail. I keep a hand on the tree trunk, trying to breathe, and then walk in a slow, silent circle around it, looking for a hint of movement, of anything that might signal where he's gone.

Nothing.

Then I realise that I'm not entirely sure of the direction from which I came either. There's a patch of leaves that looks like the one I stumbled through – but there's another that's almost identical in a slightly different direction. The overcast sky offers no clues and, even though it's summer, the ground is sticky underneath the cover of leaves.

I see my footprints but nobody else's and, for a moment, I wonder if the figure was ever there. Is it possible to imagine a person for real? To see someone where there is no one? When I think about what's happened to me, it feels silly to imagine that anything is impossible.

'Hello?'

I don't know why I call out but the sound echoes around the trees, rebounding back towards me until it sounds like someone else with my voice is here.

'I only wanted to talk.'

Nothing.

'My name's Ellie.'

I'm not completely sure why I say it but telling somebody else your name seems like a human thing to do.

Still nothing.

I head towards the first pile of leaves, looking for a hint of a footstep that might mean I'm going in the right direction. I'm crouched on the floor trying to figure out if the gentle indentation in the soil came from my shoe when a chill falls across me.

I'm still kneeling when I look up to see the shape of the Hitcher standing over me, hands in his pockets.

'Ellie,' he says. 'That's a nice name.'

Chapter Thirty-Seven

Although I'm not religious, I did go to a Church of England primary school, mainly because that's the only one in the village. After passing through the main doors, there was a reception hall, the centrepiece of which was a large cross with an even larger painting of Jesus next to it. Of course, I now know it was an artist's impression of what Jesus may or may not have looked like but I didn't know that then. I thought the white man with long dark hair and a beard was what the *actual* Jesus looked like.

For a moment, I flash back to primary school because the Hitcher looks so much like the painting. He's not scruffy at all, not really, he's just a little rough around the edges – like he'd know how to put up shelves or build a house extension, that sort of thing.

'You're him,' I say, meaning the Hitcher, not Jesus.

He offers his hand but I stand without it, backing towards a tree.

'I'm who?' he says. His voice is soft, almost like a woman's.

'The Hitcher.'

'What's a hitcher?'

'Like a hitchhiker. Y'know, thumbing a lift…?'

He looks at me blankly, so I explain that someone who looks like him was seen in the village a week or so ago – and that the locals went into meltdown, thinking he'd broken into the post office.

He scratches his head. 'People think I broke into a post office?'

'Sort of – someone who looks like you.'

'Why would I break into a post office?'

'I don't know.'

We're standing and looking at each other, seemingly not knowing what the other is talking about. It's like speaking to someone who doesn't understand English. I can't pick his accent, either. It's not from anywhere around Westby, but then it's unlike anything else I've heard. He pronounces his words very deliberately, over-pronounces, perhaps. He sounds posh but down-to-earth at the same time.

'You're going to have to explain this to me,' he says. 'A couple of people see me in the village and then everyone's saying I broke into a post office…?'

'That's pretty much it.'

'I don't get it.'

'I'm guessing you never grew up in a village…?'

He scratches his beard. 'London.'

'That's a pretty big village.'

He breaks into a smile, which completely changes his look. Without it, he could easily seem intimidating, mainly because of his size. When he grins, he seems child-like and mischievous.

'If I'm supposedly a bad guy who broke into a post office, why did you follow me?' he asks. 'Wouldn't you be scared?'

I open my mouth but don't know how to reply. He's right – I *should* be frightened but I'm not. It hadn't even crossed my mind to be afraid.

'What's your name?' I ask.

'Melek.'

'Melek? Like dalek?'

'What's a dalek?'

'How do you spell it?'

'M-E-L-E-K. Melek.'

'I've never met anyone named Melek before,' I tell him.

He nods and then grins again. 'Thank you.'

'Does it mean something?'

'Dunno. Does Ellie mean something?'

I'm not sure why I'm telling him but he seems harmless. Friendly, even. 'My full name is Eleanor,' I say. 'It means Shining Light.'

He lets out a low whistle. 'Do you do much shining?'

I laugh, properly laugh, unable to stop myself. 'No,' I manage.

'You're letting yourself down, Ellie,' he replies.

With that, he turns and starts to walk through the trees. 'Hey,' I call after him, but all he does is peep over his shoulder and smile.

For a moment, I'm alone – and then I make my decision, chasing after him, skipping across the twigs and bracken until I'm at his side. He seems surprised that I'm there but continues to walk effortlessly, as if he's on a perfect athletic track.

'Where are we going?' I ask.

'*I'm* going home.'

'Where's home?'

'Wherever I lay my hat.'

I have to quickstep to stay at his side. He's a fast walker. 'Is that a song?'

'Marvin Gaye – then Paul Young.'

'I think they've played it at the Deck.'

'What's the Deck?'

'A place where we go to eat.'

Melek rounds a tree and then heads into a semicircle of bushes. A rucksack is lying under another tree and he heads straight for it, sliding down the trunk and then fishing into the bag until he pulls out an apple.

'Want one?' he asks.

'I've not been eating recently.'

'Suit yourself.'

Considering we're in the woods, Melek has found himself a cosy-looking spot. The bushes provide a barrier against the wind, while the trees above are tall and have grown into each other, providing a natural cover if it rains. We're probably only ten minutes' walk from Westby and yet this could be the middle of nowhere.

'Didn't the search parties find you?' I ask.

'What search parties?'

'No matter.'

Melek takes a large crunchy bite of the apple and chews. 'So, I'm the Hitcher,' he says.

'I guess.'

'I kinda like it – but I wasn't even hitchhiking.'

'Are you the person people saw in the village?'

He shakes his head and then nods. 'Perhaps. Maybe it was my twin.'

'You have a twin?'

He shakes his head. 'I'm joking – it probably *was* me. I go to that toilet block every now and then to wash up. I didn't break into your post office, though. I've never sent a letter in my life. They can trace everything if you do that.'

Melek takes another bite of his apple.

'Who's they?' I ask.

'Them. The government, MI5, MI6, big business. I'm off the grid. Ain't nobody spying on me.'

I wonder if he's joking again or if this is serious. He takes a third bite of the apple, not laughing, so I can only assume he means what he says.

'Where did you get the apple?' I ask.

'Thought you didn't want one?'

'I don't – I was just curious where it came from.'

'Not your post office. I don't do stealing.'

'I never said you did.'

He takes another bite, watching me the entire time. Eventually he nods past me. 'There's an apple grove that way.'

I look over my shoulder, even though there's no reason to. All I can see is trees. Melek is now nibbling the top part of the apple around the core. 'What's the difference between a grove and an orchard?' I ask.

'No idea, all I know is that there's free apples that way.'

Melek finishes the fruit by pecking at the leftover bits around the bottom, and then he throws the browning core into one of the bushes. He wipes his hands on the ground and then reaches into his bag and takes out a battered paperback.

'Do you live here?' I ask.

It looks like he's reading and he replies without looking up. 'I live here and there. Place to place.'

'But you've been here for a week or so?'

'I don't know. The sun rises, the sun falls.' He peers up from the book, looking at me from bottom to top. 'Why are *you* here?'

Something about the way he asks compels me to answer. 'A girl's gone missing,' I say.

He takes a moment to process it, brow rippling slightly. '… and you think—?'

'No, I don't. But people in the village were talking about seeing this long-haired man with ripped jeans and some people were thinking…'

He nods. 'I don't get what's going on here. You live in one weird place, Eleanor. Folks see someone they don't know, then assume he's breaking into post offices and stealing girls?'

I shrug. 'People round here aren't such fans of outsiders.'

'Well, I ain't an insider.'

He says it with a firm full stop and then turns back to his book.

'Don't you want a roof to live under?' I ask.

He stares up again, this time as if I'm an alien with three heads asking the stupidest question imaginable.

'Why would I want a roof?'

'In case it rains.'

'Pah! That's crazy talk. I have free water in the river. Free apples in the grove. Books in my bag. What else do I need? I'm only passing through. A few more sunrises and sunsets and I'll be on my way. I still have a job to do.'

'What job?'

He looks directly at me and I shiver. It feels as if he can see everything I am. That he knows my problems, understands everything about being me. I'm trembling as if someone has trampled across my grave. In my case, that could perhaps be true.

He doesn't answer, instead turning back to his book and releasing me from my frozen state. The spine of his book is full of creases, the absolute philistine.

'Were you by the river very early on Sunday morning?' I ask.

'I do not know one day from the next.'

'A few days ago – were you by the river?'

'What are you really asking me, Eleanor?'

There's the briefest moment in which I shiver once again – and then the words inexplicably fall from my mouth. 'I died on Sunday morning.'

Melek doesn't flinch, folding his book closed and returning it to his bag before looking up. 'Yet you're here in front of me,' he says.

'You don't seem surprised that I'm telling you I'm dead,' I say. 'Most people would tell me I was being silly, or deny it was possible.'

He continues to stare unmovingly.

'Is it down to you?' I ask.

'Is *what* down to me?'

He's so calm that it's infuriating. It feels like he's taking the piss... *Giving* the piss. I don't know why the thought occurs to me, where the words come from, but I've said it before I can stop myself. 'Are you my guardian angel?'

Still he doesn't react. 'Do you believe in angels?'

'I don't know... I don't think so.'

'If you don't believe in angels, then how could I be one?'

I breathe in through my nose, out through my mouth. Thinking. 'Someone recently explained to me about faith. He said that if a person believes in something, *really* believes, then it doesn't matter what others say.'

'This person sounds wise.'

Melek and I continue to stare at each other and I will him to say something, even if it's to say I'm talking nonsense.

'Did you bring me back from the dead? I ask.

Melek turns his head slightly to the side, eyes narrowing. 'Back from the dead? And you think I'm crazy for living without a roof.'

Chapter Thirty-Eight

After making a fool of myself, there's little else to say to Melek. When I tell him I have to go, he doesn't argue, nor does he ask me to keep his location a secret. Instead, he points me past a spindly grey tree and tells me to keep walking for ten minutes. I do just that – and then emerge onto the car park next to the river, in almost the exact spot through which I entered the woods.

I wonder if he was being honest about not seeing the search party – they would have walked right past his spot, after all. The entire experience feels like something that isn't real.

The overcast skies have brought dusk to the early evening, so I cross the bridge once more and walk home along the exact route I took when I pulled myself from the river what seems like months ago. When I reach the house, I'm left standing on the pavement, staring towards the shock of red graffiti across our front door. The idiot who sprayed it has gone for 'MUDEROR' as an insult, which would have more impact if he or she could spell correctly. The paint seems relatively fresh as the lower parts of the letters are running down the wall.

I stop at the end of the path and turn in a circle, peering towards the windows of the surrounding houses. Nobody is watching that I can see, though it is dusky enough that anyone could be standing a little back from their window, eclipsed by shadow.

I head into the house but no one has been here since Mum and I left this morning. If that mystic from the seaside really can do anything about auras, then she should have a pop at sorting out the house. The echo of the door opening ripples around the empty building, leaving a spooky, unnatural impression. The aftermath of the police team's search is still on show, with the kitchen drawers pulled out and so many little things out of place that it's as if I'm in the alternative dimension Naomi mentioned.

After filling a bucket with warm, soapy water, I return to the front of the house with a sponge. It's not easy but because the paint it recent, it comes away with half a dozen hard scrubs. As I dig into the wall, pressing as hard as I can, I feel the eyes of the neighbours upon me. Perhaps they're there, perhaps not – either way, I won't give them the satisfaction of turning to show how annoyed I am.

By the time the water in the bucket has turned pink, I've managed to get rid of the 'M' and half the 'U'. The water sloshes into the drain and I head back inside for more. While the water swills into the bucket, I check my phone – but there are no further messages or calls. Whatever's going on at the police station must be significant, because I can't think of another reason why Mum would spend so much of the day out of reach. I try calling anyway but it goes straight to voicemail.

With her not answering, I call Jim instead – who's still named 'Uncle Jim' in my phone. He answers straight away: 'Ellie?'

'Yeah.'

'Where are you?'

'At home.'

'Your mum's been trying to call you for the past hour.'

He rattles out the words, rat-a-tat-tat.

'My phone's been on.'

'She gave up after a while, because…'

He tails off and sighs, during which time it dawns on me that I've been in the woods with Melek during the period he mentions. There's every chance I was in a mobile black hole and, by the time I was out, she'd given up.

'Did you say you're at the house?' he adds.

'Yes, somebody's graffitied "murderer" across the front door. I'm trying to clear it away before Mum gets home.'

'Okay, do me a favour – stay put and I'm going to send a car for you. It'll bring you to Langham police station, which is where your mum and I are.'

He sounds grave.

'What's going on?' I ask.

'Your mum needs you, Ellie.'

'Why?'

He sighs again. 'I'm sorry for having to tell you this on the phone – but it's Ollie.'

'What about him?'

'He's confessed, Ellie. He says he killed Sarah Lipski and Helen James.'

Chapter Thirty-Nine

Langham police station is ablaze with light. It's a strange thing to notice as I head through the main doors at the front but the bulbs above are so white – and there are so many – that I find it hard to see.

The officer who picked me up from the house leads me through a maze of corridors. The walls are covered with various posters adorned with slogans like 'THINK' and pints of beer with long lists of facts… because that's the one thing drinkers *really* like: facts. Eventually, I end up in a small room with half a dozen blue canvas chairs, a low table covered with battered magazines, a water fountain, and a vending machine that's humming away in the corner. Mum jumps to her feet when she sees me, striding across the room, her face a mask of red and tears and she wraps her arms around me and squeezes so tight that I start to cough.

'Ellie,' she says, a single word, my name. It's so harrowed, so haunted, that it sounds like she can't believe I'm in front of her.

'I'm here, Mum.'

By the time she releases me, the door to the room has closed and we're alone. She stands, wiping her eyes, but it has little effect. She pulls a tissue from her sleeve and blows her nose long and loud, then dabs at her eyes.

She's a mess.

'I tried calling,' she says.

'I must have been somewhere with no service. I'd called you before that.'

She points at the ceiling. 'No reception. I had to keep going outside. Did Jim contact you?'

I nod, even though I called him. For a moment, it looks like she might break again. She collapses onto the seat and leans forward, head in hands. 'Why would he do this, Ellie? *Why?*'

'I don't know.'

'Why would he confess to something he didn't do?'

I was about to say I don't understand – and then I realise what she's said. I thought she was asking why he'd kill two girls – but she's actually wondering why he gave a false confession.

It's still not hit her yet.

I'm not sure I understand it all but I've spent the journey here thinking about Ollie's reasons and can only assume it was some sort of anger fuelled by… I'm not sure. Perhaps Sarah dumped him? I don't know. It still doesn't *feel* like something my brother might do and yet there was a time when I suspected him myself.

My mouth is dry but I find myself licking my lips anyway, unsure what to tell her. Who else could have killed Sarah, probably Helen as well, and tried to drown me? I don't believe it's Robbie, nor Ben or Naomi. It's not Melek, the Hitcher; or Ash, so who else is there? The Ravens? I can't picture it. Ollie's the connection to all of us, and now he's apparently confessed.

Mum seemingly reads my thoughts. She peers between her fingers at me. 'It's not him,' she says.

I'm saved from having to answer because there's a double knock at the door and then Jim appears. His face is more wrinkled and haggard than last night and it doesn't look like he's slept since then. His shirt-sleeves are rolled up, his top button undone.

'I'm sorry I've been so long,' he says, talking to Mum.

She stares at him blankly but says nothing. Jim steps into the room and quietly closes the door. He waits for a moment, possibly to see if anyone's going to knock, and then crosses to sit next to Mum.

'Things are out of my hands,' he says. 'Because of my connection to you both, plus the seriousness of the case, there's nothing I can do. The Langham police might even end up handing it over to the wider authority. Everything's up in the air at the moment.'

Mum says nothing, so I reply instead. 'What happened today?'

Jim reaches to the water fountain and fills up a plastic cup. He holds it to his forehead, rolling the condensation across his skin, and then downs it. 'I'm not certain for the reasons I mentioned. I've been doing other work from this station today and then asking officers I know the odd question. I've been checking in on your mum, too.'

She doesn't dispute it as he has another drink. 'Oliver hadn't been talking all day,' Jim adds. 'That's possibly because of the legal advice he was given, or perhaps for other reasons. I don't know. I went down to the cells to check on him a few hours ago – not to question him, just to ask if he was all right. He'd been offered a chance to talk to your mother but refused. He wasn't eating but I managed to get him to drink some water. He was down, obviously – shocked, probably – but as normal as you might expect given the circumstances.'

'If he wasn't talking, how did he end up confessing?' I ask.

Jim shakes his head. 'I have no idea. After making sure he was as all right as he's going to get, I came back up to finish my shift. I had some paperwork and the next thing I know, someone came in and said Oliver had requested to be brought up from the cells for interview. Apparently, he confessed then.'

'What do you mean, "confessed"?' I ask. 'What did he say?'

'I don't know, Ellie. I don't know precise details. The guys on the floor say he admitted he killed Sarah a year ago and that he's responsible for Helen's disappearance, too. I can't push for too much of the details. I told you – things are out of my hands.'

The room feels colder. 'Where is Helen?' I ask, careful not to ask where her *body* is.

Jim shakes his head. He doesn't seem to know much more than we do. I can only assume this is a detail Ollie is keeping to himself.

So little of it makes sense.

I want to see Ollie myself, to ask him what's going on, but I don't think I'll get the chance any time soon, if ever. I'm still not sure if I believe he did all this. Could he really have faked the affection with which he talked about Sarah? Or was that some sort of guilt?

The one thing I really want to ask him, sister to brother, eye to eye, is if he held me under the water and drowned me.

'He won't let his solicitor in,' Jim says. Mum sits up straighter, as this is apparently the first she's heard of it.

'Since when?' she asks.

'Since the time he confessed. He said he wasn't going to say a word until the solicitor left the room. He wouldn't accept the duty lawyer, either.'

Mum stands and steps towards the door. 'I want to see him.'

Jim jumps up and takes her hand. She doesn't pull away and the two of them stand in the middle of the room, neither looking at each other, nor me. They're both staring at the walls, which are covered with more posters. One has the slogan 'RESPECT', followed by a list of the penalties for attacking a police officer.

'He won't talk at all,' Jim says. He refused to see his solicitor, or me – and when they asked if he wanted to talk to you, he said no. He's gone back to his cell. They're hoping to question him more in the morning.'

Mum staggers slightly and Jim wraps an arm around her front, pulling her to him. She doesn't struggle this time, their argument from yesterday seemingly forgotten. She buries her face in his shoulder and sobs the word 'why?'.

It takes a minute or two for her to pull away. Her face is streaky and lined with tears both dry and new. It's hard to see her like this but I feel empty inside, unable for whatever reason to feel angry or upset. I don't know what I feel... probably confused more than anything else.

'I'm going to take you to a hotel,' Jim says, talking to Mum and then glancing towards me as well. 'As soon as news of this gets out – which won't be long – your house will be under siege from journalists and the like. The B & B from last night is too obvious, so I'll find you somewhere around Langham where you can go unnoticed, for tonight at least.'

He steps away from my mum, leaving her hand dangling in the air as she reaches for him, wanting his comfort. '*Why?*' she sobs, but Jim turns to me and then the door.

It's the question to which no one but Ollie has the answer.

FRIDAY

Chapter Forty

I'm lying in bed, desperately wanting to sleep but unable to get past that sinking feeling of being held under the water. Every time my eyes close, I'm in the river again, choking and swallowing, gasping for air. There's a hand on my chest, the other on my head, the person's weight holding me under, pressing hard as I fight back until...

It's impossible for me to keep my eyes closed for longer than that.

I sit up in bed, gasping, my head swirling. A part of me thinks that if this is all over – if it *was* Ollie whose hands I feel – then why am I still here? I can't sleep, can't eat. I'm a shell of a person, so what use am I?

I'm not sure if it's down to Jim, my mother, or some kind soul at the hotel, but I have a room to myself. It's not that much bigger than my bedroom at home, though there is a small bathroom in the corner. It's still a space where I can be by myself. Between the bed and the bathroom is a door connecting my room to Mum's. At first, she was panicked that we were apart, that she's already lost one child and I might go the same way. I spent a while assuring her I was going nowhere and then she took a tablet, one of the ones left over from after Dad died. It wasn't long after that she fell asleep.

It's a little after midnight and I know there's no chance of me sleeping. The television is muted, beaming bright images that leave the room in a blue-grey haze. I don't want to watch it but it's hard not to – and the twenty-four-hour news channel is about the only sane thing on at this time of the night anyway. There are photographs of Ollie and Sarah, the iconic one of her with the flowing blonde hair that everyone knows. There's another of Helen, too – smiling in her school uniform on the final day of term from a year ago. Her red hair is bright in the brimming sun and it's hard to comprehend that a person who is a part of me has wiped out these two bright souls.

I still don't know if I believe it, even though he confessed. My thoughts veer from one extreme to another; from, 'he didn't do it', to 'why did he do it?'. He confessed, after all.

The silent images on the screen change to Langham police station, then the sleepy centre of Westby to signify that we're all yokels from the middle of nowhere.

After that, it is Rebecca the Raven – who else? – who is solemnly holding it together for the reporters. She's as pristine and porcelain as ever, but I struggle to feel too much anger towards her because, in this instance at least, she has as much right to mourn Helen as anyone else. Helen was a success where I was a failure because, in the end, who cares about such petty feuds?

Robbie and I had a heart to heart about going our separate ways, about the end of our era, as he called it – and it was touching and heartfelt. The same applies with Rebecca and me, though. Our lives will split in different directions and, before long, we'll forget why we hated each other anyway. Why any of it mattered.

The television is showing another photo of Helen, this time her taking part in some inter-school debate competition that I don't remember. They're reporting it as if she's dead, which might be the case – although, from what Jim said at the station, Ollie hasn't told them where the body is.

I sit zombie-like, watching the footage on a loop. It's not long before the same photos and graphics are repeating themselves. Ollie, Sarah, Helen, Rebecca, Helen again. And repeat.

Still not tired.

It's only on the fourth loop when it occurs to me that I might be able to help. It was on a smaller scale but I discovered the bracelet Ollie had hidden by thinking in a way I thought he might. If I did it once, I can do it again – and this time I might be able to find Helen, or at least a trace of her.

I've been in the same clothes all day but fashion sense is low on my priorities. My phone battery is low, which is the result of being in a hotel while the charger is at home. The only other thing in my pocket is the bracelet I found in the river.

Sarah's bracelet, if Ollie was telling the truth.

I hold it, running my thumb across the smooth leather and then, because I feel an urge, I tie it around my wrist.

I don't want to risk being recognised by anyone on reception, so creep along the corridor, following the blue arrows marking the fire exit. Aside from the odd muffled voice and a creaking lift, all is still. As far as I can tell, I reach the door at the far end of the corridor without being seen. The fire exit door pushes open with a clunk and then I'm outside. I can't tell if the air is cold or if it's simply me. It might be both but it bites either way. My teeth chatter but I don't have a wardrobe of clothes here to pile on the layers, so I close the door quietly and continue down the metal stairs until I'm on the ground.

It's cloudy – no stars, barely a moon – but I know the way back to Westby, even in the dark. The hotel is part of a retail complex on the edge of Langham, close to a cinema, bowling alley and obligatory McDonald's. I think there's a law about McDonald's being mandatory on retail parks. I skirt around the edge of the largely deserted car park, sticking to the shadows until I reach the main road. From there, it's a straight walk to my village while keeping a few metres into the treeline.

Not that any cars pass anyway.

It takes an hour for me to reach the village, then another ten minutes to reach my street. Any thoughts of returning to the house are immediately dispelled because Jim was more right than I could have imagined. Three satellite trucks are parked outside the house, with a handful of people whom I assume to be reporters milling on the pavement. A cameraman with a bright white light fixed to the top of his camera is filming our front door, which still has 'DEROR' spray-painted across it.

I stand for a few moments, watching the surreal sight of the house in which I've grown up become the centrepiece of a television show. I want to stomp over there and tell everyone to get lost but know it will do no good. I'll end up being the deranged sister on camera and they won't leave anyway – they'll camp on the pavement until a different story comes along.

The walk back to the village centre is slow as I try to think like Ollie. If there are any clues in the house, they're off-limits. The police have already found Helen's clothes at the college changing rooms, so where else does Ollie spend time?

It's not long before I find myself on the bridge again. Since waking in the river, this is the place where I constantly find myself drifting. The river shimmers in what little light there is, the deepest parts in the centre a thick, intimidating, impenetrable black. The only noise is the gentle babble of the water over rocks, until an owl hoots somewhere past the car park, into the woods. When I look up towards the public toilets, I see a shadow next to the block. It's hunched under the trees, stretching towards me, unmoving.

'Hello?'

My voice echoes softly and then disappears. I take a few steps towards the car park but the shadow doesn't move.

'Melek?'

The final 'K' of his name reverberates around the open space but still the shadow doesn't move. It's so dark that I'm wary of moving too far from where I am. I should be scared – this village hardly has a good record when it comes to teenage girls out by themselves – but, as before with Melek, I don't feel anything.

I think about his choice of lifestyle, bumming around the countryside and living off the land. Some nomadic figure drifting through life. Is that a way to live? I'm not sure. Some of it seems appealing, the absence of responsibility for one, but there's also the loneliness and lack of security.

'Hello?'

The shadow still doesn't move, even when I'm on the far side of the bridge, and I reason that it's a trick of the light – a misshapen tree or bush.

I re-cross the bridge, unsure what to do with myself. The village centre is deserted, though it won't be for long. Soon the media trucks and morbid onlookers will arrive. When Sarah died last year, it only took a day for the tourists to arrive in their ones and twos, cameras and phones in hand to take selfies in front of the river. I always wondered what they were doing with the pictures. Posting them on Instagram with the caption: 'That spot where that girl died! #dead #deadgirl #rip #withdaanglesnow #drowned #sosad #deadgirlsofinstagram'?

It can't only be me who thinks that's weird.

I weave in and out of the village cut-throughs and then, as if I was drawn there, I'm in front of my father's old newsagent. The wooden boards are blank, yet I can't help but picture the shop the way it used to be. At Christmas, there would be fairy lights rimmed around the glass, with toys and games on display. I would sit under the counter amusing myself while he dealt with customers. It's one of my earliest memories, perhaps my happiest – and I wonder how he would feel about all of this. About how Mum has gone to pieces; about Ollie. In many ways, everything that's gone wrong for us links back to when he got ill – not that it's his fault. Would Ollie have done this if Dad were around? I can't say for sure but I doubt it.

The path at the back of the shop is littered with rubbish – shattered wooden pallets, crumbling bricks and the usual array of chocolate wrappers and crisp packets. The gate that leads into the yard at the back of the old newsagent is secured with a wooden board that's taller than me – except that it's only been slotted into the gap between the two gateposts and not secured. I slip it to the side and then replace it before heading into the area where Ollie and I used to play together.

A cement mixer caked with dried grey sludge is in the corner, next to stacks of bricks and wooden beams. There are three or four bags of sand in another corner, with at least two of them spilling onto the floor. A thin layer of dust sits across everything. Even with the mess, the yard seems a lot smaller than it did when I was a kid. Ollie and I would play one-on-one football from wall to wall. I was never that bothered but he'd agree to play hopscotch with me if I played football with him – and so we did. With so little difference in age between us, we were evenly matched at most things until we got to eleven or twelve years old. Before that, we could play for hours in this enclosed space. Recently, Ollie claimed it never happened – not the hopscotch part anyway. I know the truth. Well, that *particular* truth.

Aside from the wooden boards, the front of the newsagent is barely distinguishable from when I was growing up – but the back is a mess. Riveted metal boards block the windows, with signs on all the lower ones reading 'do not enter'. Another wooden board is barricaded across where the door should be, but there is a graffiti tag across it. I edge closer, wondering if the markings are some sort of insult, but it's only when I'm close enough to touch the wood that I realise it's not attached. Much like the one blocking the gate, it's simply resting in place.

Someone has been here recently.

I move the board to the side and then step through the back door of the building, before replacing the wood behind me. Inside, it's dark, *really* dark, to the point that I kick something accidentally and send it spiralling across the floor without knowing it was there. It clangs and echoes as it bounces off the wall, making me jump. Something is dripping, though it's hard to tell from where the noise is coming.

The flashlight on my phone isn't great – but the beam of creamy light is better than darkness. I turn in a circle, taking in what used to be the delivery room, where boxes of crisps and chocolates would be dropped off. The edges are coated with sawdust and grime, while the walls are bare of any sort of plaster, exposing the crumbling brickwork.

There used to be a door leading from the delivery room to behind the counter but the frame is no longer there. Instead, it is simply a gap that looks as if the bricklayer has missed a bit. I head through anyway, into the main area of what used to be the shop and, to my surprise, the counter is still there. It's not as high as I remember but I can picture myself sitting underneath, banging Lego bricks into each other. The shelving hasn't been ripped out, either – and I can almost recall the order of the sweet jars that used to sit there. Bonbons were always on the top shelf, with chocolate mice on the bottom. Dad said it was because he put the least-popular sweets at the top so he didn't have to reach for them so often.

Bonbons *are* a bit rubbish.

There is more dripping, with two puddles forming close to where the postcard spinner rack used to be. The rest of the unplastered walls are crumbling. The newspaper racks that used to sit by the front door have gone, as have the long shelves that housed the magazines. It feels like the final memories of my father belong to this place but they're almost gone, too.

The final door also has a board resting across it but it is easy to move out of the way. The storeroom is where Dad would keep everything that was out-of-season. Unsold Christmas cards and wrapping paper would be boxed up and put away until November came around again. It wasn't like now, where the build-up to Christmas begins in August.

There was a box marked 'Mother's Day', another for 'Father's Day' – plus Easter cards and gifts. Luckily for Ollie and me, unsold Easter eggs would not keep for a year, so we always ended up with free chocolate after Easter Monday. On one occasion, there was a large Smarties egg that Ollie really wanted. He hid it in the storeroom, ensuring it couldn't be sold, and then moved it into view when the Monday had gone. He got his free egg but offered me most of it, saying it didn't taste right. The chocolate was fine, of course – it was the dishonesty that got him.

That's the brother I remember. How did he become whatever it is he confessed to being?

The air in the storeroom feels sludgy, thicker than in the rest of the shop. I shine the light from my phone into the first corner but the device dims and beeps in annoyance, warning me again that the battery is low. Shreds of light creep down from above anyway and, even though it hasn't rained, there are more puddles on the floor from the gaps in the unfinished roof. Everything is a murky, milky grey.

My phone beeps once more and starts flashing an extra red light. It makes sense to start beeping *and* flashing when the battery is already low, right?

It is as I'm trying to make the flashlight come back on that I spot it. In the corner of the storeroom, shrouded in shadow, is a fold-down cot-type camp bed. Rails run around the edge and there is a lumpy mass underneath a white sheet.

I gasp, knowing what's underneath but having to see for myself. Of course this is where Ollie would hide something. He had the same upbringing around this place that I did. In so many ways, it makes everything worse. This will now muddy those memories of our father.

The sheet isn't a sheet at all, it's a thin, fleecy blanket: warm and soft. I hold onto my phone, using the light to illuminate the corner of the room, as I steadily pull back the cover. I see the long, wavy red hair first, then the pale-grey waxy skin that is unmistakably Helen. Her lips are pressed together, eyes closed. I've never seen a dead body before... not counting my own. She seems peaceful but then, as I pull the blanket down further, I see the twisted indentations in her neck from where someone has strangled her.

From where *Ollie* has strangled her.

I close my eyes, unable to look at the horror any longer.

The poor girl.

I turn, still staring at the blankness of my eyelids before a stone skittles across the floor and clatters into the wall. I shine my torch up and the figure in the doorway shrinks away, blocking it with his hand. I expect Ollie, somehow out of his cell – but it's not him at all. It's too tall, the features too wrinkled. It's not Ollie, nor Robbie, Ben, Naomi, any of the Ravens, or the Hitcher. It's no one from my list.

It's Jim.

He takes a step forward but I can't see him properly because he's still blocking the light from my phone. I angle it away from his face, pointing it towards his midriff, leaving his top half in shadow. I want to ask how he knew about Ollie bringing Helen here but then, from nowhere, I'm in the river again. I'm fighting for air, pushing against those hands. One on my chest, one on my head.

And then I remember.

Chapter Forty-One

Robbie's battered Vauxhall chunters into the night and I'm alone on the road, barefooted and furious at myself for kissing Ben. I don't know why I did it. It's easy to blame him for suggesting we go upstairs, but I went willingly. I was upset because I know Robbie and I are coming to an end – the end of our era – and I don't want to be alone.

It's not a good enough reason.

I stumble along the pavement, trying to avoid the tiny stones that scratch my feet, but when I reach the house, Jim is there, sitting on the low wall, shaded from view by next door's hedge. He says he was called out to a party because of neighbour complaints about noise. After calming things down and making sure the neighbours were happy, he drove here – to my mum's house – where she was waiting up for him.

Or so he thought.

She was really waiting up for me.

Jim and I sit together on the wall. It's dark and there's an edge to the breeze, even though it's not cold.

'Do you know the first thing your mother asked me?' he says.

I'm tired, confused and emotional. It's been a long day but he's Uncle Jim and, for whatever reason, he wants to have a conversation.

'No,' I reply.

'She asked if you were at the party,' he says.

'What did you say?'

'That I didn't see you.'

'Oh.'

I think he's telling me this because he wants me to be grateful for him covering but it's not that at all. His voice is low and controlled, but bristling with something else.

'She didn't ask if I had a good day,' he says. 'She didn't ask if it'd been hard, if I'd had a lot on. She didn't ask about anything to do with me. She didn't even say it was nice to see me. The first thing she asked was how you were.'

I'm on the wall, unsure how to reply. 'Sorry,' I manage, although I'm not sure why I say it. I stand, ready to head inside, but then there's something clamped over my mouth and a hand on the back of my head. After that, there's only black.

I blink back into the storeroom. Jim is a couple of metres from me. He glances towards Helen's body and then focuses back on me. His eyes almost glow in the dark and when he speaks I can't see his lips moving.

'Why are you here, Eleanor?' he asks.

He's close to one of the pillars of light that is shining through the half-finished roof, his toe edging one of the puddles. He's wearing a backpack, which looks so bizarre for someone of his age. He's not super old and yet rucksacks seem like a young person's thing. A bag to carry to school.

It suddenly seems obvious. Robbie and I have talked about going our separate ways, about leading different lives and seeing where we end up. But what if I was determined *not* to do that? To keep the life I had?

Who would be friends with a woman for thirty-six years unless there was something else there? Apart from the school girlfriend my mother mentioned, Jim has always been single, so much so that I thought he was gay. As soon as my father died, he was there. He's been pining for my mother his entire adult life.

You know you and your brother will always be my number one, don't you?

I can still hear my mother's words and I know they're true. But Jim knew they were true as well. When he got home from his late shift and Mum asked about me instead of him, he realised once and for all that he would never be her priority. He had to get in line, the way he had his entire life.

My phone beeps once more and then the light dies. My eyes have adjusted somewhat but it's gloomy and the shafts shining through the holes in the roof offer little. There is a thump as Jim shrugs his backpack onto the ground – and then I see something cylindrical in his hands. A pipe or a bat. I'm not sure.

Silence – except for a slow, methodical drip.

'Did you kill Helen?' I ask.

The question hangs, echoing and unanswered. Jim doesn't move and then, even though I still don't see his lips part, the reply comes.

'I think the real question is, how are you still alive?'

I shiver. The water is in my mouth.

'You left me in the river?' I say. A question.

'I *drowned* you in the river,' he replies. 'You stopped breathing. You had gone. What a surprise it was the next morning when your mother called, babbling about a ceiling fan and telling me you were up and about. It was a good job she called, else I would've struggled to keep it together when I saw you in the house later that day.'

He adjusts the grip on whatever's in his hand and it clinks on the ground. Other than a vague shape and his eyes, I still can't see anything of his top half. There's no way I can get around him to the door, not without getting a whack from whatever he's holding. For now, all I can do is keep him talking.

'Why did Ollie confess?' I ask.

'Because, as I told you, I went to see him in the cells. I told him I'd slit your throat and your mother's if he didn't.' Jim speaks calmly, matter of factly, as if he's telling a story of what he bought at the supermarket. 'Your brother must really care for you. He was surprisingly pliable.'

'You were at the college,' I say.

'What?'

'On the morning after the party in the woods. I bunked off but Naomi said you were there. That was when you got into the kit room and planted Helen's clothes. You either stole Ollie's key, or used one from reception.'

'Right little police officer you are,' he says. 'Anyway – I'll ask you again. How are you still alive? I waited all those years for your mother and then, when she's finally free from your wretched father, she tells me her kids come first.'

He spits the final word as if it's a piece of rotten food. He's disgusted by it.

'You killed Sarah,' I say, trying to put together the puzzle pieces. It feels like bits are still missing. 'You wanted Ollie to be blamed for it and thought it would get him out of the way.'

There is a small shuffling and it feels like Jim has moved closer to me, even though it doesn't look like it.

'Your mother wouldn't have handled the loss of your father and brother so closely to one another. I had to look for an alternative way to get him – and then, ultimately, you – out of the way. I shouldn't have counted on my colleagues, though. The detective lot came in from Langham, as I knew they would, and blew it. Lack of evidence and all that. They didn't even charge him. But there was no way he could escape that twice. When I followed his car and saw him dropping off that ginger bimbo, I knew it was time.'

His weapon jingles on the floor once more and then he raises it until it's resting on his shoulder. 'I'll ask you one more time. Why are you still alive, Eleanor? *How* are you still alive?'

I glance backwards at Helen's body, trying to gulp away the pain of seeing her like this. She didn't deserve it. Jim's eyes burn through the darkness and I edge towards him, keeping my voice low.

'I could tell you – but you won't believe me.'

'Try me.'

Another half-step. 'You really won't.'

One smaller step and he raises the weapon. In the slim shaft of light, I can see that it's a hammer with a long handle. It's above his head, ready to crash down – but then there's another scuff of sound from behind.

Jim turns but not quickly enough as Melek hurls himself rugby-style into his chest.

Chapter Forty-Two

There is a loud masculine grunt but I'm not sure from whom it comes. All I see is a flash of movement through the glimmer of light. The two men bounce off the walls with a crunch and then they're on the floor. A silhouette is on his knees – and then, sickeningly, there is a blur as the hammer crunches down. I wince as something squelches. I don't want to know what. The shadow groans a swear word and pushes himself to his feet.

It's Jim.

I have no time to hesitate, to question, to do anything other than run.

For the first time since waking in the river, I feel alive. Those days of skiving off cross-country belong to somebody else because, boy, do I run. I'm through the door, round the counter and out of the delivery room before I can even think. The gate is open at the back and I barrel through that, then sprint along the path until I'm on the high street. My lungs should be burning, my legs screaming, but they're not. It feels like electricity is simmering through me as I pump my legs and run for all I'm worth.

Jim is not far behind. He has longer legs and is more used to this than me – but I have a head start.

I don't know why but I head towards the river. It feels as if it's pulling me, calling me, and I bound onto the towpath, racing towards the bridge. There is a clatter of footsteps behind, the gruff breathless gasps for air. They're getting louder but I feel invincible. The river is the scene of my greatest triumph, my most incredible trick. Jim held me under the water until I stopped breathing, yet here I am. Beat that.

I continue to run but glance over my shoulder as I move. Jim is a couple of metres back, gaining… gaining.

Except that he doesn't have to.

As I turn back to look where I'm going, my foot slides over a small rock on the side of the path. My ankle crunches sideways, my knee buckling and then I'm falling. I groan, though there's no pain – I've forgotten what that is – but I still can't stop myself from slipping down the bank. I grab at stones, roots, anything to stop my fall, but it's too late. Before I know it, my feet are in the water and here I am again.

Jim's sliding down the bank towards me but his feet are controlled. Before I can haul myself out of the river, he grabs my collar with one hand, covering my mouth with the other. I can see him clearly now, lip snarling, eyes dark with anger.

'Second time lucky,' he says emotionlessly and then he launches me backwards, not letting go as he continues to cover my mouth with one hand, using the other to push down on my chest.

I'm under the water, trying to fight my way up, but he's too strong. I kick and flail but connect with nothing. I try to scratch him with my arms but the water is heavy and the best I can do is grab his wrist with my hand. I try to prise his fingers away but it's no use and I can feel the darkness coming for me.

It's coming.

It's coming.

It's here.

Everything is black but there is a hand on my head, another on my chest… only they're not Jim's. The fingernails are longer and there are fewer hairs on the wrist. They're not pushing me under – they're pulling me up.

I realise that, in my vision, the hands were *always* pulling me up.

With a gasp, I emerge from the water, expecting to see Jim's insect limbs around me, to see his fury-ridden face. But it's not him at all.

Her hair is long and golden with a gentle kink, her eyes are beaming, beautiful blue. Sarah Lipski is a few metres away from me in the river. She has both hands in the water – and then I see Jim. His arms are flailing as she forces his head down into the river. His back is like a large stepping stone in the middle of the water, bobbing up and down, legs flailing before his body sags and goes limp. Sarah lifts her hands and turns to me, water up to her hips, as Jim's body floats lifelessly towards the bank.

I whisper 'no' but it's already too late.

She's ghoulish yet beautifully angelic at the same time. Her skin is white and waxy, like Helen's but glowing with life. She smiles sadly, head at an angle as she puts a finger to her lips.

'Sarah?' I say, but she doesn't reply.

She takes a step towards me and then drops her hands into the water.

'Did you save me?' I ask. 'When I was dreaming, it wasn't someone's hands pushing me under the water, it was yours pulling me out.'

She smiles again but the rest of her face is unmoving. For a moment, I think the water level is rising but then I realise she's sitting down. The water burbles over her chin, then her lips, her nose, before she disappears under the surface completely. I wade towards her as quickly as I can but my legs are heavy and I have to take huge, hulking footsteps. When I reach the spot where she disappeared, I crouch until the water is at my chin and then fumble in the murky depths, wanting to pull her clear of the river.

There's nothing there. No one.

I take another step, turning back the way I came, and then inhale deeply, dunking myself under the surface. It's useless because the water is dank and dark and I can neither see nor feel anything. I gasp my way back to the surface and it's then that I feel something on my wrist. I fight the urge to pull away, feeling the gentle tug and then… it's gone.

When I pull my wrist free of the water, the bracelet is no longer there.

For a few moments I stand still, turning in a circle and hoping to see Sarah. All that's there is Jim, his face and legs in the water, his back like a giant rock.

I wade back the way I came but it takes a long time to reach the bank, even though the distance is short. It feels as if everything has caught up with me – the lack of food, the days with no sleep, the walking, running, wading in the river. By the time I haul myself out, I'm exhausted. I should go for help, tell people it was Jim all along, and yet all I can do is lie flat on my back and close my eyes. For the first time in days, I know I can sleep. Know I *will* sleep. But first I say a silent thank you to the girl in the river.

My saviour.

Sarah.

ONE WEEK LATER

Chapter Forty-Three

Naomi sits opposite me, pressing back into the booth that has tapes from Gary Numan on my side through to Siouxsie and the Banshees on hers. She tries to suck her strawberry thickshake through the straw but it's a losing battle so she grabs a spoon instead.

'I really am sorry,' I say – again. 'I don't know what happened.'

She swallows a mouthful of thickshake and then picks up a second spoon from the table, twists it in her hand, and offers it to me. She's not smiling but I guess that would have been a lot to ask.

As olive branches go, I'll definitely take a spoon.

'You sure?' I say.

'I don't give away strawberry thickshake lightly,' Naomi replies, 'especially not at the Deck – and *especially* not at linner-time.'

I dip the spoon and swallow a bit of the gooey ice cream mix. I even get a small dark chocolate chunk – Naomi really knows what she's doing when it comes to anything ice cream related.

Something strange happened after I came out of the river that final time. I closed my eyes as I lay on the bank and, when I woke a short time later, I was hungry. In the way I once knew for certain that I'd died, I knew then that I needed food. I'm not sure I can explain it better than that. You know what you know. You believe what you believe.

Since then, my skin has regained much of its colour. I'm almost looking back to my old self – and I can eat again. I've had everything on the Deck's menu in the week since it all happened with Jim… including the four-bean burger. Ash sorted it especially for me, even though it's no longer the special.

For the record, it contains kidney beans, green beans, butter beans and pinto beans (I don't know what they are). Not a baked bean in sight.

'What did you do to your finger?' Naomi asks.

I hold it up to show the small clip over the end. 'The doctor said it was broken, so he reset it. They gave me something to help me sleep and I was out for fourteen hours. It was amazing.'

Naomi doesn't ask how I did it, probably assuming it was while fighting off Jim. I'm the centre of attention in the village, with so many stories going around about me that I can't keep up. The truth is, it was broken when I fell off the shed roof. It was only after I got out of the river the final time, after I woke up from my nap on the riverbank, that it started to ache.

'Do you want to know what *actually* happened with Jim?' I ask.

Naomi has another spoonful of the thickshake.

'I want you to know that I had already forgiven you for kissing Ben,' she says. 'It's not because you nearly died, or because of what happened to your brother. It was before that. It's because you're my friend and, however many years down the line, neither of us will even remember Ben's name. We'll still be friends, though.'

I open my mouth but she cuts me off. 'And don't say you're sorry again. I get it.'

'Okay.'

She leans in, the hint of a mischievous smile creeping across her face. 'So… what *did* happen?'

I tell her most of what occurred. Stumbling across Melek in the woods, going to the newsagent, finding Helen's body, being confronted by Jim, Melek trying to be my hero, running and then ending up in the river. I leave out the part about Sarah.

Naomi oohs and aahs while continuing to eat. When I finish with me on the riverbank, she slides the rest of the thickshake across the table towards me. The ultimate act of friendship.

'I still don't understand how you escaped,' she says.

I shake my head. 'Me either. I think Jim might have slipped in the river, perhaps hit his head on a rock?'

Naomi eyes me sideways. It's not convincing but what else can I tell her?

'Is that what you told the police?' she asks.

'What else is there to tell? I don't know. One minute I was trying to get away from Jim in the river, the next I looked back and his head was under the water.'

She nods, acceptingly. It's a shame I have to lie but she wouldn't believe the truth. I'm not sure if I believe it. Seeing Sarah feels like a dream. There was something about the way she pressed her finger to her lips that still haunts me, though in a good way. It's comforting. I'm not sure I'll ever forget it.

'How do they know it was Jim who killed Helen?' Naomi asks.

'They found indents in her neck that matched his fingerprints. They also found the hammer in the river that had Jim's fingerprints and Melek's blood.'

'They think he killed Sarah as well?'

'I guess.'

She whistles low. 'Wow… all because of your mum.' She stops and then wafts her hand. 'Sorry – I didn't mean it like that, I—'

'I know what you meant,' I say.

Naomi takes a moment and then stands, straightening her skirt. She looks from me to the counter. 'You reckon that Ash guy's not that bad…?'

'He's harmless. He just has a strange way to him. Ask him something about movies. He loves it. You've probably got a lot in common.'

Naomi peers between us again and then shrugs, before marching to the counter. I watch her, in awe that she still wants to be my friend after everything. The past few days have blurred by, with police interviews, hospital appointments and needing to be there for Mum and Ollie. This is the first time I've seen Naomi since Rebecca let on about Ben and me. It feels as if none of that happened. Little things become insignificant when big things come along.

Naomi says something to Ash behind the counter and he smiles – *really* smiles and then laughs. She laughs too and it's not long before she's heading back with two thickshakes.

'I figure this is a three-shake kinda afternoon,' she says.

I stick to the strawberry and chocolate chunk one. She doesn't even bother with a straw, going directly into hers with the spoon.

'How's Ollie?' she asks.

'Back at home. Not himself, obviously – but he's still talking about going to uni. It'll be a new start where nobody knows him.'

'He can reinvent himself.'

I nod. 'I hope he does. Once they told him Jim was dead, he told the police that Jim had threatened him in the police station cells. They were reluctant to release him at first but found one of Helen's hairs under the back seat of Jim's car. At his house, there was a small key to access the kit room at the college. They had no reason to keep Ollie in – plus they were too busy fielding queries about why they hadn't looked at Jim in the first place.'

Naomi nods along. 'And the Hitcher turned out to be a hero. I bet the village biddies didn't expect that.'

I smile but say nothing. The memory of talking to Melek in the woods, of hearing how peaceful he was, is too much. He saved my life but lost his own.

I realised days later that Melek never answered one of my questions. I told him that Eleanor meant shining light – but he never told me, or didn't know, what his own name meant. Luckily, there's Google for that. There's Google for everything. It might be a coincidence but there's very little I take for granted nowadays – and Melek *can* be translated as 'angel'. He didn't react when I asked him if he was my guardian angel and I'm still not sure why I had that thought in the first place. What I do know is that he was in the right place to save me when I needed saving.

Naomi senses I don't want to talk but shuffles around our shakes until there's a caramel one in front of me.

'There are Creme Egg bits in there,' she says. 'They keep them in the freezer at the back so you can have them all year round.'

I shovel a spoonful of caramel Creme Egg thickshake into my mouth and it's wonderful. I can smell it, taste it, and the world is alive again.

'Is your mum okay?' Naomi asks.

'Not really. She keeps saying she loves me – and Ollie. Hard to complain. I don't know how she kept it all together. Want to know the strangest thing? Well, perhaps not *the* strangest, but…'

'Go on.'

'Jim left her everything in the will. After everything that happened, she owns his house, his car – everything. She says she doesn't want it but I don't know. It's too weird.'

Naomi puts down her spoon and leans across the table. She takes my hand in hers and it's cold. Ice cream cold. The best kind of cold.

'I'm glad we're friends again,' she says.

'Me, too.'

She nods towards the door and I turn to see a man entering, sandals with socks pulled up past his ankles. I don't need to say anything because Naomi's grin says it all. It's so nice to be able to give the piss again.

In the week that has passed since I awoke in the river, I've wondered how much of it was true, or how much is down to my stunted memory. Was I ever really dead, or was it my imagination? Could I have really gone five days without food or sleep? Did the necklace from my grandmother somehow protect me? Was Melek my guardian angel? Did I really see Sarah in the river? Did she put her finger to her lips and then take that bracelet back?

Ultimately, I don't know – so I decided my dad was right all along. Or *almost* right.

Life *is* a lot like a well-made sandwich. The two ends are kinda boring and what matters is all that fancy stuff in the middle. What he forgot is that sometimes those sandwiches are triple-deckers and that, every now and then, you get two goes at all that fancy stuff in the middle.

A Letter from Kerry

I don't know how much of my work you'll have read over the years. I've dabbled through genres and tried a few different things. I never wanted to write the same type of book over and over. It feels a bit safe. A bit easy. A bit *boring*.

The initial idea for this came while I was working on one of my 'regular' crime books in the Jessica Daniel series. I liked the thought of someone investigating their own death and it eventually became this ghostly-supernatural-teenagery-crimey-wimey-coming-of-age story that you've hopefully just finished.

With books, movies, TV shows and probably most kinds of entertainment, one of the first things anyone wants to know is the genre into which things fit. It's neat and tidy if something can be labelled in a certain way. Easy to market and know the target audience. Look at how many reviews or posters say things like, 'It's *Die Hard* meets *Mean Girls*!' (which sounds amazing, by the way). Everything is compared to everything else. If you like *Die Hard* and/or *Mean Girls*, you might like this new movie (which still sounds amazing). It would definitely star The Rock… or Chris Pratt! (I love Chris Pratt).

Anyway, I never knew if *The Death and Life of Eleanor Parker* would be published because I never had a good answer to the question of what, precisely, it is.

Is it a crime book? Sort of. Is it a coming-of-age tale? Kind of. Is it a supernatural story? Maybe.

I figure that, probably above anything else I've ever written, this book is whatever you, the reader, want it to be. All I tried to do was write something I hoped would be interesting. I really hope I succeeded.

On that note, please do leave a review on your platform of choice. As ever, it's the best way us authors have of getting our work out there in front of new readers. It's people like your very selves who have enabled me to find audiences in countries like Canada and Australia, where nobody had really read my stuff before.

If you want to keep up-to-date with all my latest releases, just sign up at the following link. Your email address will never be shared and you can unsubscribe at any time.

www.bookouture.com/kerry-wilkinson

Thanks to, in no particular order, Claire, Natasha, Nicola, Kim and Noelle for their help with this.

If you're wondering where the idea for Tape Deck comes from, I was listening to a lot of Frank Turner's *Tape Deck Heart* at the time. The album has nothing to do with the diner I thought of – but did provide a name. Oh, and Frank Turner is great. On the day I am writing this letter, I am literally off to watch him tonight.

If you want to ask me anything, you can email me through www.kerrywilkinson.com – or at facebook.com/kerrywilkinsonbooks – I try to reply to everyone but sometimes that pesky spam filter grabs your legitimate emails, while allowing through ones trying to make me slimmer. Perhaps someone's trying to tell me something?

Cheers for reading,
Kerry

 @kerrywk